EDUCATING AVIVA

Other Books by
REBECCA MARKS

The Dana Cohen Mystery Series

On the Rocks
Four Shots Neat
Stone Cold Sober
Old Fashioned with a Twist

And the following novels

Time Out
About Time
Paint it Black

Educating Aviva

REBECCA MARKS

LUMINARE PRESS
WWW.LUMINAREPRESS.COM

Educating Aviva
Copyright © 2022 by Rebecca Marks

All rights reserved. This book or any portion thereof may not be reproduced or used in any manner whatsoever without the express written permission of the publisher, except for the use of brief quotations in a book review.

Printed in the United States of America

Luminare Press
442 Charnelton St.
Eugene, OR 97401
www.luminarepress.com

LCCN: 2022901158
ISBN: 978-1-64388-917-7

*I dedicate this book to Footsteps,
the only organization in the United States providing
comprehensive services to people who have chosen to leave
their ultra-Orthodox communities and begin new lives.
Based in New York, Footsteps provides a range of services,
including social and emotional support, educational and
career guidance, workshops and social activities,
and access to resources. Information about
the organization can be found online at
https://footstepsorg.org.*

CHAPTER ONE

Aviva and David

As Aviva Stern walked to the corner of Seventy-sixth and York, her eyes burning with salty sweat, she saw it—the "Bagels" banner, with a small neon sign flashing "Kosher" underneath. Reaching up and blotting the perspiration off her forehead with her long-sleeved shirt, she felt a wave of relief, felt her breathing relax. She was sure she couldn't walk much farther without collapsing from dehydration and exhaustion. It must be at least eighty-five degrees out, ninety percent humidity, and she'd been walking for what seemed hours. July had been sweltering even for July, but at home in Brooklyn she rarely walked this much.

Today, she'd had to get away, anywhere, so she'd walked to the Marcy Avenue subway stop, determined to get on the first train that arrived. It was a Manhattan-bound Z train, so she'd boarded and just ridden, changing trains for the Q at Canal Street. Then she'd ridden that to the end of the line, Ninety-sixth and Second, and had gotten out and started walking again, downtown on Second Avenue. But she'd had no idea where to go—no idea really where she was, except that it was Manhattan, and it felt different here than it did at home. The air felt different. Smelled different.

She reasoned that if she walked toward the river, the air might be a little cooler, so she'd made a left on Seventy-sixth, determined to head all the way east, but when she noticed the bagel shop sign, she decided that might be a better destination. It was likely to be air-conditioned. Making her way across York with the bagel shop in sight, she was so drained and sweaty, she didn't pay attention to the oncoming traffic, and a cab flew past her—so close she could almost touch it—honking its horn, the driver yelling something in a language she didn't understand and shaking his fist at her. She recoiled, her hands flying up around her face, and by some miracle managed to get back on the curb without being hit. She was breathing hard, and now the perspiration was seeping out from under the heavy wig and hairband, so she couldn't help herself—she started to cry. People—young people in flip-flops and shorts, older people on canes, dog walkers with their charges in tow, women pushing baby carriages—simply brushed by her without paying attention. She backed up to the corner of a brick building and leaned against it, still breathing heavily. What was she doing here? But then she caught her breath and decided that no matter what, she had to get into the shop and at least get a glass of water.

Finally, wiping away the tears and gaining a little composure, she pushed herself away from the building, but as she started to cross the street, she felt a searing pain in her ankle. She must have twisted it during her escape from the taxi. No matter, she forced herself across the street—this time looking both ways before she stepped off the curb, making sure she was walking with the light—and limped into the store. It was blessedly cool, and she sat down at a small table close to the door, rubbing her ankle, which ached. It smelled good in here, like freshly baked bread and cake.

She hadn't noticed hunger before, but the aromas inside this place made her realize she was starving. She'd run away from home before she'd eaten anything—it had been impossible to eat anything this morning after—that. But then she remembered she had no money at all. She'd begged someone emerging from the subway station to swipe their Metro card so she could get through the turnstile. The woman had taken pity on her and obliged. But she'd spent all the money she'd made working at the bakery in Williamsburg on food for the week. She felt like crying again, but she bit her lip. There were quite a few people in this bustling place, sitting at tables or on line at the counter. She'd just sit here until she figured out what to do. She put her elbows on the table and her head in her hands.

"Excuse me, Miss?" An older man, possibly in his fifties or sixties, was looking down at her. Her head jerked up. He was standing directly over her, and the only thing she could see was a double chin, from the neck up, and some gray stubble. He was wearing jean cutoffs and a disheveled shirt that hung down on one side. She could see his belly jutting out over the pants. She gasped.

"Yes?" she managed to say.

"Are you done eating here? There are no tables left, and it looks like you're just sitting." He was juggling a newspaper and a paper plate with a bagel in one hand and an overfilled cup of coffee in the other. He began tapping his foot as if he was very impatient. Aviva didn't know what to say. She stared up at him. "I asked if you are leaving?" he said. "I need this table."

"Excuse me, sir." A disembodied voice came from somewhere behind the counter. Aviva looked around, but the man with the belly was standing directly in her line of vision. "She's waiting for her order. You'll have to find another table. I'm sorry."

The man huffed but walked away, scanning the small room for signs of an empty seat. Aviva had no idea who had spoken out for her, but she began to panic. If he was actually going to bring her food, she had no money to pay for it. She thought she should just get up and slip out of here before she could be embarrassed, but her ankle was throbbing, and she was sure she couldn't move fast enough. Before she could think of another solution, someone had walked over and sat down across from her. She felt the blood rush from her head. If it was possible to feel dizzy sitting down, she did.

"Aren't you going to say thank you?" The young man had put a cup of coffee on the table, with three small creamers and a spoon. He'd also brought over a sesame bagel and a small container of cream cheese. Aviva felt the saliva starting to form inside her cheeks.

"No—oh, I—" She hadn't had the courage to look up, but finally she did. She couldn't tell how old he was. A little older than she, likely, but he had a beautiful smile, straight white teeth, a well trimmed beard, and twinkling deep brown eyes.

"It's okay," he said. She noted a pleasant accent she couldn't place. "You like coffee?" He raised his eyebrows, as if he might have made a mistake.

"I do, but—"

"You don't like *our* coffee?" He laughed.

She shook her head. "No, it's not that." She was going to have to confess that she was penniless, but that was harder than she thought.

"We have tea also, if you want that?"

"No, no," she said, finally. "I love coffee."

He smiled again, and this time she noticed the crows' feet at the corners of his eyes. They were somehow comforting, gave the message that he smiled a lot. She wanted to bathe in his smile. "Good! Then what's the problem?"

"I don't have any money," she blurted out, her hand in front of her mouth. He had obviously heard her. He continued to smile, and then reached out as if he was going to touch her hand, but she pulled it back with a quick jerk.

"I'm sorry," he said. "I didn't mean anything. Please, go ahead and eat and drink. It's on me."

On me, she thought. She'd never heard that expression before. She hoped it meant he was paying. She pulled the bagel closer and took a bite. She couldn't help thinking at that moment it was the most delicious thing she'd ever eaten.

"When's the last time you ate?" he said, this time, his mouth straightening out, the twinkling eyes narrowing.

"Oh, it's okay, I'm not starving," she said, trying to suppress a giggle. "I was just a little hungry." She poured one of the creamers into the coffee and swirled it around with the wooden stirrer he'd brought over. "This coffee is delicious."

"Well, it's not Starbucks or anything," he said, "but it's not too bad." He sat back in his chair and watched her intently as she chewed the bagel and took sips of coffee in between. "You feel better? You looked very sad when you came in."

"Yes. Thank you." Suddenly she felt a wave of shyness, like a little girl getting caught devouring a huge bowl of ice cream. "I, um, I twisted my ankle."

"Ouch," he said. "You want an Advil or something?"

Now he was offering her medicine for her ankle. She couldn't figure out where this angel had come from, but she felt as if he were looking inside her, and it made her feel uncomfortable. She pushed the rest of the bagel away. "No thank you," she said. "It's all right."

"It's no good?" His brow furrowed. "The bagel?"

"Oh, it's fine. I just—I just felt a little embarrassed all of a sudden."

"Please don't," he said. "Go ahead, eat. Sometimes I forget to eat too, and then I wonder why I starve." He laughed, pushing the paper plate with the bagel back until it touched her hand. She couldn't help watching his eyes crinkling with the brilliant smile. She wasn't embarrassed about being hungry—it was about not being able to pay. She took another bite of the bagel, another sip of the coffee.

"So," he said, "what's your name?"

She blushed now, trying to avoid his steady gaze but not succeeding. She'd never in her life spoken so many words to a complete stranger, at least not one from outside her neighborhood. If she forgot herself for a moment, it surprised her that it wasn't even difficult. "Aviva Stern," she said.

"What a pretty name, Aviva," he said. "In my language, that means to revive or to enliven. Maybe you're here to revive me. I'm pretty tired." He laughed. She did too, because she had no idea her name meant anything of the sort. She'd never thought of herself as lively. She'd been told she was named Aviva because she was born in April and her name meant "springtime" in Hebrew.

"What is your first language?" she said.

"Spanish," he said.

"Oh, you are from Spain?" She must have had a surprised expression on her face, because he put his hand up to his face and laughed again. It was hard not to notice how much he laughed.

"No, no," he said. "Not Spain. Can you guess what country I'm from?"

The Yeshiva where she'd been a student for eight years didn't teach anything like geography, but Aviva had frequently snuck out to the library to read secular books, although it was strictly forbidden. She couldn't help herself. She loved to read, especially about other countries and cultures. The community where she lived was so insular, it was fun to dream about exciting places in the world and the people who lived there. She had looked at picture books about Mexico and South American countries. But there were so many of them, she had no idea where he might have been born.

She shook her head. "I'm not sure," she said. "Mexico?"

He shook his head.

"I'm sorry," she said, feeling stupid. "I have no idea."

"Colombia," he said.

"Oh, my," she replied. On her frequent clandestine trips to the library, she'd looked at pictures of coffee plantations in Colombia, and they looked green and lush and beautiful, but she didn't know much about it other than that.

"Now are you going to ask if I'm a drug dealer?" he said, his lips slightly turned up in a bit of a mocking way.

This time it was Aviva who covered her face with her hand. "Oh my goodness, no!" she said. "Why would I ever say that?"

"Well, that's a relief," he said, drawing his hand across his forehead. He never stopped smiling. "And where are you from? You have a little accent."

"Brooklyn," she said. "Williamsburg."

"You were born there?" he continued, pressing her. She felt herself squirm a little. It wasn't that he was mean or that his questions were asked in a mean spirited way, but she suddenly felt very "other."

"Yes, born there."

He raised his eyebrows. He'd been in the country long enough to recognize an accent other than a New York accent, so it hadn't occurred to him that she had been born in the United States. "So your first language isn't English?" She shook her head. "Yiddish," she said.

"How old are you?" he continued, as if it had suddenly occurred to him he should ask.

"Nineteen."

"Oh." He looked down at her left hand, which was gripping the coffee cup. "Is that a wedding ring?" He pointed with his chin toward the plain gold band she never took off.

"Yes."

"That's young to be married," he said.

"I was married a week before my eighteenth birthday," she said, lowering her eyes. Her grandmother had been pressuring her for some time even before that to marry. It wasn't something she'd wished for. It was just expected.

He gasped a little. "Really?" he said. "Wow!"

She wanted to change the subject, to talk about anything else. She'd been married now for a year and a half, but there were no babies—not even a pregnancy ending in miscarriage. Everyone in and outside the family said this was her fault. It seemed to be a popular topic of conversation. It was always the wife's fault. Aviva was sensitive about it—not that she particularly wanted a baby right now, but she knew she was supposed to start having them, and there was definitely a problem. "How old are *you*?" she said, looking him in the eye now, feeling emboldened because she'd answered his questions.

"Twenty-eight," he said. "But my birthday is soon."

"Oh. What is your name?"

"David," he said. "David Delgado."

Aviva brightened, as if some sort of weight had been lifted from her shoulders. So many men in her community were named David. "So—then—are you Jewish?"

Now he threw his head back and laughed out loud—the crows' feet in the corners of his eyes deepening—as if she had made a very funny joke. "Why would you ask that?" he said, once he'd regained his composure.

"Oh, I'm sorry," she mumbled. She felt herself start to blush. "Your name. That's all. That's a name from the Bible. I just thought—"

"No, I'm Catholic," he said.

Aviva couldn't help it—her mouth flew open. She put her hand in front of it.

David continued. "Most people in my country are Catholic. But there are many people named David in my country as well." He winked at her. "Catholics read the Bible too."

"But this place—it's kosher. The sign says." She pointed to the window.

"Yeah," he said. "I'm allowed to work in a kosher place." The small smile never left his lips.

"You make me feel a little—a little stupid," she said.

"Oh, no, no. I didn't mean to." David's mouth turned down for the first time. "Really, I'm sorry. I just joke around a lot. I like laughing better than not laughing. Sometimes it cures—you know, people's sadness." He reached for her hand, which was on the table, but she pulled it away again. "You have very beautiful eyes, Aviva," he said. "They are the deepest green eyes I've ever seen. But they look sad. I hope they laugh sometimes."

Aviva could relate. There was much laughter in her community too, sometimes laughter she couldn't understand. Mostly the men laughed, as they walked about in groups, their fur hats and black wool coats serving as a frame for the long side curls they wore. It seemed to her most of the women were not so jolly. But then, it was up to the women to take care of all the children, to cook, to clean, to serve their husbands' urges whenever their husbands "required" it, to stay mostly at home and to shave their heads and cover whatever hair remained with wigs. Modesty for women was the most important thing, she'd been told, to God. So anything to keep men from feeling sexually aroused the sight of a woman was what a woman had to do.

To Aviva, although it was all she knew, it was definitely not a happy life. Her sister-in-law seemed happy with it, or at least resigned to it, as did her grandmother. Neither approved of Aviva's quest for more knowledge, which they reminded her frequently. So Aviva never told them about her frequent trips to the library. And she knew she would never admit to having traveled here or to talking to a strange man. She knew that would create a huge uproar in the community, that she would be castigated and her husband chastised for having no control over his wife. So this little journey to the Upper East Side of Manhattan and especially the talk with David would remain her secret always. She would cherish it forever, although she knew it could never be repeated.

"Where do you live in Williamsburg?" he asked.

She wondered whether she should tell him, but he was so nice, she decided it couldn't hurt. "South Ninth Street," she said.

"Oh, I've ridden by there on my bike," he said.

"You ride a bike?" She felt her eyebrows go up again.

"All over," he said. "When I first moved here, I rode all over the city because it was fascinating. There are so many different nationalities and cultures living side by side in this city, you know? Very different from my home city. I think it's amazing to look at all of them, to learn about their way of life. It's not really like that so much in Bogotá. You have a bike?"

She laughed. "No, I don't know how to ride one. It's frowned on in my community, especially for women." Before David could ask her why—remind her it was 2018—Aviva glanced up at the clock on the wall. "Oh goodness, I have to leave," she said, pushing her chair out from the table. "It's late." Without realizing it, she'd finished the snack and the cup of coffee. Her stomach had stopped growling.

"Would you like a bagel for the road?" he said, winking again.

"For the road?"

"You know, to take home with you? In case you get hungry on the way?"

She smiled. "No, that's all right. Thank you so much for taking care of me. I feel much better now. I'm sorry I didn't have any money."

He waved her comment off with a gesture. She stood up and started to walk toward the exit, but the ankle pain she had forgotten about as she sat, shot up her leg. "Oh," she said, and bent down to rub it.

"Are you sure you don't want to take something for that?" He bent down too, but the look on her face told him he'd better not touch, so he stood up straight again, putting his hands in his pockets.

"I—um—no, that's okay," she said, standing up but not being able to stifle a little groan. "I couldn't take anything else from you. I'll be all right." She pointed to the bus stop across the street. "I just have to make it over there." She laughed softly.

He pushed the heavy door open and stood over to the side so she could pass through without brushing against him. "I hope you will come back and talk some more," he said, as she limped out. "I enjoyed our conversation. I'd like to know more about you and your people. Are you sure you don't need any help? I could walk you across the street." She shook her head. "I'll be fine," she said.

"Wait—you have money for the bus?"

Aviva put her hand over her mouth. She felt the blush creeping up again. She looked up at him but averted his concerned gaze.

David dug into his jeans pocket and came up with a handful of change, which he thrust into her free hand. "This should be enough for a couple of rides," he said. "You have a long trip home."

Aviva nodded her head without saying a word. She felt like a lost child, but she didn't want to cry. A bus passing in the downtown direction caught her eye. "I'll just take that bus when it comes again," she said. "I'm fine. Thank you for the money. And the food. I—I will pay you back." She walked away from the shop, trying not to limp, not turning to look at him. She wondered whether he was watching her as she went. She had never met anyone like him before. She waited until the walk light came on, and then she made her way carefully across the street.

CHAPTER TWO

David

"Hey, Delgado—you working here, or you gonna moon over that chick all day?"

"Sorry," David said. He kept looking as Aviva disappeared onto the bus, and then he watched it pull away from the stop onto York Avenue. He wondered whether she was looking out the window at him. "Right there."

"You're supposed to work longer than you take breaks, you know, man? Lots of people would love to have this job." He made a clicking noise with his teeth on his tongue.

"Sorry, boss—coming." He backed away from the door and took his place behind the counter. Something about that girl was anchored in his consciousness, and he couldn't stop thinking about her. He couldn't get the vision of her beautiful, sad eyes out of his head, and if he could figure out a way to get her to remove the wig and let him see her without it, he might sell his soul.

"So, you got a crush on that broad?"

David tried to ignore his boss, who wasn't a bad person but was obviously enjoying giving him grief for getting involved with a customer. Luckily, this guy wasn't the owner, but when his boss turned around, David dug out a five-dollar bill from his pocket and put it into the cash register. He wondered whether his boss had seen him giving her the food, whether he'd noticed David hadn't taken any money from her. He needed this job. Life as a struggling musician in this city was enriching for the soul but not for the pocketbook. This job had been a godsend, at least tiding him over until he could somehow get a steady teaching job or establish his band. Right now, they played as much as they could, but it wasn't going to pay the rent. Hopefully, someday it would.

"Did you hear me? You know her?"

David shrugged, shook his head. He really didn't want to get into it. He knew it wouldn't help him to be insubordinate, but he had no intention of being friends with this guy. Come here, do the job, and then go home to Queens to his real passion in life, which was wall-to-wall music.

"Can I help you?" he said to someone who had come in and was looking at the baked goods behind the glass counter.

"Yeah, how about an egg bagel with a schmear," the man said. "Be a little generous with the schmear, okay?" He raised both arms to the side at the same time. David nodded and smiled.

"Toasted?"

The man shook his head. "No, just as is."

David got busy preparing the bagel. "For here or to go?" he asked the man.

"Here." The man pointed toward an empty table.

"Three fifty-nine," he said to the man, who put a ten on the countertop. Blessedly, his boss had gotten busy with another customer, so the one-sided conversation about Aviva had run its course, or so he hoped. But that didn't stop his mind from dwelling on the beautiful young woman who had more than piqued his curiosity.

By the time the store closed, David had rehashed the encounter with Aviva at least a hundred times in his head. The entire thing was absurd. She was married, she came from a completely different world, there was something going on with her he couldn't put his finger on, but the more he thought about it, the more determined he became to see her again. All he had of her were a first and last name, and a street. That was it. He took off his apron and hung it on the hook in the back room.

"You okay, man?" A co-worker came up behind him and slapped him on the back. "You've been awfully quiet today."

"Oh, yeah," he said. "Fine." He laughed, but he knew it was an embarrassed laugh.

"Okay, well, see you tomorrow?"

"Yeah, see you. Chao."

He went out to the street, unlocked his bike, put on his helmet, and headed down York toward the Fifty-ninth Street Bridge. He'd always loved this ride, especially on such a hot day when there was at least a cooling breeze as he rode across the bridge. Usually he would use the ride to think about what he was going to practice that night, or some composition he was working on, or to think about any gig he might be playing in Brooklyn or Queens or Manhattan. No gig tonight. And the only thing on his mind was the girl who had managed, in a very short time, to crawl into his brain and lodge herself there like super glue. When he got home, he couldn't even remember how he'd gotten there. Aviva was the only thing he was thinking about.

"Hey, you want to go to the movies or something?" David's housemate Miguel had come down the stairs as David walked in. "You got anything doing tonight?"

"No, man, but I just want to practice. It was kind of a strange day."

David had just saved enough money to move into his own apartment in the three-story house, which was a relief. Four of them, three musicians and an artist, had been sharing a two-bedroom, before. There were five other apartments in the house, and after David moved out, Miguel, a saxophone player, stayed in the larger apartment on the third floor with Francisco, an artist they called Pancho, and Juan, a guitarist. All four of them were originally from Colombia, now trying to make their way in New York City. Juan had a steady girlfriend, so he was rarely around these days. Pancho had been living here already when the three others found the house, so he wasn't really a good friend, just a roommate.

But Miguel and David had known each other since they'd come to the United States to go to music school. They'd bonded quickly, both coming from rather sheltered lives in good families in Bogotá, not knowing too much English, clinging to one another until each of them felt fluent in the language and comfortable in their surroundings. So they freely shared with each other not only music but also hopes and fears and frustrations and dreams.

"Strange?" Miguel cocked his head, his hand on his hip.

"Yeah. You know anything about those people who live in Williamsburg? Those really religious Jewish people? The ones who wear those odd clothes?"

Miguel laughed. "No, man. I've seen them around, but I don't really know anything about them except that they dress weird and hang around together like a swarm. They talk a different language, too. And they don't seem to go far away from where they live. Why?"

"So, this girl came into the shop today."

Miguel paused at the bottom of the staircase, trying to bend closer to David, as if he wanted his friend to share a deep secret. "Yeah? *Dímelo todo!* Tell me everything!" His mouth curled into a half smile.

David waved him off with a gesture. "No, nothing really to tell. She was just—she's one of them—and I don't know, she seemed pretty sad. Very sad, actually."

Miguel's smile faded quickly. "Oh," he said. "I thought you were gonna tell me something more—interesting." He winked. "Why was she sad?"

David shrugged. "It's like, she told me she just got on the subway and rode and rode, and then she got off and walked for blocks until she saw my shop, and then she was hot and exhausted, and she hurt her leg, and she had no money."

"Whew, slow down," Miguel said. "I'm already feeling sorry for her."

"And she was—beautiful," David continued. "I mean *really* beautiful."

"What's going on with you, man?" He reached out to touch David's shoulder, but David pulled away.

"Nothing," David said, pushing by his friend. Miguel followed him upstairs and into the apartment.

"Doesn't sound like nothing. You gonna see her again?"

"I doubt it," he said, hoping with every part of his being that he *would* see her again, even though it seemed unlikely.

"That's too bad. Sounds like you really liked her."

"She's married."

"Oh, man, what are you getting yourself into?" Miguel walked toward the kitchen. "You better look out. Maybe the husband will come after you with a gun."

"Not getting myself into anything," David said. "I don't even know anything else about her. Never saw her before."

"You want something to drink, or are you going somewhere?" David walked to the refrigerator and opened the door. Miguel reached around him, pulled a bottle of soda out of the refrigerator and started drinking from it.

"Why do you do that?" David said, pointing at his friend. "That's disgusting."

"Why? You think I have cooties?" Miguel laughed. "I thought you didn't drink this stuff anyway. Why do you have it?" Miguel said, taking another large gulp. "So why do you care?"

"Yeah, but it's still disgusting." He was grateful he lived alone now, but that didn't stop the other guys from barging in and acting as if they lived here too. This roommate situation had been fine for the college years, but he was almost thirty, and it was annoying to have to act like the only grownup in the room all the time. He sighed.

Miguel laughed. "Take a chill pill," he said, slapping David on the back and burping as he walked out of the kitchen. "You're too uptight, amigo. Look, I finished it. You don't have to worry about my germs." He dropped the bottle on the kitchen counter, then walked to the apartment door and put his hand on the knob. "Come on, go out with me. We'll get a few drinks—go see a flick? I don't know where everyone else is."

"No, I gotta practice," David answered, relieved his friend was planning on leaving him alone. There was a gig in Brooklyn in two days he hadn't even prepared for, but other than that, he just didn't feel like being the object of anyone's teasing tonight. He knew it was foolish to be mooning over a very young married woman who lived in an isolated community—a complete stranger—who seemed to have a great deal of unhappiness in her life, but his heart wasn't letting go, no matter what his mind dictated. Maybe banging hard on his drum set would relieve some of the feelings, whatever they were, and allow him to move on, get her out of his head.

"Suit yourself, man," Miguel said, "but I bet there are gonna be some great looking chicks out there tonight. You know what I mean." He raised his eyebrows.

David waved him off. Until he managed to stop obsessing about Aviva, the last thing he wanted to do was go trolling for women, although that might take his mind off her for at least a little while. But it wouldn't be fair to the other women. "No, I'm good," he said.

"Suit yourself, amigo! More for me!" Miguel waved and walked out the door.

CHAPTER THREE

Aviva

The apartment didn't look any different. Aviva tiptoed in, but the only sound she heard was silence. Her anxiety had begun to kick in, even before she got off the bus and walked toward her house. Now she felt the perspiration starting to bubble up on the bridge of her nose, and her breathing was fast. She wondered whether her blood pressure was high. The worst thing that could happen would be that her husband Nachum would be here waiting for her, angry, and even worse that his uncle Eli might be with him. Neither was here, though, so she thought she might have dodged a bullet. She'd spent the entire bus ride trying to decide where she'd tell Nachum she'd been. She glanced at the clock on the kitchen wall. Five-thirty. She might have time to throw together some food for dinner. That way, he'd never have to know anything.

The harsh knock at the door made her jump. "Coming," she called out. Whoever it was continued to knock, and the knocking became more intense, even though only seconds had elapsed. Praying it wouldn't be Eli standing there, she walked to the door and opened it halfway.

"Where *were* you, Aviva?" Her sister-in-law Ilona stood there, her face chiseled into a deep frown, her hand on one hip, her foot tapping at the floor. "You were gone for hours! What were you thinking? Nachum came home for his meal, and you were nowhere to be found. I had to bring food for him." She stopped to take a breath, but didn't leave enough time for Aviva to answer. "Are you stupid? What were you thinking?" The foot tapping became harder and more insistent.

"Do you want to come in, Ilona?" Aviva said.

Ilona pushed by her, emphatically shoving her out of the way, and walked into the middle of the apartment. She stood, arms akimbo, looking around at the walls, floors, and ceiling as if this were the first time she'd ever been there. The apartment was neat, but the furniture was dark and shabby, literally coming apart at the seams. Most of it had been donated to them after the wedding by people in the community. Like Aviva, Nachum had very little money. He spent his time studying Talmud with the rest of the young men, while Aviva made minimum wage working at the bakery. She hated it there. It was hot, and she was on her feet the entire time, wishing she could be sitting in the air conditioned library learning about the forbidden things she'd always craved to learn about—history, science, literature. She worried that if their furniture fell apart, they wouldn't have the money to replace it.

"So, I asked you—where were you?"

"I—um—I was walking," she said.

"Malka said she saw you getting off a bus." Malka was another resident of this building, a good friend of Ilona. Aviva didn't like any of them. They all looked down on her with some sort of hatred in their eyes, but when she had mentioned that to her husband, he laughed it off and told her she was just being paranoid.

Aviva cleared her throat. "No, she must be mistaken," Aviva said. "I was walking. I walked a long way."

"Why?"

"Thinking."

"What in the world do *you* have to think about?" the sister-in-law said, making a guttural sound in her throat. "Thinking is bad for you. You just need to do what you're supposed to, and that includes making food for your husband. Is that too much to ask?"

"I'm sorry," Aviva whispered.

"*What*?" Ilona's dark eyes were focused like laser beams on Aviva's own. Aviva lowered her gaze. She raised her voice slightly. "I said, I'm sorry."

"You *should* be sorry. Nachum is a very good man. You're lucky to have him. Your life could have been very bad, if he hadn't been willing to take you. It's a good thing you're a little bit pretty. Otherwise, who knows?" She snorted again.

Take me, Aviva thought. *As if I were a coffee cup or a piece of furniture. Take me.* She felt the tears rising, but she didn't want to cry in front of this woman. Somehow, that would feel like a kind of defeat. As for Nachum, Aviva didn't really know him, whether he was a good man or not. He never really seemed to care to talk to her. He wasn't that good looking, not that that had ever bothered her particularly, although for a moment she allowed herself to think about David, his handsome face with the full lips and beautiful sparkling brown eyes, his room brightening smile, his kind voice and manner. She shook herself to get him out of her head.

And in terms of a physical relationship, both she and Nachum were—well, they were both so unskilled at that activity, it was almost a joke. After all these months of being married, the marriage had still not been consummated.

Nachum wasn't abusive—not like his uncle—but every once in a while, he would point to the bed and make her lie down. Then, without undressing, he would unzip his pants, push up her skirt, and try to have sex, grunting as he did, never being able to hold an erection or penetrate. She would just lie there, silent, and hope it would be over soon. He'd leave her on the bed, her skirt up almost over her head, and walk out of the room, zipping up his fly. Sometimes she cried afterward. Sometimes she was sure she heard him cry. She felt nothing at all except relief when he left her.

Then, when she didn't get pregnant, all the women with their multiple children and their wagging tongues would snicker that there must be something wrong with *her*. Once she'd asked Nachum whether he loved her, but he had just laughed. There was no love in this marriage—never had been, never would be. He'd never even tried to get to know her, to see if he liked her. She wished she had the courage now to bark back at her sister-in-law, but it wasn't worth it. Ilona would just yell louder and tell Aviva what an ungrateful girl she was, how she didn't deserve everything she had. The story never changed, but now it was making her angry. Sometimes it made her feel like ending her life, but some small voice inside kept her from doing that, made her believe that somehow there was a way out of all of this.

"So? Do I have to keep reminding you about your duty to be a good wife? To serve your husband the way you should, not to go strolling around for hours ignoring your obligations? And, let me mention, to provide him with many children." She stressed the word children, making it hang in her mouth for several seconds.

Aviva knew she would never confide in Ilona about anything like what she had experienced today at the bagel shop, or for that matter about what had happened this morning with Ilona's uncle Eli. At times like this, she missed her mother desperately. She still remembered those times when she was a small child, before her father had died, when her mother was there for her, loving, strong, and sweet—before she lost her mind. What Eli had tried to do to her—right in the living room, when he knew no one would be coming to interrupt them—she could hardly think about it without crying. He'd pushed her against the wall, pulled down her underclothes, pressed her shoulders so hard she thought her back would break, and began to force himself on her. She managed to find a cache of super strength, and kicked back at him until she somehow hurt him and he backed off, tripping on the frayed floor mat and cursing. Then he had left her crying and terrified, gripping the wall for support. "So, if *he* can't get you pregnant," he had said as he slammed the door, "you should let me see if a real man can do it. But what do you do? You attack me. You are a stupid girl."

 The only thing that had given Aviva any hope that there was life outside of the confines of these few blocks in Williamsburg where people like her lived, were her clandestine trips to the library whenever she could sneak one in. She'd been going there for years, since her mother had been whisked away—out of sight, out of mind—to Aviva's aunt in Kiryas Joel. After that, she'd hardly ever heard from her mother again, and her aging grandmother—her father's mother—had grudgingly taken on the task of raising Aviva.

 Aviva would sneak away when her grandmother dozed off, especially after the senility began to set in. She'd always loved to read, from the moment she learned how, but in this community, they weren't allowed any "secular" books, only religious ones, and mostly only for the boys at that. Girls "had no need" to read or learn anything, her grandmother had always reminded her. Their righteous role was to be a good and obedient wife and to give birth to many children to "make up for the loss of so many Jews in the Holocaust." Nothing else was ever explained—the concept of love, the concept of pleasurable sex, the concept of self fulfillment— these were left alone like hot potatoes, as if dealing with them would somehow make one a sinner against all of God's laws.

But each time Aviva entered the library, she found those vilified secular books made her feel alive, and with the help of a kind librarian, she first discovered authors like Louisa May Alcott, Laura Ingalls Wilder, L.M. Montgomery, later Jane Austen, Charles Dickens, and the Brontes, and so many contemporary authors who wrote of other times, places, and people. She was torn, because she felt perhaps she was truly evil for wanting more than what her life offered, so when she was approached for marriage by Nachum's family, she decided to acquiesce. Her grandmother was well beyond being able to care for her anymore, and it seemed this was the logical next step. And although she had only met Nachum a few times before the marriage, he seemed like a pleasant enough young man, even though he never had much to say to her.

"Where are your children, Ilona?" Aviva was tired of being scolded. "Did I hear them yelling in the apartment when you opened your door?" She hoped changing the subject would stop Ilona in her tracks. At twenty-seven, Ilona had five children—three boys and two girls. The boys were wild and kept their mother running in circles all the time. It seemed to Aviva that Ilona always looked tired and older than her years.

"My children are just fine, Aviva. Their care is none of your business. Don't change the subject."

"Why do you hate me, Ilona? What did I ever do to you?" She wanted to remind Ilona that she had been willing to marry Nachum, despite his physical challenges—a short, weak leg that had been caused by incorrect treatment of a congenital defect when he was a baby, which gave him a permanent limp. She'd heard some of the other girls gossiping that the only reason Nachum's family had approached her grandmother for her hand, was that none of the other eligible girls would give him a second look. She would never bring that up to his sister, who was fiercely protective of Nachum.

Ilona threw her head back and laughed out loud. "I don't hate you, Aviva. I don't know why you would think that. I just worry about my brother. You don't care for him well and you don't get pregnant. And you should feel like the luckiest girl in the world that someone as good as him wanted to marry you at all."

"I think I care for him fine," she replied, slightly under her breath.

"I heard that," Ilona snorted. "If you care for him so well, then present him with a baby." That said, she turned and headed out the door, with no goodbye. Aviva was relieved to see her go. Ilona's nattering only made Aviva want to run as far away from here as she could, but even imagining that made her feel guilty. It was a vicious circle.

She couldn't remember Nachum ever smiling at her. But through it all, the image of David kept entering her mind, his beautiful smile, his kindness, his friendly concern, even his curiosity. Since her father's death and her mother's banishment, not one person in this community had ever made an attempt to act that way, and yet a total stranger, a Catholic one at that, from South America, had shown her the kindness that she didn't even realize she so desperately craved. She couldn't stop thinking about the handsome young man in the bagel shop with the name from the Bible.

CHAPTER FOUR

David

David tried to get settled with his drums, knowing he needed to practice for the gig that was coming too soon. There was a part of the music he just didn't feel comfortable with yet, especially since his concentration had been sabotaged by thoughts of the beautiful Aviva. He'd only met her today, only talked with her for a short time, but there were certain things he knew—the attraction had been instant, and his concern for what he believed was her deep unhappiness just as fast. Her beautiful sad green eyes, the softness, almost musicality, of her voice, the dimples when she smiled, the round feminity of her body that was apparent even through the dark shapeless clothing that covered her from the neck almost down to the ankles. Everything meshed together to draw him in, to trap him. He'd had relationships before, had even fallen in love a couple of times, but nothing like this had ever happened in the past.

He questioned his sanity. He had nothing in common with her. She was so much younger, ten years. She was married, but so childlike, so naïve, and at the same time carrying a certain kind of sad wisdom. Although he'd never been married, he had had enough experience in the world to feel like a true adult—he'd been well educated in Colombia and then had graduated from a prominent music college in Boston, very far away from his home. She came from an entirely different, cloistered, almost foreign world that existed right in this city, only several miles away. He was also from a different world, but his culture had let go, had allowed him to move to a different continent and explore the possibilities of his freedom. So it was almost as if he had become more native than she.

But something about her—certainly her beauty, but also her sweetness and her vulnerability—made him want to protect her, to guide her, to help her out of a situation he knew hardly anything about, except that it was obviously making her very unhappy. That wasn't all, though. The sexual attraction was as strong as the protective one. He wanted to know what color her hair was—her real hair. He wanted to know what she looked like out of all those clothes. He wanted to kiss her, to smell her, to touch her, to have her touch him back. It didn't matter that she was married. He wanted to make love to her over and over again, in every way imaginable.

He shook his head, hard, banged a drumstick down on the rim of the snare drum, as if the harsh noise might eradicate the thoughts. But they continued to swirl. She was married. Married! Although his family were practicing Catholics, David had never been particularly religious. But he'd always had a strong moral code—don't go after women who weren't available, don't go after friends' exes, don't do anything that you wouldn't want someone to do to you. His parents had raised him like that, and he strongly believed it was the right way to act. But for some reason this circumstance was different.

Aviva hovered beyond his usual ability to intellectualize a situation away. Just thinking about her made his heart beat a little faster. And the worst part was that he had no way of getting in touch with her. She had told him where she lived—the street, even. He could go and stand there, waiting for her to come out of one of the houses, but that was absurd. That's what stalkers did. He certainly wouldn't blend in to the scenery in that neighborhood. People might be freaked out to see a stranger lurking around waiting for—what? It wasn't an option.

His active mind was preventing him from getting any practicing done, so he decided to take a bike ride—somewhere, anywhere. It was a pleasant night, no rain, a little cooler than it had been the past few days, with a calm breeze. He put down the drumsticks and glanced back at his little practice room as he walked out the door, feeling guilty about the paid gig for which he wasn't going to be prepared if he didn't spend some hours learning the music.

"Hi. Nice night," his next-door neighbor said, as David unlocked the bike and put on his helmet. This guy complained constantly about the "noise" coming from David's place, so he'd usually tried to avoid the guy. He turned around and gave a little half wave.

"You giving us a break tonight?" the neighbor continued, his lips curled up slightly in a smile. "No drumming?"

David shrugged, got on the bike and rode down the street. As usual, the Queens streets were busy, active with traffic and buses and people. David snaked around the parked cars, waited at the light for some pedestrians to cross the street. "Thanks," one of them said. David nodded and drove on. He didn't have much of an idea where to go tonight, just wanted to get some physical activity, because he was hoping that might help settle down his thoughts. He wasn't paying much attention to where he was going. He turned left onto Fiftieth and then merged onto Greenpoint Avenue. From there he navigated across the John Jay Byrne Bridge to Brooklyn, and then turned left onto Leonard Street, right onto Driggs Avenue, and then found himself driving up South Ninth Street. *Como una polilla a la llama*, he thought, *like a moth to the flame*. In a sense, he was annoyed with himself for giving in to his intense curiosity, yet on the other hand, he was also satisfied in a smug way that he had.

But once on Aviva's street, David couldn't help notice the almost unnatural quiet. Even in the dusk, he could tell the street was neat, well kept, the bushes trimmed and the lawns mowed. There were hardly any people outside, nor was there more than the occasional car. It was so unlike Queens, where people poured out of little clubs onto the streets and you could hear music coming from everywhere. All the people he saw here were in small groups—maybe four or five—of Orthodox men, their side curls blowing in the breeze under their high fur hats, their long black coats looking incongruous in the summer heat. Even though the sun had mostly set, the temperature was still in the high seventies, and even though there was a wind, the air was muggy and heavy. He didn't know how those men could stand wearing all that clothing. He looked down at his shorts and tee shirt and felt grateful he didn't have to dress in dark wool in the middle of the summer.

Whatever had possessed him to come here made him drive up and down the length of the street two or three times, trying not to look as if he were peering into the windows of the houses, which he was. Anyway, they were too far back from the street for him to see anything except shadows. He wondered where she was, which house was hers. In his heart of hearts, he longed for her to come out the door of one of them, but he was quite sure that wasn't going to happen. He didn't see any women on the street at all. He even had a fleeting impulse to ask one of the men passing by whether they knew her, but something told him not to. That it might get her in trouble. He felt like a school kid with a teenage crush. After a half hour or so, he turned around and drove home the same way he'd come.

"Hey, where you been?" Miguel had beat him home and was sitting outside on the porch.

"What happened?" David said. "No hot girls?"

Miguel shrugged. "All the skanks were out tonight," he said, laughing. "Where you been?" he repeated.

"Just riding around, bro," David said.

"Thought you had to practice?" Miguel raised an eyebrow. "For that gig?"

David put both arms out and shrugged, as if to say, "Whatever."

"So we're two fuckin' losers," Miguel said, laughing again.

"You got that right," David said, thinking about Aviva's beautiful eyes and the promise of a sexy body under all the shapeless clothing.

"Want to come in for a beer?" David pointed his thumb toward the house.

"Sure, why not." Miguel followed him upstairs and helped himself to a beer from David's refrigerator.

The two men stood in the kitchen drinking in silence.

CHAPTER FIVE

Aviva

Aviva took off the wig, wiping off her skin where she had been perspiring under its weight. Then she took all her clothes off. The house was very warm. They had window fans, but no air conditioning. They hadn't had the money to buy window units, and Ilona wasn't willing to loan them one of hers. "You can come over my place and sit for a while if it gets too hot in there," she'd said. "My kids need the cool." So frequently in the heat of the summer, it was so hot, it was hard to sleep, but Aviva preferred dealing with the heat over subjecting herself to her sister-in-law.

She stood naked in front of the mirror in her bedroom, staring at herself from the top down. The hair on her head was coming back nicely in thick blonde spikes. Her hair was a little wavy, and it had a lot of body. When she was young, and it was so blonde it was almost white, people had always commented on how beautiful it was. One of these days, she knew, Ilona would be over here with the clipper, demanding to shave off what had grown in, but Aviva had already made up her mind. She wasn't going to shave her head again. And if the hair grew too long to cover with the wig, she was determined to rebel against the hateful thing.

She'd put it down on her dressing table haphazardly, secretly hoping it might fall off and get damaged, which would never happen. She picked it up and smelled it. It smelled musty and awful. She made a face and dropped it on the table again. She played with the hair that had grown in. At this moment, she was in love with her hair, and she would never let anyone shave it again, even if it grew down to her ankles. She didn't even realize she was humming a tune.

She continued to look at her nakedness. Her breasts were high and full, her waist very small, her bottom round but not fat, and her legs long and shapely. She had nothing to compare it to, but she was fairly sure she had a pretty body. She ran her hands down the front, from her neck down to her pubis, and watched as the nipples hardened. She wondered what it would feel like to explore her vagina, how it would look inside there, but she was never brave enough to experiment. That had always been forbidden territory, her grandmother warning her that if she touched herself down there, very bad things would happen. Her grandmother had never elaborated. But Aviva had been too terrified to try.

Nachum was still studying, out with the other men. It wasn't really that late, but Aviva was exhausted from the heat and her very long walk. She hoped she'd be fast asleep by the time he got home, so that she didn't have to have sex with him. Even if he got home before, she would pretend to be fast asleep. It wasn't like him to wake her for sex. He seemed to dislike it almost as much as she did, which confused her. No one really spoke about sex in their community, other than saying you had to do it to get children. But she had read books in the library, as many as she could get her hands on, and more of them than not described wonderful sex scenes that were exhilarating and felt good, for both the man and the woman. This was definitely not the case with her and Nahum. He didn't seem to like to touch her, or at least he never really did. Nor did he ask her to touch him. She was never undressed when they had sex, nor was he. He'd undo the front of his trousers and motion for her to lie down and pull up her skirt. Frequently, he simply couldn't get an erection, so he just rolled off her and went to sleep. Those times were the best for her. Other times, he might ejaculate, making a sticky mess that she hated, all over her legs and clothing. Or, he might get an erection, only to lose it immediately.

Every so often, her mind wandered back to the bagel shop and the handsome young man with the beautiful smile who had been so kind to her. Tomorrow she would finish her morning chores quickly, and then sneak off to the library while Ilona was distracted taking care of all her kids. She wanted to know everything about the country Colombia—where it was, what the people did there, how they lived, how they enjoyed themselves. She wondered whether they were all as handsome and sweet as David. She would continue her geography studies with an in-depth look into David's country. Now that she'd met him, she was hungry to know about the place where he was born. She wondered whether God would seek retribution against her for her sinful thoughts. She tried to slough off her worry. What had she done? Talked to a young man who'd helped her when she needed help, that's all. What was so sinful about that? Nothing. Except she knew her grandmother and Ilona would feel differently.

She slipped her nightdress over her head and sank into the bed. As tired as she was, she tossed and turned for close to an hour. She couldn't fall asleep. Everything that had happened today swirled through her head. Wasn't it more sinful what Nachum's uncle Eli had wanted to do to her? He had warned her not to tell anyone, warned her that terrible things would happen to her if she did, that he would poison the family against her, shame her until she wanted to die. She felt so embarrassed, she wasn't sure she'd *ever* be able to tell anyone about it. She was a nobody in this community, with no family to back her up. He, on the other hand, was an important man with a great deal of power.

She was, however, determined it would never happen again. If she had to kill him, she would never again let him near her, never let him touch her. Before she'd run away on her expedition to the Upper East Side, she'd spent forty-five minutes in a hot shower, scrubbing herself raw to get Eli's smell and touch off her body. The thought of what he'd done to her still made her feel like retching. She knew it was something she would never forget.

She was still awake when Nachum got home and walked into the bedroom. He wasn't a terrible person. That much she had to admit. He certainly wasn't abusive like his uncle. He was mildly pleasant to her most of the time. It was just that she had the distinct feeling he didn't really like her, or at least that he didn't care one way or another, which was almost harder to take. But he seemed to be supportive of her learning to cook, and he sometimes thanked her for the meals she made him. He also told her he appreciated her bringing home leftover bread and cake from the bakery on the days she worked. But she couldn't remember their ever having a serious conversation about anything. She didn't know whether he cared about politics, or if he did, what his political views were. At the library, she sometimes read the news magazines, so she had some knowledge of the government, although she found it a little confusing. She knew that if Nachum was troubled or worried about something, he always ran across the hall to Ilona's apartment to talk to her, never to Aviva.

She often thought—wished—he should talk to her as a partner, discover that she was an intelligent person with something important to say. Then, maybe he would like her better. But that never seemed to happen. Over dinner, he always sat with his books open, spread in a semicircle around his plate, so their mealtimes were silent except for his noisy chewing and asking for more food or coffee or an extra napkin.

She didn't like her part-time job at the bakery very much, but at least it gave her a chance to be with other people—to talk to them—and it helped pay the bills. There was no way she could tell ever tell Nachum what his uncle Eli had done to her. She knew over and above the threats Eli had made, neither Nachum, Ilona, nor anyone else in their family would believe a word of what she said. And Eli was such an important man in the community, she couldn't even go to the rabbi.

"Are you awake?"

Nachum was standing close to her side of the bed, looking down at her. She wasn't sure whether she should answer him, but his tone was rather urgent, so she decided not to act as if she were asleep. "Yes, why?" she said, trying to sound drowsy.

"Could I talk to you?"

"Okay," she said. Something in his voice frightened her. She pushed herself up, and her head jammed against the headboard. A shooting pain lodged in the back of her skull, and she was almost relieved to have something else to think about beside what he was going to scold her with. "Is anything the matter?"

"Ilona told me," he said, clearing his throat, "that Malka down the hall saw you getting off a bus today. She said she saw you get on it, and then hours later, she saw you get off it. Did you go to work today?"

Aviva was wide awake now. It infuriated her that the neighbors took it on themselves to spy on people. Now both Ilona and Nachum had indicted her just for getting on a bus. What business was it of Malka's? She was a nosy, annoying woman, constantly distraught about her seven children, who shouldn't waste her time butting into other people's business. "No, it wasn't me."

"Did you go to work?"

"No, I was off today. It's my day off." She sighed. "Is that all right with you? That I have a day off? Or would you like Malka to follow me around? Let her crazy children raise themselves?"

He ignored her crack but wasn't taking no for an answer. "Are you sure it wasn't you, Aviva? She knows you pretty well. Certainly well enough to recognize you." He shook his head from side to side. Aviva felt like a small child being yelled at for stealing a cookie.

"Why does she even care where I go? And why is she reporting my supposed whereabouts to Ilona?" Aviva said. She felt her face draw into a frown. "If she has a problem with me, she should come to me."

"You shouldn't be going off on the bus like that. Didn't you have housework to do?"

"Does it look as if I didn't finish my housework?" she grumbled.

He shook his head.

"Then why are you angry at me? Why am I the villain here? You're my husband. You are supposed to take my side. But you never do. It feels like you and Ilona spend your lives trying to catch me doing something wrong." Despite her desire to remain unemotional, the words began to spill out, as if she had no control over them. Then she started crying.

"Are you crying because you feel guilty?"

Aviva's eyes had adjusted to the light he'd switched on. He was standing with his hands on his hips, as if she were a bad little girl and it was his job to correct her. "I have nothing to feel guilty about. I'm crying because I don't know why you hate me."

"Oh, Aviva," he sighed, "I don't hate you."

"What *do* you feel about me? You have never said. I know you don't like me."

Nachum sighed. "You're my wife. I married you. Maybe if you wouldn't go galavanting around, you might manage to get pregnant." He slapped the side of his head with his hands and limped out of the room. Aviva felt her entire body tense up, felt her breathing quicken.

"How can I get pregnant if you—" He either didn't hear her or was ignoring her. "It's not magic." He turned and walked toward the bathroom, waving his hand in the air as if he were dismissing her. It didn't matter really. She wanted to scream, but she knew it was probably a waste of time being angry. Anyway, she was just happy to get rid of him. In any event, she wasn't in the mood to get into a serious argument with him right now. She was too tired, and he always made sure he had the last word before storming away, so there was no use. She turned off the light and rolled over on her side, her back facing the door.

If he came back, she would pretend to be asleep, whether or not she was.

Every time she started to drift off, a noise would make her start, and she would flash back to Eli's unwelcome visit. She even had a nightmare about him and woke up shaking. It made her cry and laugh at the same time that she couldn't escape the horror, even in her dreams. Nachum slept deeply all night, snoring lightly. The snoring didn't usually bother her, but tonight, it made her angry that she had to lie here and listen to it. Anyway, it was competing with the two fans whirring in the bedroom windows, and it annoyed her that the rhythm was off.

As the first ray of sunlight peeked through the old Venetian blinds, she crept out of bed, showered, dressed, and went into the kitchen to prepare breakfast.

"You were up awful early," he said, after he'd gotten ready in his traditional three-piece suit, the *tzitzit*[1] peeking out from under the vest.

"I couldn't sleep," she said.

"Why?"

She shrugged and turned her back to him as she went to the stove to get the coffee pot.

"What are you doing today?" he said.

"Going to the bakery to work," she replied. He never remembered which days she worked, although they never varied. This was yet something else she regarded as lack of respect. He didn't have time for her trivial life. Nor did he care much, although she was the only one bringing money into the household. "I work the same days every week."

---

[1] Tzitzit are the knotted fringes worn on traditional or ceremonial garments by Orthodox Jewish men, per Biblical references in Deuteronomy and Numbers.

He put a forkful of eggs into his mouth. "These eggs are too well done."

"I'm sorry," she said. She actually wasn't that sorry. She wondered whether she unconsciously wanted to have a way to get back at him, mostly for his crimes of omission, also for his uncle, although to be fair, she didn't think he had any idea what his uncle had tried to do to her. She also knew he was still angry at her because of what Malka had reported to Ilona. Anyway, she had no desire to argue with him. "I'll try to get it better the next time."

"After all this time, you should know how I like them," he muttered under his breath.

"What are *you* doing today?" She knew full well he'd be on his way to the study hall to study Talmud. It's what he did every single day, at least after *shul*[2].

He looked up at her, a piece of scrambled egg hanging precariously from the corner of his mouth. "You know what I'm doing," he said, returning to the plate of food.

"Do you need anything else from me? I want to get to work."

"It's seven-thirty, Aviva," he said, his fork midway between the plate and his mouth. "When does the bakery open?"

"Not until nine, but they're training me to make the dough, and that starts very early." This was a bald-faced lie. Aviva's job was to stand behind the counter and serve customers. That was because she was one of the few young women who worked there who knew how to make change without making mistakes. She'd asked whether she could learn how to make the dough, but her boss had told her that wasn't going to happen. She was way too valuable at the front of the store, to prevent the bakery from losing money. Today, however, her only desire was to get out of the apart-

2 The synagogue.

ment before Nachum, so she wouldn't be alone here, in case Eli had any thoughts of visiting again. She shuddered, and then hoped Nachum hadn't noticed.

"You're not going to clean up the dishes and the kitchen before you go?"

"I'll do it when I get home," she said.

"I guess that's all right," he sighed.

She planned to leave here and see if her boss would let her in the bakery, even though she wouldn't have anything to do until the first customers arrived. She'd tell them she didn't have to get paid for the extra time. Maybe they'd let her watch them make the dough.

"Aren't you eating?"

She was not very hungry yet, although she figured she would be ravenous a couple of hours from now. There was always something to eat at work—overdone bread or misshapen cookies that couldn't be sold. She wouldn't starve.

"I just don't have an appetite," she said. "I'm going to leave now, if you're all set."

"I guess so," he said. "Whatever." There was no sign of affection or curiosity in his voice. It was its normal dispassionate monotone. She was sure that when she returned, all of his dirty dishes and the remainder of his breakfast would still be sitting on the table. It was as if he had no concept nor did he feel obligated to help out with anything. That's just the way it was here. It wasn't that he was evil or nasty, but men simply didn't do those "homely" things. That was all "women's work." She thought if he ever put his dishes in the sink, she might faint dead away. She giggled to herself.

"Something funny?" he said.

"No, it's nothing," she said. "I'll see you later."

"Yeah," he said.

She walked out of the apartment, looking up and down the hallway before she felt comfortable leaving. If Eli were anywhere around, she wasn't sure how she'd react. But the hallway was empty. No sign of him. She took a deep breath. It was the first time today she'd felt comfortable even breathing.

CHAPTER SIX

David

The gig went okay, but even though the audience didn't seem to notice, David felt a little embarrassed because he knew he could have done better. He just hadn't been able to get his head around learning all the music as well as he liked to. He was too preoccupied with Aviva, thinking about her, wondering why she'd been so sad at the shop. After the show, the band hung around the bar drinking some beers and schmoozing, and a couple of women came over and looked very interested in hooking up with him. One of them, a cute brunette, rubbed up against him and put her hands everywhere she thought he'd react. He pushed her off.

"Sorry, not in the mood tonight," he said. Even the beer didn't taste right.

"Well, *be* that way," she snorted, flicking her bright red fingernail on his chin. "I don't need you either." She started on one of the other band members, who was much more receptive.

David had hoped Aviva might come back to the shop, but he was getting teased there because he went to the window to look out every time he had a free moment. Several days had passed since their meeting, but he was still trying to be hopeful about seeing her again.

"Your girlfriend dump you?" one of his coworkers chided him as they took a break one day. "Why don't you give her a call?"

"I don't have her number," he said, his head in his hands. "I just have this feeling there's something wrong. She's in trouble." He ran his hand through his hair.

"Why? Because she's not drooling all over you?" He laughed, spurting some coffee out the corners of his mouth. "Your head is getting so swelled, you're gonna have trouble walking out the door."

"No, you don't understand," David said. He waved the man off with his hand. "Anyway, she's not my girlfriend." The guy pointed at David and laughed. But no one could understand his seeming obsession with her, the least of all, he himself. The next day, his day off, he decided to take another bike ride to Williamsburg and see if he could find her. She'd said she worked in a bakery there, although she hadn't mentioned which one, and he suspected there were at least a few in her neighborhood. No matter, he'd ask people on the street or even go from one to the next if he had to, until he found her.

It felt a little strange to David, in his shorts and sandals, being in the midst of Aviva's community. Most people ignored him, but he got curious looks from others. He tried to hide behind his dark glasses, but that was a little silly. It was obvious he didn't belong here. He found a small bakery right away and walked in. The girl behind the counter looked a little embarrassed, staring down at her feet as he stood there, shuffling back and forth.

"Can I help you?" she finally said.

"I'm looking for someone. Wondering whether you know her? Or if she works here?"

The girl raised her eyebrows. Now she looked him up and down, tilting her head to one side. "Who?" she said.

"Aviva?"

The girl laughed. "There are quite a few Avivas," she said. "Do you know her last name?"

David cleared his throat. He was on a detective mission with the scantiest of information. "Aviva Stern."

The girl shook her head. "I'm here two years, and no one by that name has worked here since I've been here."

"Are there other bakeries in the neighborhood?"

Now her face seemed to darken. "What do you want with this girl?" she said, looking him up and down. He noticed that she was wearing a wig and a hairband too, similar to the one Aviva wore.

"Nothing, she stopped in at my shop, and—um—she left something," he lied. "I wanted to return it to her. That's all." Stupid thing to say, he thought to himself, but it was the only thing that had popped into his head on the spur of the moment.

"You mean Jewish bakeries?" she said.

David nodded. He didn't want to give her any more information, especially because he really didn't have any to give.

"There's a couple," she said. She pointed down the street, gave him the names of two others.

"Thank you so much!" he said, smiling broadly. Then he worried he was making too much of it, but just knowing Aviva could be in one of those places excited him. "Sorry to bother you."

"No bother," she said, turning away from him to go back

to her counter duties. But he was sure he felt her gaze burning into the back of his head as he walked out of the store.

It hadn't specifically occurred to him until now, but he laughed as he got back on his bike at the fact they both worked in bakeries. At least they had something in common. He tried two more bakeries in the area with the same lack of success. Part of him thought it was silly to pursue this, whatever it was. Another part of him wouldn't let him stop. He made a pact with himself that if she wasn't at the next one, he'd ride back to Queens and forget about her.

The fourth bakery was small, an old-fashioned looking shop with a worn and tattered, green and white canopy over the front window. He parked and locked the bike, and approached the place, shielding his eyes against the sun, which was blazing down as he looked in. There were two women standing behind the counter, but, alas, neither of them was Aviva. He walked in anyway. *Nothing to lose*, he thought. He decided to start the conversation, because he was tired of being stared at. He'd give them something to think about.

As he pushed open the heavy door, the aroma of fresh-baked goods seemed to circle his head. The smell was delicious. It didn't match his nervousness. "I'm looking for someone who might work here," he said. At this moment, he was the only customer in the store. The two women looked up. The older one spoke.

"Why?" she said.

David thought that was a strange question, and he hadn't been prepared for it. The woman stared straight at him. "I—um—I heard she worked here," he said. It was obviously a lie, and he felt his face flush hot. He hoped he was far enough away for them not to notice. He hadn't answered the question. "Her name is Aviva," he said, quickly, trying to make it seem like a normal statement. He knew immediately from the looks on both their faces that he'd hit paydirt. "Does she work here?"

At that moment, as if his words had evoked her appearance, Aviva came out from the back of the shop, carrying a large tray of pastries, balancing it carefully as she walked. The tray looked heavy. David wished he could jump back there and help her, but he stood still, his hands buried deep in his shorts pockets. She looked up and saw him, and for a moment, he was sure she was going to lose her balance and drop the tray. Her hands were shaking, and all the color drained from her face as she gasped. The other young woman turned and somehow managed to save the tray and put it down safely on the counter, as Aviva seemed almost paralyzed, her eyes unfocused. For a minute or so, no one spoke. David felt as if time had stopped. He was sweating, but it wasn't only from the heat. He wiped his brow on his sleeve.

"Aviva!" he said, but then he was sorry he'd spoken at all. She still looked unsteady on her feet. "I—um—I just wanted to buy something here. One of those." He pointed to the tray she'd just brought in. "I heard the pastry here is delicious."

"Do you know this gentleman?" The older woman spoke each word as if it were followed by a period.

Aviva shook her head. "Not really."

"He asked for you by name."

"Just an acquaintance," she whispered.

"Well, go ahead then. Sell him what he wants." She wiped her hands on her white apron. "I have to go in the back and see about the rest of the bread dough," she said. She walked off, raising her eyebrows at David, who continued to stand there with his hands in his pockets shuffling back and forth from foot to foot. The other young woman put her hands over her mouth and giggled. To David, she looked even younger than Aviva. Then, as if she knew she wasn't wanted there, she turned and walked toward the back room.

"What are you doing here?" Aviva whispered after a moment.

"I—I was worried about you," he said, speaking almost as softly as she.

"Why?"

"You were so unhappy when you came to my shop. And you had no money. And your leg was injured." He tried to peer over the counter to see if she was limping, but he couldn't see anything.

"I'm okay," she said, looking down at the tray of pastries.

David pulled out his wallet. "Give me two," he said.

For some reason, that seemed to break the ice, and Aviva giggled a little. "Two what?" she said. The tray had four or five different varieties of cake.

"You pick them," he said. "If you sell them to me, I will like them."

Aviva shook her head, at the same time plucking one lemon and one blueberry confection off the tray and wrapping each one separately before putting them into a white bag. "You like fruit?"

"Who doesn't like fruit?" he said.

"How did you find me?" she continued, handing the bag to him over the counter.

"How much do I owe you?"

Aviva shook her head. "No, this time it's on me," she said, smiling as if she'd discovered a new phrase and hadn't had the opportunity to use it until now, which was true.

"No, I couldn't," he said. "You might get in trouble."

She touched the old fashioned cash register, which made a zing sound and then a ding sound. The drawer opened, but she closed it quickly. "I won't get in trouble. This is to pay you back for your kindness the other day."

David shrugged. It was the first time he'd seen her really smile. "I was only doing what anyone would do," he said. He turned, scanning the small room with raised eyebrows. "No place to eat this here?" he said.

"I'm sorry, this is much smaller than your place." The smile faded from her lips.

"No worries," he said. "I don't want to complicate your life anyway." He pointed with his chin toward the back room. "Seems as if they keep a watchful eye over you."

She shrugged. "I guess so," she whispered more than said.

David hesitated, passing the bag from one hand to the other. "I should be going," he said. She nodded. As he backed away and walked toward the door, he turned his head toward her. "Any chance I might see you again?" he said. This time he was whispering. Aviva threw her hand over her mouth. She didn't say a word.

"Are you coming or going?" A woman was pushing on the door. "I'm in a hurry," she said.

"I'm sorry," David said, moving over to one side. He gave a little wave to Aviva, who bowed her head as if to acknowledge it. Then he lowered his head to sniff the bag she'd given him with the pastries. "This smells so good," he said.

"Can I help you?" Aviva said to the woman.

David slipped out the door. Once he was outside, he paused and looked back into the window one more time before he walked to his bike.

CHAPTER SEVEN

Aviva

Aviva tried to act as if it was a normal day, but her mind kept wandering to David. She made mistakes, giving one customer change for a twenty when the woman had given her a ten. The customer was honest.

"Honey, you gave me too much back," she said. Aviva flushed red, her hand springing across her mouth. Aviva's boss looked up, the little frown lines across the bridge of her nose marching to attention. She walked over to Aviva.

"Is everything all right?" she said to the customer.

"Fine," the woman replied. "She just made a small mistake with the change. All set now, no problem." The woman left the shop with her bread.

"You haven't been right since that man was in here this morning," Aviva's boss said to her. "I never saw you make incorrect change before. What's going on with you?"

"Nothing," Aviva said, but she knew that was not much more than a lie.

"Well it's something," the woman said. "Who is he?"

"I'm sorry, I'll do better. He's no one."

Her boss shook her head and moved back to the other side of the counter. "You'd better, Aviva. This is a business."

For the rest of the day, Aviva tried to force herself to think only of her job, and not of David. It was amazing he'd found her, amazing he'd come here at all. She knew she'd been thinking about him, but she was shocked he had been thinking about her. She was sure, however, that she would never see him again, so every time his face flashed through her mind, she tried to shake it away and pay attention to the customers, placing a rubber band on her wrist—something she remembered from her childhood that her mother used to do when she was anxious—and snapping it every time she thought of David, which was often. Luckily, it was a fairly busy day, so she didn't have much freedom to daydream. When it was time for her to take her thirty-minute lunch break, she noticed her wrist had a round circle of red skin, and it was beginning to sting. *Perhaps that is God making me atone for thinking of David so much*, she rationalized, snapping the rubber band again as she ate the sandwich she'd brought.

On the way home from work, she wondered whether Nachum would be able to tell she'd been having thoughts of another man. Of course he wouldn't. He never paid enough attention to her to know any of the emotions she might be having. Aviva had fretted about that frequently. Today, she was almost grateful that her husband was so distant.

She walked into the apartment, which was empty and silent, and removed half a leftover chicken from the refrigerator. She planned to cut it up and make chicken salad for dinner. It was too warm to cook tonight, so she'd chop celery and onions into the chicken, add some oil and vinegar, and serve it over lettuce leaves. She was proud of her creativity. Ilona had brought over two cupcakes that her kids hadn't eaten, so dinner would be fine. She enjoyed preparing food. It gave her something interesting to do. Dusting and sweeping the apartment was definitely not interesting, but if she missed a day, Nachum would always notice. She heard the door click open and continued working on the meal. Nachum was home early. That was nice. She jumped when the voice addressing her wasn't Nachum's.

"So, pretty little wife, making dinner? But your husband is very busy studying. He told me to tell you he will be two hours late tonight." Eli had walked up behind her and put a hand on her shoulder. Then the hand slid down her side, and he tried to slip it between her arm and her body. She held her arms tight to her sides, but suddenly, her fingers lost all of their strength. She watched as the knife she'd been using to cut the chicken slipped out of her hand and crashed onto the linoleum, bouncing and splattering oil and chicken blood in its path. Time slowed, and it felt to Aviva as if minutes were passing, not seconds. She wanted to scream, to run, but her throat was closed and her feet cemented to the floor.

With his other hand, Eli began lifting her skirt from the back. He'd become completely silent, breathing heavily. She wanted desperately to look into his eyes, to communicate in some way that this was evil, that she was angrier than she'd ever been. But he was behind her, and he was strong. "Let me show you who's a man, not that sissy nephew of mine. He can't even get you pregnant. I can show you what a real man is."

He started to push her against the counter, and the drippings from the chicken that had splattered there began to seep into her blouse, dying it a yellowish pink. He was holding her so tightly that the edges of the counter were digging into her breasts, causing searing pain. She kept eyeing the knife on the floor, but there was no way she could extricate herself from his strong grip to retrieve it. She fantasized picking it up and plunging it into his body. So what if she went to jail. It would be worth it.

As he began to pull down her stockings and her panties, suddenly she got her voice back. The scream that emanated from the depths of her being was raucous and shrill. The word "no" escaped from her lips. It shocked him, and for an instant he loosened his grip on her and let go. He was stronger, but she was much faster. She jerked herself out from under his hands, bent down to scoop up the knife, and despite being hog-tied by her underwear, got to the door, her stockings around her ankles, her skirt disheveled, her wig displaced so that it sat on her head at a strange angle. She opened the door and continued to scream, holding up the knife, because she knew he'd follow quickly to try to shut her up.

He did follow to the doorway, but when she continued to brandish the knife, he zipped up his pants and walked out the door and down the hallway. All of this took less than five minutes, but time had become slow motion for Aviva, and it might as well have been five hours. Then Ilona opened her door and stuck her head out.

"What in the world do you think you're doing?" she called. "Are you crazy? You're going to scare everyone on this floor. What's wrong with your clothes?"

Never letting go of the knife handle, Aviva bent over and pulled up her underwear. She said nothing. Eli, who had ducked into the stairwell, now came walking back toward Aviva's apartment door, as if he'd just arrived.

"What's going on here?" he said, looking over at Ilona but then back to Aviva, the corners of his mouth turned up. "Did something happen? Did I hear a scream?"

"I have no idea, Uncle," Ilona said, sighing. "This girl is very strange." She sighed again. "I keep thinking maybe she'll end up like her mother." She lowered her head and shook it slowly, as if to mock a show of pity.

Eli walked past Aviva, making sure to leer at her. At Ilona's door, he said, "I agree with you. She is going to end up insane like her mother. I'm sure of it. She definitely has mental problems." The two of them stood there, watching, as Aviva struggled to put herself together. She didn't know whether she'd be able to talk, but she decided she had to.

"He's the one with the mental problems," she said, after she had managed to regain her composure a little. It was amazing that no one else had come out of their apartments. Aviva realized with a jolt that she was completely unsafe here. Eli had the key. Ilona would never protect her. They would report to Nachum that his wife was a mental case, just like her mother. And not a soul would come to her aid.

"What in the world are you talking about, Aviva?" Ilona said, one hand on her hip. There was yelling coming from her apartment, the kids acting as they usually did. Ilona didn't pay attention to the noise.

"He tried to—," Aviva screamed, feeling more tears welling up in the corners of her eyes. She hadn't realized she had so many tears.

"Tried to *what*? You *are* crazy, my ridiculous sister-in-law. You are living in a delusion. What is wrong with you?"

Aviva had stood up straight now and was facing the two of them, still holding the knife. "Don't you dare ever touch me again, you bastard," she snarled, her voice lower now. She said the words, but she wondered how she could protect herself in the future. Today she'd gotten lucky. What if she were asleep in bed, and he let himself in with the key?

Nachum was often out late, and she seriously wondered whether Nachum would even protect her if he were here. But she knew, of course, that Eli wouldn't try anything if Nachum were home.

Eli shook his fist at her and said, "*Shteyner zol zi hobn, nit kayn kinder.*"[3] The two of them laughed at Aviva, as she stood there at her door, disheveled and furious.

"Come, Uncle," Ilona said, pulling him by the elbow and sputtering with laughter, "that girl is never having any babies at all, is she?" Then, her voice dripping with honey, "Please come in and have some coffee and cake. I'm sorry this girl is acting like a lunatic. We will have to tell my brother, her husband, this can't go on. But I'm not sure what he can do. For now, just come and sit with me." As the two of them made their way into Ilona's apartment, she turned back and shook her index finger at Aviva. "I'm telling Nachum he has to fix you," she spit. "You have to stop acting like a lunatic." Then she slammed the door and was gone.

Aviva sighed. She walked back into her own apartment and closed and locked the door. She dragged a heavy chair from the living room and managed to jam it under the doorknob. When Nachum finally got home and couldn't get in, she knew he'd bang on the door, and only then would she remove the chair. She couldn't breathe until she took a shower and washed the taint off her body, but even scrubbing as hard as she could didn't remove the feeling of his hands on her. It nauseated her.

After the hot shower, she wrapped herself in her long bathrobe and went back into the kitchen, but the thought of preparing food made her gag. If Nachum was angry there was

---

[3] A Yiddish curse that means, "She should have stones and not children."

no dinner prepared, so be it. She scooped up the chicken into a plastic container and shoved it haphazardly into the refrigerator. Then she sponged the counter and the floor clean with bleach, as if Eli's taint had implanted itself in those places. She wasn't sure she'd ever be able to eat chicken again. Then she ran her fingers through the still-wet hair that was beginning to grow out, sat down at the dining table, and put her head in her hands. Finally, she allowed herself to cry freely. It wasn't a loud cry, but the tears flowed until her hands were wet and salty. She was heaving sighs that made her feel as if she couldn't breathe. There was really nothing else she could do. She hoped Eli would stay away now—if he'd gotten the message—but she had no reason to believe she'd scared him off for good. A chair under the doorknob was anything but a permanent solution.

She couldn't get over the thought that Eli had keys to her place and Ilona's, and that one night when she was in bed and Nachum was still out studying, Eli would sneak into her house and attack her again. She determined to keep a long knife in the drawer of the night table, but the man was strong. There was no good way to ensure she'd be safe, no way to ensure he wouldn't turn the knife on her. She supposed she could run away to Kiryas Joel[4], to her aunt's house, but her aunt didn't have much money—was always on the brink of destitution. Aviva understood her aunt was financially stretched just caring for Aviva's mother and her own large family. She wouldn't want an extra mouth to feed. Besides, Nachum or some of the men from the *shomrim*[5]

---

4   Kiryas Joel is a community about an hour north of New York City, founded by a rabbi in the 1970s as a home town for Satmar Hasidic Jews who had outgrown the small area in Williamsburg, Brooklyn where they had mostly settled.

5   A volunteer neighborhood watch group who protect ultra-Orthodox Jewish communities in the United States and many other countries.

would track her down and try to force her to come back. She was sure of it. And if she even thought of calling the NYPD, it was likely they would defer to the Hasidic patrols, at least that's what she'd heard. Aviva had never felt so trapped.

She wasn't paying attention to the passage of time, but she finally got up and went into the bedroom. Physically, she was too keyed up to be tired, but emotionally she felt as if the only escape would be into sleep. She turned out the light and lay down on her bed, but sleep escaped her. As much as she tried not to, she couldn't help running the incident with Nachum's uncle through her head over and over. Each time the memory of his hand on her body ran through her brain, she gagged and felt like retching. After an amount of time that she wasn't sure of, she decided the only way to fight back was to tell Nachum everything. If her husband was willing to believe her and protect her, she decided she would make the decision to stay and fight. At the moment, there was no other option.

She must have dozed off, because she dreamed someone was banging on the door, but when she awoke the banging was real, and she heard Nachum's raised voice coming from the hallway.

"Aviva, what is going on? Open this door right now!"

Aviva stumbled out of bed, too groggy to remember to turn on the light or to put on her slippers. "Just a minute," she called out as she pulled the chair out from under the doorknob. The heavy wooden chair leg jammed into her foot, and she cried out in pain. Finally she managed to free the door, but her foot was throbbing so much she could feel her heartbeat in it.

"What the hell?" Nachum pushed his way by her. She had bent down to rub her foot, but at least that had awakened her. "What do you think you're doing? Is there anything to eat? I'm starved. I didn't realize it was so late."

"I need to talk to you," she said, her voice still rough from the crying and the short sleep she'd had. "Now."

"Why? What's going on? Why did you have that chair in front of the door?"

"Please sit down with me, and I'll tell you." She pointed to the dining table.

"Can I at least have a glass of water first?" He jutted his chin out in the direction of the kitchen. Aviva went to get him the water. She was already angry at herself, because she'd wanted to address the situation immediately, but now she was just following orders as usual. She filled the glass and brought it to the dining area. Then she sat down and beckoned for him to do the same.

"Something terrible happened here earlier tonight," she said, as Nachum began to drink the water. He looked up at her, not saying anything, his eyebrows raised, his eyes two question marks.

Aviva cleared her throat. "Your uncle was here."

"So?" he said, knitting his brow as if he was going to get angry at her.

"He is not a nice man." Aviva felt her resolve weakening. She had to get the words out quickly, or she would lose her nerve.

"What do you mean? He's always been nice to us."

A little too nice, she thought. She cleared her throat again. "He was here tonight. He just walked right into the apartment."

"Yes, we agreed that he should have an extra key, in case of emergency."

"This was not an emergency. Nachum, he touched me."

"So, he's our uncle. What's the problem."

Finally, Aviva's anger overtook her frustration. She pounded one fist on the table. Nachum jumped.

"Aviva?" He pushed his chair slightly back from the table, as if he felt she might threaten him with her fist.

"Nachum, he would have raped me."

"*What?*" Now Nachum stood, and Aviva thought that maybe, hopefully, he would be horrified for her. "That's the most ridiculous thing I've ever heard," he said, laughing derisively. He wiped his sleeve across his forehead, which had broken into beads of sweat. "I've known him all my life. He is important in the community. Why do you want to hurt him by saying these things?"

"I am not lying. He tried twice. Remember the day you scolded me for taking the bus? Well that's why I took the bus. I just wanted to get out of here. That was the first time."

"You're saying he did this more than once?"

"He tried to do it again tonight. I managed to escape for the second time. That's why I put the chair against the door."

"Aviva, are you going crazy like your mother?"

Aviva screamed. She hadn't planned on screaming, but the sound came out of her, rising from the bottom of her belly and coursing through her body before it left her throat. "What is wrong with you," she said, after she'd caught her breath, "that you do not believe me, do not feel it's your duty to protect me? You are supposed to be my husband, but you don't even like to touch me, and you can't even—" She looked up at him, moving only her eyes. He had no reaction. "And now, you doubt me? You think I would make up something like that? Do you think it's easy to tell you this?" She was breathing so hard, she thought she might hyperventilate. Nachum stood there, both hands in fists planted on the table, glaring down at her.

"He said he was going to try to get me pregnant, because you couldn't," she added, wanting to insult her husband in the worst way possible. But he didn't react.

"I'm sorry, Aviva, but I just cannot believe any of this is true. I don't know why you are saying any of this, but I think it's cruel and terrible of you. Eli is a fine man. No one will believe you. Now where is my dinner?"

"Get your own damn dinner," she hissed, and she pushed the chair away from the table, scraping hard on the old wood floor. Her entire body was shaking. She rushed back into the bedroom, slammed the door, and got into bed.

CHAPTER EIGHT

Aviva

Aviva had fallen asleep almost before her head hit the pillow. Now that she'd gotten everything off her chest, she was finally able to relax enough to close her eyes. Her sleep was undisturbed by dreams. She had no idea when Nachum had gotten into bed. He never tried to touch her, because she was sure he knew that if he had, she would have pushed him away. Nevertheless, she felt safe because Nachum was there, despite the fact that he'd ridiculed her report of the assault. It didn't matter. Tomorrow she would call the bakery and tell them she was taking some time off. She would leave the apartment before Nachum did, so she wouldn't have to worry about another surprise visit by Eli. After that she would decide where to go. Wherever it was, it wasn't going to be here.

Perhaps because she was so intent on getting out of the apartment before Nachum, she awoke almost with the sun. Looking through the gap between the window blinds, she could see the first streaks of a pinkish, yellowish sky. Her clock said five-forty-five. Nachum was sleeping deeply, snoring as usual. He often arose around seven, expecting his hot breakfast to be on the table by seven-thirty. She got out of bed carefully, trying not to disturb him, and although he stirred, she was relieved he didn't wake up. She tiptoed out of the room to the bathroom, taking clothing for today and a couple of changes of underwear with her, and then took a quick shower and got dressed. She did not pull on the thick tights meant to cover a woman's legs under the long skirt. Modesty was of paramount importance here. Men should not be able to get a sexual thrill by seeing a woman's bare legs or her upper arms or her hair. But Aviva's legs without the tights felt as free as her head, as if for the first time her skin could breathe.

Not stopping to eat anything, she moved toward the front door, catching a glimpse of the wig on the dining room table where she'd flung it the night before. She was determined to honor her resolution not to put it on again, but she felt a slight tinge of guilt. She threw it into her bag with her toothbrush and a couple of changes of underwear. Then she ran her fingers through her hair, trying to fluff it out, although it was still wet from the shower. She looked at herself in the mirror, and she had the urge giggle at herself nervously, but she put her hand over her mouth before she made any noise. She decided that excitement was winning over guilt.

Then she walked past the kitchen, trying not to look in, knowing her husband would be furious to find her gone and no breakfast waiting for him. It didn't matter. She had no desire to stick around or to serve him anymore. It might have been different if he'd believed her or at least had been at all sympathetic. And although his reaction to her telling him about Eli had been disappointing, it wasn't so much that she was angry at him. She just felt nothing at all when she thought about him, and that was somehow the difference between staying and going. Although she felt a pull to the life here because she'd never known anything different, her trips to the library as well as her fear of staying gave her the impetus to get out. There was life beyond Williamsburg, and the books she'd read did nothing but confirm it.

Finally, she opened the jar where she kept the money from her job that she used to buy groceries, took it all, and put it in her purse. She had no idea how long it would last, but she didn't care. It would be enough to get out, and she couldn't think of long-term planning right now. She'd read about the "fight or flight" impulse, and at this moment flight was winning over fight—not even a contest. The money didn't matter. As they vilified and detested her, Nachum's family would pity him and make sure he didn't starve.

When she opened the apartment door, she looked up and down the hallway twice to make sure no one was around. It was so quiet, you could hear a low, almost silent, hum that she figured was the electricity. Only the sound of the building. No human noise at all. She tiptoed toward the staircase and made it outside without seeing a soul. Then she began to walk fast.

She said a silent prayer of thanks there was no one yet on the street to yell at her for showing her hair. Any later in the day, and the modesty patrols would have been out in force, if one of the neighbors didn't catch her and tattle on her first. Those modesty patrols that guarded these blocks had no compunction about grabbing a woman who they deemed was dressed "provocatively," or with short sleeves or skirts that didn't go down at least to the mid-calf. She walked several blocks away from her building. The bakery wouldn't be open yet, but she walked by there anyway. There would be activity in the back very soon, preparing for today's trade. Her experience there hadn't been terrible. They appreciated her for her excellent mind and her honesty. She made a mental note to call them later, somehow, from wherever she could find a phone.

She wasn't paying much attention to where she was going, but she found herself heading for the subway. Then it dawned on her. She would get on the train, leave Brooklyn, and transfer to the subway that would take her uptown in Manhattan. She would go to David's bagel shop. Once there, she was completely unsure what she would say to him or how he would feel about her being there. But he had made the effort to find her at the bakery. He was obviously concerned. She longed for his smile, wished she had let him touch her hand. She'd never had anyone make her feel as cared for as David had, even though she'd been with him only twice, for a very short time.

The subway ride seemed to take forever. Her growling stomach began to remind her she'd left the apartment without eating or drinking anything, so she knew she would order a bagel and a cup of coffee once she got to the shop. Even a single cup of coffee would be wonderful now. After she'd changed lines at forty-second street, she knew she had only a few stops, but between fifty-seventh and sixty-third, the train lurched and then came to a grinding halt in the dark tunnel. For a moment the lights went out, and Aviva grasped the seat and began to breathe hard. She had a momentary fantasy that Eli had followed her and somehow caused the train to stop and the lights to go out. She shook herself to try to wipe that out of her brain. It was obviously a delusion.

Finally there was a garbled announcement over the intercom, but Aviva was fairly sure the voice said there was a short delay but that they would be moving soon. She loosened her hold a bit on the seat. Her hands throbbed from gripping so hard, the knuckles white as a sheet.

"Are you all right, honey?" The older black woman sitting next to her had turned toward Aviva and was trying to get her attention.

"I—I," Aviva stammered. She didn't know what to say. She was embarrassed that someone had noticed her fright.

"It's okay, this happens all the time on the subway, you know?" The woman laughed, a deep belly laugh. "NYC public transit. Ya gotta love it. Where you goin'?"

"Seventy-second," Aviva managed to blurt out.

"Oh yeah, two more stops. You in a big hurry or something?"

"No, I was just—" She stopped again, not sure whether to admit she had been frightened.

"It's okay. Really. We'll be there soon." The woman reached over and patted Aviva on the shoulder, and although she had the urge to move away, she didn't. The pat was reassuring.

"Thank you," she said.

"It's okay, honey. Stuff happens." The woman turned away again and went back to looking at her phone.

The subway started moving again with another lurch and Aviva put her hands in her lap. She was relieved, but nevertheless, when the doors opened at seventy-second, she sprang out of the car as quickly as she could and sprinted up the stairs. She couldn't wait to get out onto the street. Once there, she took several deep breaths. It wasn't even seven o'clock yet, but the streets were fairly busy with people walking, cars and taxis honking their horns. She was happy to disappear into a crowd in the open air.

Today, she knew where she was going. She walked fast down seventy-second to York, and then uptown until she reached the bagel shop. She was breathing faster, and it wasn't only because of the brisk walk. The place was full of people at this hour, but Aviva made a beeline to the counter and stood on line, shuffling from one foot to the other. Her heart was beating fast at the thought of seeing David again. Finally, someone said, "May I help you?"

"Yes, I was wondering if David is here?"

"David who?" the man said. "We got a couple Davids here."

"Delgado," Aviva said, her eyes widening.

"Oh, Delgado. Sorry, Miss. This is his day off. He'll be in tomorrow though."

Aviva's heart sank. No way she could go back home and then come back tomorrow. She felt the blood drain out of her face, but she didn't know what to say.

"Maybe I can give him a message for you?"

The whole point of coming here was to have been to ask David for help, for guidance. She had hoped at least to talk with him and have him work through the situation with her so she could figure out what she should do next. She wasn't sure why, but for some reason, she trusted him—to see her with the wig off, without the heavy stockings, as she really was. Somehow, she was positive he would be at least a sympathetic ear. He'd sought her out, found her at the bakery, which with very little information was remarkable. She attempted to convince herself she was not attracted to him, because that was a feeling she knew well was not allowed. But the feeling that came over her when she thought about him was unmistakable. She had never felt that way before about anyone. She tried to avoid panicking. She was aware she needed to communicate with him, but she had no idea how.

"You want to leave him a message?" The man behind the counter repeated his offer. His face looked sympathetic, not angry. She felt he seemed to relate to her distress. So many people outside her community had been kind to her, it was astonishing that people cared or even noticed her discomfort. Contact with these "others" was so strictly forbidden by her people, it amazed her that strangers might be good to her. That went against everything she'd always been told.

She finally regained her voice. "Would that be all right?"

"Sure, what do you want me to tell him?"

"Could I write him a note or something?"

"Sure. Do you have a paper and pen?"

"No." She looked down at her feet. Again, she was embarrassed that she was living in a world of people able to navigate it, but she always seemed to come up short.

"Just a minute," he said. He reached behind him and pulled an order blank off a pad. "Here. And here's a pen. Just bring it back to me when you're done."

"Thank you so much," she said, taking the pen and paper and heading over to an empty table. But she wasn't sure what to write. She sat there, the pen poised above the paper, for minutes. But every time she thought of what to say, she immediately decided it was not appropriate. Finally, she took a chance. *Dear David,* she wrote, *I am sorry I missed you today. I would like very much to talk with you, if that is possible. I need your help. Thank you. Aviva.* She read what she'd written several times. It made her feel a little guilty that she hadn't been specific, although in her own mind she didn't have specifics, and she was too embarrassed to write anything about what Eli had done to her. She was just confused. She hoped David wouldn't think she was in terrible trouble, because she knew he'd be concerned. And although she really *was* in terrible trouble, she hesitated to get him involved, because she realized it might put him in danger. Below her name, she added, *I am sorry to bother you. I am really all right, but I just need to talk.*

She walked back to the counter and gave the man the note and his pen. "Thank you," she said.

"No problem," he replied. "I'll give it to him tomorrow."

"Oh," she said, suddenly remembering the bakery. "I have another favor to ask?"

"Sure," he said.

"May I use your phone? I have to make a quick call, and I don't have one." She almost expected him to tell her no, but instead he produced a phone and placed it on the counter. She looked at it. She'd never used a cell phone before and wasn't sure how to make a call.

"You need help?" he said. He continued to smile at her.

"I—um—I never used this kind before," she stammered. Her face had flushed red.

"Oh, easy," he said. "Just press the keys and then when you're done press the green button. Okay?"

Aviva nodded.

"And don't forget the area code."

Aviva took the phone and sat down at one of the empty tables. Her boss at the bakery seemed concerned when Aviva told her she was not feeling well, but she tried to reassure her she'd be better in a few days. She returned the phone.

The only thing she could do now, unless she wanted to go home, which she did not, was to take a bus to Kiryas Joel and throw herself on the mercy of her aunt. And try to communicate with her mother. She hoped her mother was not too sick at least to hug her and tell her things would be all right. It had been years since she'd been there, possibly almost ten years. She had spoken with her mother on the phone during those early years, because her mother had seemed a little less ill. But recently, she'd stopped even calling, because her aunt was always very harried with all the kids, and her mother was too ill to talk.

CHAPTER NINE

Aviva

The one-hour bus ride seemed interminable. Aviva had sat by a window, but it was making her dizzy to look at the scenery speeding by. Her stomach was so empty, she worried the growling might disturb others on the bus. She'd been so taken aback that David hadn't been at work, she'd forgotten to eat or drink something. She felt a little faint, hoped she could remember how to get to her aunt's house from the bus stop. She would have to walk, and the dim memories she had told her it hadn't been too long a walk.

The bus stopped with a lurch, and everyone piled out onto the street. It seemed even hotter here than it had been in the city. All Aviva could see as far as her eyes could reach was a sea of Hasidic costumes—fur hats, long black coats, heavy shoes, women in long heavy skirts and either wigs on their heads or scarves tied around them so securely it was impossible to see any hair. She hadn't remembered the town's being this crowded the last time she was here, and on every street corner were children playing, running, making noise—mostly Yiddish noise—and women managing them as if they were herds of sheep.

As she stepped off the bus, Aviva almost tripped and fell. Her head was spinning, and she was sure she was on the way down, but a strong arm grabbed her under the shoulder and righted her.

"Are you all right?" It was a middle-aged woman, thin but so strong she had managed to prevent Aviva from hitting the ground. "Do you belong here?" The woman was speaking in Yiddish. Now she had pushed Aviva gently away at arm's length and was staring at her from top to bottom.

"Oh, I forgot," Aviva said, fishing around in her large bag and retrieving the wig, which was disheveled. She tried to fix it with her hand and put it on, although she thought it might be lopsided.

"Who are you?" the woman asked. Her voice didn't sound angry, just curious. "Where are you from?"

"Williamsburg," Aviva said, finally getting her balance.

"So you don't live here?"

"No. But my mother and my aunt do."

"Where do they live?"

Aviva gave her the address.

"Come, follow me." The woman raised an arm over her head in the direction she wanted Aviva to go. "I'll take you there. You look a bit unwell."

"Thank you," Aviva said, allowing the woman to lead her by the elbow. They passed a large sign Aviva didn't remember, but the last time she'd been here she had been a young girl. The sign said, "Welcome to Kiryas Joel. A Traditional Community of Modesty and Values. In keeping with our traditions and religious customs, we kindly ask that you dress and behave in a modest way while visiting our community. This includes: Wearing long skirts or pants; Covered necklines; Sleeves past the elbow; Use appropriate language; Maintain gender separation in all public areas. Thank you for respecting our values and please Enjoy Your Visit!"

"So, you like our sign?" the woman said as they passed it.

Aviva shrugged. The sign epitomized everything their community demanded. At this point, after what she'd been through, it made Aviva a little angry. The final exhortation, "Enjoy Your Visit" seemed nothing if not ironic.

"Okay, so you walk three blocks down there." She pointed her index finger down a street. "Then you turn left, and it's the second building on the right. They're on the third floor. Got that?"

Aviva nodded. "Thanks again," she said. Thank heaven it wasn't too far. The woman gave a little wave and turned back where she'd come from.

The closer Aviva got to her aunt's house, the faster her heart beat and the more she felt the perspiration forming on her forehead and around her temples. Several scenarios played in her head, none of them pleasant. Either her mother would be too sick even to see her, or her aunt would castigate her for having the nerve to leave her husband without a word, or if she even got the courage to tell her aunt what had happened to her, her aunt would tell her to go back and just tolerate it because there was no other choice.

She wouldn't say a word about David. She was sure they'd disapprove of her behavior anyway, and the fact that she had been talking to a young man outside the community would be completely unacceptable. Aviva was positive of that. But she also knew there was no way she would ever return to the apartment and let herself be abused by her husband's uncle. She wondered how many girls went through such abuse without ever saying anything about it.

She couldn't believe she was the only one, although a year ago she wouldn't have believed this could happen to her.

At the house, she stopped at the front door. There were four names on the buzzer, and she reached her finger out to press the one that belonged to her aunt, but her finger froze before she pressed it. Then, taking a deep breath, she pushed it hard and held it down for a long time.

"Who's there?" A woman's voice piped out over the intercom. It had been so long since Aviva had been here, she couldn't even have sworn to the fact that it was her aunt's voice.

"Aunt Rachel? It's me. Aviva." Her voice shook as she whispered the response.

"Who?"

"Aviva." She said her name a little louder.

"Aviva? Is that *you*? Why—" But before her aunt finished her question, she'd pressed the button, and Aviva pushed open the door and began climbing the stairs. Her aunt was waiting for her, the door to her apartment open halfway.

"Oh, my. It *is* you!" She opened her arms, and Aviva fell into them and began to sob. "What in the world is going on? I'm so surprised to see you. What's wrong?"

"Can I come in?" Aviva's voice was coming in gasps. She'd been doing so much crying lately, she wondered how she could still have tears.

"Of course, come on in." Her aunt threw open the door and ushered Aviva into the threadbare but clean living room. "Sit down, sweetheart. Would you like a glass of water? Coffee? Anything?"

"Thank you, Aunt Rachel. Water would be nice. And do you have a Kleenex?"

She watched her aunt walk toward the kitchen. She'd seen her aunt last at her wedding, but she hadn't really had a chance to talk to her. She looked around the room. It was exactly the same as it had been the last time Aviva had been here, which had to have been the better part of ten years and several children ago. Rachel came back with a glass of ice water and a tissue.

"What's going on? How is Nachum?"

Aviva's silence told a story. She had no idea what or how much to tell her aunt, didn't know whether she could hope for the older woman to support her, or whether Aunt Rachel would be as harsh and unbending as Nachum's sister Ilona.

"Problems, Aviva?" Rachel raised her eyebrows. "It's all right. You can tell me. I know you don't have anyone else."

Aviva sighed. "First," she said, "I want to know about my mother. Is she any better? Can I see her?"

Now Rachel sighed. "I'm afraid not," she said. "She seems to go deeper and deeper into some kind of silent asylum. She has not spoken in a year."

Aviva's mother had not even attended her daughter's wedding. Aviva was not surprised by Rachel's news, but it was still painful to hear. "Is she—is she here?"

"No, dear. There is a, well, it's a kind of home in the village. There are some kind ladies who take care of people with mental issues."

"Can I visit her there?"

"I suppose you could, but I don't think she'd communicate with you. Her face is carved in stone. She doesn't speak, she doesn't move. They feed her through straws, and sometimes she won't even accept the food."

Aviva felt herself beginning to cry, again. "Isn't it expensive to keep her there?"

"The community chips in whatever they can for this place. It's actually a godsend."

"I think I'd like to see for myself," Aviva managed to say. Rachel was Aviva's oldest aunt. She was in her fifties, and all her five children were grown and married now with children of their own. So Rachel spent much of her time taking care of her own house and caring for her grandchildren. "Well, I suppose I could take you if you really want to go. But I worry about how it will affect you."

"My mother's illness has affected me all my life, Aunt Rachel," she said. "I don't think it could do much more."

"I suppose so," she said. "But is seeing your mother the only reason you came here? Don't you have a job?"

Aviva sighed. "Things—" she said, but stopped. She wiped perspiration off her forehead and then took the wig off and put it down on the sofa next to her.

"Why?" her aunt said, her gaze traveling from the wig to her niece's growing hair. "What's going on with you?"

"I just can't—" she started again but couldn't finish. She put her head back onto the cushion. "I don't think I can go back there."

Rachel's face turned white. "What are you talking about? You've been married less than two years. What do you mean, you can't go back there?" Rachel stood and began plumping the cushions on the chairs, and then she picked up a duster from the top of a table and began walking around the room running it over surfaces. Aviva realized it was just something to do, because her aunt was shocked. As if cleaning might help that.

"It's very hard for me to talk about," she said.

Rachel stopped in her tracks. "Did something happen to you?" Her stare, the knitted brow, the sucked in lips, made Aviva think she must be imagining that Aviva was on the verge of losing her mind, just as her mother had. The duster was raised as if Rachel was about to lower it onto a surface, but she held it there—looked like a statue in the game of statues Aviva had played as a child. Aviva nodded.

"Don't you think it would help to talk about it?"

"I don't think I can," she said.

"I can't help you if I don't know what you need help with," Rachel said. There was a tremor in her voice, as if she only half wanted Aviva to tell her.

Two or three times Aviva opened her mouth to talk, but the words wouldn't come out. "I'm sorry," she said, hanging her head.

"What are you doing here, Aviva? You never came to visit your mother before, but now you are here, and there's something wrong, but you won't tell me what it is."

"I can't go home," Aviva said, her voice not more than a whisper.

Rachel put the duster down, threw her head back, and laughed out loud. "What are you talking about? Of course you can go home. You must go home."

Aviva shook her head hard. "No. I would rather live on the street."

Rachel's eyes grew very wide. For several moments neither of them spoke at all. "Does Nachum know?"

Aviva shook her head again.

"Is he the one who did something to you?"

"No."

Rachel sighed as if a weight had been lifted off her shoulders. "Then why can't you tell him?"

"I just—can't," she said. "Would you tell him? Please?"

"What do you want me to say?"

"Tell him I want a divorce."

"*Aviva!*"

"I mean it, Aunt Rachel. I will never go back. First I am going to visit my mother, and then I hope you will let me stay here until I figure out what to do next."

"You know you can't stay here long, don't you?" She looked away for a moment. "I'm sorry, I don't mean to be harsh, but we don't have the money to keep you. What about your job? Weren't you working in a bakery?"

Aviva shrugged. "I'll just have to get another job. Somewhere."

"You hate Nachum that much?"

"I don't hate him. He isn't a bad man. I am just very unhappy."

"You're leaving because you're unhappy?" Rachel slapped the side of her head and made a choking noise that sounded like the combination of a cough and a laugh. "If everyone could leave their marriage because they were unhappy, no one would be married."

Aviva stared her aunt in the eye. "You realize what you just said, Aunt Rachel? Do you realize how insane that sounds?"

"We don't use the word insane around here, Aviva. Not with your mother—um—the way she is."

"I'm sorry. But I am not willing to stay in a marriage when I am miserable."

"But you said Nachum is not a bad man."

"It doesn't matter whether he's a good man or a bad man. I've made my decision," she said. She tried to get the feeling of Eli's hands on her out of her head, but that was almost impossible. "You can't talk me out of it."

"What will you do?" Rachel's face looked so gray that Aviva was tempted to put her arm around her aunt to comfort her.

"I'm trying to take it one day at a time."

"You don't have any plan? Where will you live?"

Aviva's eyebrows shot up, and her eyes widened. She didn't speak.

"I told you, there's no way I can afford to have you stay here. Besides, you are my niece and my flesh and blood, but to be honest—we have an obligation." She stressed the word obligation as if it had eight syllables, not four. "Anyway, I have no desire to deal with the castigation of the community, that I am harboring someone who ran from her marriage and from the life." She looked at her hands, which were in her lap.

"Harboring? Do you feel I'm some kind of criminal?"

"No, no, you know I don't feel that way."

"It sounds as if you do from what you said."

"You are very young," Rachel said. "But I am not. I have been in this life for over fifty years. I have accepted the way we live, and whether I agree with everything or not, I have made the choice to conform to the rules. It's important. Happiness is not necessarily the goal."

Aviva wished she could probe her aunt's statements, but this wasn't the time. Besides, she didn't want to get into a serious argument, because she needed to be here at least temporarily. "I never thought you'd take me in for good, but could I just stay here a few days? Until I figure out what to do?"

"Did you call your job today?"

Aviva nodded.

"Did you tell them you're not coming back?"

"No, I just said I'd be out today."

"Don't you think you should call them? And what about Nachum? Don't you think he'll be worrying about you?" Rachel had lifted her index finger, as if she was about to point it at Aviva in a scolding way, but as soon as she had it in midair, she changed her mind and put her hand back in her lap.

"Honestly, I don't think he'll even notice I'm gone."

"*Aviva!*"

"At least not until he finds out there is no dinner waiting for him."

"This is really not fair to him."

"What about *me*, Aunt Rachel? Why doesn't it matter to anyone what's fair to me?"

"All you've told me is that you're unhappy in your marriage. But that Nachum is not a bad man. So honestly, Aviva, I have no idea what this is all about."

"It's more than that," Aviva said.

"Then what is it? Help me understand."

"I can't talk about it."

Rachel threw up her hands, and shaking her head slowly from side to side, she stood up and walked toward the kitchen. "I don't know what your problem is. I'm almost glad your parents don't know this is going on."

"That's a cruel thing to say," Aviva said, her voice almost in a whisper.

"I'm sorry, I didn't mean to be cruel," her aunt said. "But there has been talk from people who visited here from Williamsburg that you were always a little unmanageable."

"What does *that* mean?"

"They said you were always sneaking off to the library, reading God knows what in there. No wonder you have these wild ideas."

"The library is a good place," Aviva said. "Because someone wants to learn about their world and the history and science of it doesn't make them unmanageable, or bad for that matter. What are our rebbes worried about? Why is knowledge evil? The more I know, the more I don't understand that."

"Don't you believe them? They are very wise. And don't you believe that God is watching over you?"

Aviva sputtered. "What is God, Rachel?" she said. "Can you answer that? If there is such an entity, then why is there evil in the world? Why did evil find me?"

Rachel gasped. "You say evil found you, you say this has shaken your belief in God, but you will not tell me why or what. I understand you haven't had an easy life, but then no one really has an easy life. You will find this out as you get older, I'm sure of that."

"Well my life hasn't been easy from the very start," Aviva said, starting to feel the tears gathering again. She gulped a couple of times to try to keep them from coming.

"I am very frustrated with you," Rachel said.

"So, join everyone else," Aviva shot back. "I'm sorry you're frustrated with me. That was not my goal, to frustrate you. But I can't say anything more, just that there is no way I can go back home."

"Well, I am apparently not going to be able to convince you that you're wrong. I warn you though, once you get out there in the world and realize you desperately miss your community and that the world is much harder than you thought, it will be near impossible to come back."

"I do love many things about our community," she said. "When it's joyful, there is a lot of joy. But for me, there is more pain than joy. And leaving is a risk I have to take."

Rachel stood in the archway to the kitchen, looking over at her niece, her hands on her hips. "You can stay here for two or three days," she sighed. "But I'm afraid that's it. You're going to have to figure out something or go back home."

"Thank you, that's a relief," Aviva said.

"And for now, don't you think you should call your job and tell them you're not coming back? If that's what you really want?"

Aviva put her hand over her mouth. "May I use your phone?"

Rachel pointed to the phone sitting on a side table, and then she turned and disappeared into the kitchen.

CHAPTER TEN

Aviva and David

Aviva couldn't stop her hand from trembling as she dialed the number of the bakeshop. Up until now, everything had seemed clear. She couldn't go back home, not to a husband who was totally indifferent, and not to his uncle who felt entitled to assault her whenever he wished. She knew enough to realize she'd get no backup from the community on either issue. But if she quit her job with this phone call, then Rachel was right—there really *was* no going back.

She felt jammed between a rock and a hard place. Doing this would remove any possibility of redemption between her and those people—her people. But as frightening as that was, she knew she had to get away from them now—there was no other choice. Her eyes traveled around the room, but she wasn't really seeing much. She had memories of this place from when she was a small child, and it didn't seem much different. But despite the fact that her aunt had shown her a little sympathy, and the fact that Eli didn't know where she was, Aviva didn't feel very comfortable here.

"Hello?"

Aviva's life before her marriage had been much more solitary than that of most of the children who often had four, five, six, or more siblings. She had grown up with an aging grandmother who, in her later years, began to show signs of dementia. Before she died, her grandmother had started losing her memory and with it her interest in the things and people around her. So there weren't many people for Aviva to talk to. She wondered whether the boredom and lack of conversation were reasons why she'd been so attracted to the library.

When her grandmother dozed off or later when she couldn't even remember where Aviva had been, Aviva would sneak off to the library and lose herself in the books. One of the children's librarians there, a middle-aged woman who told Aviva her name was Jeanne O'Hara, took a liking to the young Hasidic child who was constantly asking questions. Jeanne would encourage Aviva to study whatever subject piqued her curiosity, and so Aviva studied geography, history, biology, and as she got older, many of the best classic novels Jeanne recommended. The sadness and difficulties Aviva felt being a virtual orphan were tolerable as long as she could bury her nose in a book.

As a married woman under the watchful eye of her sister-in-law, working and taking care of the apartment, it was harder for Aviva to get to the library regularly. But she had made a friend at work. Miriam was a little younger, not yet married, but fascinated with what she considered Aviva's worldly knowledge. So, they talked as much as they could as they helped the customers of the bakery, and frequently their boss allowed them to take a lunch break together if there was someone else minding the counter. The two girls would joke together, complain about their respective situations, gossip about the bakery manager and the people who came in to buy.

One day, when she was feeling uncharacteristically talkative, Aviva had broken down and told Miriam about what had happened with Eli the first time. She was embarrassed afterward, because it seemed to upset Miriam terribly. All the blood had run out of the young woman's face, and she trembled. But after she recovered, she had thanked Aviva for trusting her enough to tell her, and they'd hugged. "I'm so sorry this happened to you," Miriam had said. Aviva realized this girl would be her friend forever. So, she was relieved when she recognized Miriam's voice, grateful she didn't have to talk to anyone else. "Hi. This is Aviva."

"Are you all right, Aviva? What's going on? Why didn't you come to work?" Miriam was whispering, as if someone else was there with her. "I was worried about you."

"Mimi, thank goodness you answered. I—um—I have to tell you something."

"Well, before you do, I have to tell you that man was in here again today."

Aviva was ready to say, *What man*, but then she realized it must be David. Mimi would not have referred to either Nachum or Eli as "that man," as she knew them both. Aviva's mood improved in an instant, and the mind numbing exhaustion she had been feeling seemed to disappear. If her hands were shaking now, it would be from excitement, not anxiety. David had come back looking for her. "David?" she said softly.

"He left a note for you. Will you come and get it? When are you coming back to work?"

"Would you mind reading it to me? Is it a long note?"

"No. He wrote his name and his telephone number. And he wrote, *Please call me right away*. Who is this man, Aviva?

Why does he keep coming to the shop? Does Nachum know? What is going on with you?"

One of the things a good Hasidic married woman never did was to consort with men other than her husband. Aviva scrambled to find a piece of paper. She was relieved to find the message pad and pen next to the phone. "Would you please give me the phone number?" she said, ignoring Mimi's questions. Just having his number gave her a new energy she hadn't felt for a long time. "Did he say anything else?"

"He wanted to know where you lived. He knew your street. How did he know that?" She took a breath, almost a gasp. "I told him your house number. Is that all right? Who is he?"

"He is a friend," Aviva said, worried that David might have met with some unwanted aggression toward him if he'd gone to her house. He was young and tall—looked quite strong—but she worried that someone would call the shomrim, and they would outnumber him, possibly rough him up.

"A *friend*? What kind of a man friend do you have?"

"I wanted to let you know. Would you tell the boss? I won't be coming back to work."

There was a pause. Aviva could hear heavy breathing and what sounded like fingers beating rhythmically on a glass counter.

"Did you hear me?" As much as she didn't want to upset her friend, she was anxious to get off this call and phone David. Warn him. Violence in situations like this was a distinct possibility.

"What are you talking about? How are you going to live if you don't have a job? You mean you're not coming tomorrow?"

"No, I'm sorry. I didn't mean to inconvenience everybody this way, but I won't be coming back. At all."

"*Why?*"

"I'm really sorry. I have no time to explain. I have to go now. I promise I will tell you after—"

"Oh my God, is it Eli again?"

"Goodbye, Mimi." Her voice trailed off. She didn't know what else to say. "Thank you for being my friend. I will always be grateful you listened and sympathized with me. I had fun working with you." She didn't wait for a response, hung up the phone, took a deep breath, and then picked it up again. She had to get to David before he ventured into her world and something bad happened to him. She dialed his number, and now she felt her hands trembling again, this time with excitement.

"Hello?" David's voice was strong, although it was obvious he didn't recognize her aunt's number—how could he?

"David?"

"Oh my God, Aviva! Is that you? I was so worried about you."

Despite her efforts not to, Aviva burst into tears. More tears. She couldn't speak.

"Are you all right?" he said. "Where are you?" She could hear the worry in his deliberate words. She tried to pull herself together.

She gulped some air, wiped her eyes. "I am okay," she said.

"Thank heavens! After you left me that note at the shop, I was thinking something bad had happened to you, but I couldn't reach you. Where are you?"

Aviva thought about Eli. Something *had* happened. "I am in Kiryas Joel at my aunt's house."

"*Where?*" he said. He thought maybe he'd heard her wrong. He didn't recognize the name.

"Kiryas Joel. It's a town about an hour away from the city," she said. "I am so happy to be talking to you."

"Are you coming home soon? Can I see you? I want to make sure you're all right."

Since her father's death, no one in Aviva's family, in her community, had ever shown her by actions or words that they were at all concerned about her. Aunt Rachel did care, but she was so caught up in her own life and in making sure Aviva's mother was being taken care of, she never really contacted her niece even to chitchat.

But here this man she'd met only twice, seemed to care about her well being more than any of the others. It felt almost absurd, funny. She only knew she was grateful for him.

"Are you laughing, Aviva?" he said, but there was a smile in his voice. "It's nice. You have a pretty laugh."

"I couldn't help it," she said. "I feel as if you've lifted a great weight off my shoulders."

"So, then you're all right? When are you coming home?"

Aviva wanted to tell him she was never coming home, but of course, that's not what he meant. "I'll be here a couple of days," she said.

"And then?" he pressed her.

"I don't know where I'll go."

"I'm confused," he said. He felt a strong attraction to this beautiful girl, wanted to care for her because he was sure she was suffering. But he knew she was married. He had no desire to be a home-wrecker. Was the marriage foundering? Was she leaving her husband for some reason? She wasn't talking. "You did tell me you're married, right?"

Aviva paused. "It's a long story," she said. She sighed. "I am—was." She took a breath. "I'd rather tell you in person than on the phone."

"All right," he said. To himself, he thought, *What am I getting myself into here*? "Should I meet you at your house?"

Aviva gasped. "Oh, thank goodness you said that. No, you should never go to my house. I would worry about your safety. You would not be—um—welcome there."

"Then where?" he asked. His tone of voice told her he was getting a little impatient with her.

"Please, I promise I will explain everything. Don't give up on me."

"I'm definitely not giving up on you," he said. "Sorry if I sounded annoyed."

"No, not exactly annoyed. I understand how you could be thinking I am a freak."

"I don't think you're a freak!"

"Would it be all right if I met you at your place?" She had no idea where his place was, but that seemed like the only option. At the bagel shop, there would be no way to talk to him privately and for more than a couple of minutes. She felt a pang of fear, perspiration forming on her brow. Could she ever tell him about Eli? She felt so ashamed. It would be so terribly hard to talk about, and then what if she confided in him, but he rejected her? She would have to make something up. There was no way to tell him about Eli. And what if he turned out to be like Eli, although all of her instincts told her she could trust him.

"Sure," he said. "When?"

"Are you working the day after tomorrow?"

"No," he said. "I'm actually free that day."

"Then that's when I'll come over. But I don't know where you live."

"How are you getting home from where you are?"

"Bus," she said.

"How about if I meet you at the bus terminal?" he said.

Again, someone had offered to take care of her, to meet her and then shepherd her to a safe place, or what she hoped was a safe place. Safer than her own place anyway. "I will call you with the time," she said.

"Good. I'll be there," he answered.

She sighed. Finally, she could stop holding her breath. "Thank you so much, David. You don't know how much I appreciate it."

"You're welcome."

"Goodbye then."

"Goodbye. See you soon."

Aviva hadn't noticed her aunt come back into the room. "Who were you talking to?" Rachel said.

"A friend," Aviva said.

"What friend? What did she do that you appreciated it so much?"

"Oh, it was my friend Mimi at the bakery. I asked her to let them know I'd be here until the day after tomorrow."

The answer seemed to satisfy Rachel's curiosity. "Oh, okay. So, you're staying two days?"

"Is that all right?"

"Fine."

"With my uncle too?"

Rachel waved a hand, as if to say it would be all right. "Would you like to go see your mother now?"

Aviva nodded, relieved she didn't have to do any more explaining to her aunt.

"All right. I'll take you. I just hope you're prepared for what you're going to see."

CHAPTER ELEVEN

Aviva and Rachel

The visit to the "home," or whatever it was, turned out to be much more emotionally devastating than Aviva had even imagined. It was a rather dilapidated house on the outskirts of town—what looked as if it used to be white paint had turned a dirty gray and was peeling in many places. Some of the siding appeared to have fallen off, exposing black tar paper underneath, and a blue tarp had been thrown carelessly over a large part of the roof where, apparently, the roof shingles had come loose.

Several, perhaps ten or so, people who appeared to have mental problems were living here with the woman who had taken them in as a charity. Most of the residents wandered around the place aimlessly, back and forth, some talking to themselves. Each had an ankle bracelet that Rachel explained would make a terrible racket if they tried to leave the property. That alone was hard to look at. But she really hadn't been prepared for what she found when she walked into her mother's room. Even in the two years since Aviva's wedding, her mother had deteriorated so much that she didn't even seem to recognize her daughter or to change her affect when Aviva was in the room. Aviva talked softly to her mother and tried to hug her, but the woman either didn't respond or pushed her daughter away.

The woman looked dirty, her hair unkempt, a front tooth missing, which, the proprietor of the place told Aviva, had happened when another resident decided to pick a fight with her. Aviva's mother never moved a muscle. She sat in a chair beside her bed, facing the window, staring straight ahead but obviously not seeing anything. Aviva finally gave up trying to make her mother respond in any way. The woman didn't even seem to blink.

"How long has she been this way?" Aviva asked Rachel as they sat in the room with the silent woman.

Rachel shrugged. "It just gets worse and worse. Maybe six months now, she hasn't even moved at all. At night, someone has to bring her to the bed, lay her down, and cover her with a blanket, or she would sit in that chair until she fell asleep and fell out of it."

Aviva controlled herself until they'd left the room and left the house, but then she broke down in sobs that felt as if they were ocean waves, rising up through her entire body, uncontrollable and loud. Her mother was only forty years old, but she looked sixty and looked as if she were wasting away, her bones all jutting out of translucent skin. *How could that happen to someone*, she thought as Rachel put an arm around her and led her back toward her own place. She cried all the way back to her aunt's house, and then she collapsed on the couch.

"I thought you knew," Rachel said.

"How would I know? Every time I suggested to Ilona that I go visit my mother, she shot it down with some excuse. She rules the roost in that family. And she gets in my way every time, no matter how hard I try to make her like me."

"I don't know why I'm telling you this, but you know Nachum's family was hesitant to take you on, worrying that you would end up like my sister." She sighed.

Aviva snorted. "Take me on." She blew her nose into a tissue her aunt had handed her. "As if I'm a horse or a dog. Almost two years with them, I have done nothing wrong, ever, but Ilona reminds me every chance she gets that I was not their first choice," Aviva said, clearing her throat, trying to stop the tears. "The only crime I've ever committed was escaping to the library to read books."

Rachel threw her head back and laughed, but it wasn't a happy laugh. "Well that's because your husband isn't exactly what I'd call a prime specimen. None of the first choices were interested."

Despite herself, Aviva giggled. She could laugh about it now, because she was not going back to him. She would never go back to him. "You're telling me," she said.

"You promise me he didn't do anything to you, did he?" Rachel's brow had contracted into a tableau of horizontal wrinkles.

Aviva picked her hand up, waved it as if to dismiss that notion. "No, he didn't do anything to me. Really, he's not a bad person, and the worst thing he did to me was to ignore me. It's everyone around him."

"What really happened, Aviva?" Rachel said, moving closer to her niece. "Something happened to you. You wouldn't flee your home without telling anyone, quit your job, and come here to tell me you're getting a divorce just for a lark. Why won't you tell me?"

Aviva loved her aunt. They hadn't lived close-by for years, but she always felt her aunt had compassion for her. She didn't like to think it was pity, because that felt awful, but she always felt safe around her aunt, as if, within the confines of the culture, the woman was on her side. "I'm not sure I can tell anyone."

"So, something did happen. Did you tell your husband?"

Aviva shook her head, put her hands up to her face. Her skin felt very hot. She wasn't looking in a mirror, but she could feel the blood rushing up from her neck to her face, knew her face was red.

"Why not? It's up to him to protect you. We do enough for these men. The least we can expect is to be defended by them."

Aviva laughed again. "I told you, he isn't really interested in me, Aunt Rachel," she said. "He's never been interested in me. In that house, I might as well be a chair or a lamp or a table."

"Well before you jump to get a divorce, don't you think you and Nachum should go to the rebbe for some counseling?" She had moved very close to Aviva and was tapping Aviva's knee with her index finger, as if she were making an important point. "Or how about his uncle Eli? He is an important man in the community. Perhaps he could help? You could go to him as a couple and ask for his guidance."

For the first time, Aviva's anger superseded her frustration. She pushed Rachel's hand away and stood up, shaking a fist at her aunt as if she might hit her. Rachel recoiled.

"Eli? *Eli?*" Aviva's voice had risen many decibels. "That scum? I wouldn't talk to that man if he were the last person on earth."

"Aviva? What is going on with you?"

With her voice breaking, still standing over her aunt, who had raised an arm defensively and was leaning back toward the arm of the sofa, Aviva took a deep breath of air and then said loudly and strongly, "That man—Eli, the important man—what he did—I will never go back there." She stood up with such force, the couch moved backward several inches even with Rachel sitting there. Then she marched into the bathroom, slammed the door, sat down on the toilet, and began sobbing again.

Within seconds Rachel was pounding on the door. "Aviva? What's going on in there? Please open this door. Please! We have to talk."

"The door's unlocked," Aviva whispered. Rachel opened it and stood there, keeping her distance.

"What were you implying?"

"Use your imaginaton."

"Are you *sure*?"

Aviva laughed through her tears. "Am I sure? Seriously, Aunt Rachel, you realize what you just asked me? Yes, I am sure. He made some excuse like he would get me pregnant because Nachum couldn't."

"Oh, dear God," Rachel said. "Did he actually—"?

Aviva shook her head. "I managed to get away before he did—that."

Rachel put her head in her hands. "I can't believe it."

"Are you calling me a liar?"

"No, of course not. I'm just completely flabbergasted," she said.

Rachel reached out to Aviva, who took her aunt's hand and walked back to the living room. Then, fighting her sobs, she told Rachel the entire story.

"I just can't believe." Rachel was dabbing her eyes with a tissue.

"Well, get used to it. He's an evil man, and who knows how many others—"

"Did you call the police?"

"Of course not. What good would that have done? He'd have said terrible things about me, told them I lied, and the police would have gone away."

"You don't know that for a fact."

"It's best for me just to get out of there. When he tried it again this morning, I knew I couldn't stay one day longer. Rachel, I almost stabbed him."

"Oh dear God," Rachel said again.

"I am getting a divorce, and if Nachum wants to remarry, he will have to give me a *get*[6]. I can't imagine he would refuse. Unless Ilona thinks they can't find another idiot to marry him. Anyway, even if he refuses, I was never legally married to him. So, I can go about my business away from all of them."

"You are not an idiot."

"I know I'm not. And that's why I'm leaving that horrid, dysfunctional family."

"You know about dysfunctional families? That's a big word," Rachel said.

"I read a lot. I told you that."

Rachel paused, her hand on her hip, looking down at Aviva, who had stopped crying. "Have you thought about what a terrible adjustment it will be for you? You've never known anything but the Hasidic life. It's such a strong community. Where will you go?"

"I haven't thought that far ahead yet. I know there are groups that help people who want to leave. I've read about them. I will get my GED, and then I will go to college."

"Aviva! How?"

---

6 A *get* is the divorce decree that is necessary for a marriage to be broken in Orthodox Jewish law. Only the husband is able to give a get to the wife, not the other way around, and it is issued by the couple's rabbi. The document states: "You are hereby permitted to all men."

"I'm trying to make the best of this, Rachel. Even before Eli—well, you know—I was unhappy. But this gives me the motivation to get out and make something of my life."

"You don't want kids?"

"Maybe someday. Right now, kids are the last thing on my mind. I'm just happy I don't have any. It would be so much more complicated if I did."

"I'm not sure how my husband—your uncle—will feel about this."

"I mean no disrespect, but honestly, I don't care how he feels. I have to do what's right for me, and this is right."

"I'm almost surprised I feel so supportive of you. But I do. I think I've mellowed with age. And looking at your mother, who knows what the future holds for any of us." Rachel reached her arms out to Aviva, who leaned over and accepted the warm embrace. The two women were silent for several minutes. "I do love you, Aviva, and I want you to be happy, even if I'm not sure whether you're making the right decision. And honestly, I'm worried about you. But I respect you. You are so young, but you're smart, and you know your heart."

"Thank you, Aunt Rachel. I didn't think I was going to be able to tell anyone what happened. It was so—embarrassing. It made me feel very guilty, ashamed—like I did something to deserve it."

"You must never think that way, my dear niece. Our community may be old fashioned, but no woman should have to go through that. I am shocked, but certainly not at you."

"Actually, I'm relieved that somebody knows what happened. I hope you believe me, because I am telling you the truth."

"I've known you your entire life, and I have never known you to be a liar," she replied. "But you have to start thinking about where you will go. It's not going to be easy." She shook her head slowly. "It's not going to be easy at all. You may have regrets."

Aviva thought about David's offer to pick her up at the bus terminal. She wasn't sure she could tell him. At least he would be a friend, and she knew at this moment, she could really use a friend.

CHAPTER TWELVE

Aviva and David

Despite her aunt's suggestion that it might not be a good idea, Aviva had insisted on seeing her mother one more time, telling her goodbye. Today, her mother had seemed agitated, although she still didn't speak or indicate she had any idea who was talking to her. But when Aviva got too close, her mother started to shake and turn pale, so Aviva stayed an even shorter time than she had the first day. She and Rachel had hugged for a long time, Rachel insisting on walking her to the bus station and waiting for the bus to come. Aviva sat in the back of the bus so she could see Rachel waving to her as long as possible. Then she spent the entire bus trip with images of her mother criss-crossing with images of Eli's leering face. No matter how hard she tried, she couldn't shake those images loose.

She'd worried about how she and David would connect at the bus terminal, but he'd figured out what gate her bus was stopping at, and he was waiting there at the door, tapping his foot as she finally alit. She was the last person out. She had never been so happy to see someone.

"Aviva!" he called to her as she started down the bus steps. He was waving and smiling, and he'd brought a single daisy for her, which he thrust into her hand as he grabbed her bag. She was relieved he didn't try to touch her, because she wasn't sure she would be able to let him do that. She had removed the wig halfway through the trip, and she left it on the seat. She never wanted to see it again.

Aviva blushed. "Thank you for this flower," she said. "It's beautiful."

"No big deal," he said. "I just thought it might cheer you up."

"Just seeing you here is cheering me up," she said.

"Are you hungry?" It was about eleven-thirty in the morning, and she hadn't had much of an appetite for breakfast, so her stomach was rumbling a little. Since she'd left home, she had been having trouble eating anything.

"Are you?"

"I can always eat," he laughed. "What do you like?"

Aviva thought about the kosher life she was leaving. It would still be very difficult to mix meat with milk, to eat the forbidden foods like shellfish. She hoped he would understand. "I guess just some toast or a bagel," she said.

"This is New York City," he said, "so I think either of those will be easy to find."

She couldn't take her eyes off his smiling face. She had no idea how she'd had the good fortune to meet him. He shepherded her down the escalators and out the revolving door onto Eighth Avenue. As they stopped on the sidewalk, he slipped a hand around her waist, but she jumped.

"Oh, I'm sorry," he said. "I didn't mean to startle you."

Aviva blushed a bright red. "You're going to have to forgive me," she said. "I am jumpy when someone touches me." She'd thought she was over that, especially when she allowed Rachel to hug her, but she obviously wasn't. As much as she was determined to get a divorce from Nachum, even over and above Eli's assault, this was a man, and she was still married. It would take her a while to relax and let him touch her in any way.

"Are you going to tell me what happened?" he said, putting his hand in his pocket as he carried her bag with the other one.

"I will try, but that is going to take some time as well." She thought about her aunt's reaction, but no matter how much her aunt sympathized, she had given no indication she would do anything about it. That was all right. Rachel had to protect herself too. She knew if Rachel tried to do something, she would be persona non grata for a long time if not forever. This was her own problem to deal with.

"Okay," he said, but she noticed his smile disappearing. "How about this place?" He pointed to a deli on the corner, and Aviva nodded. There was an empty table in the back. "What would you like?"

"I don't know," she said. Her money was almost gone. "Maybe just coffee?"

He raised his eyebrows. His attraction to this beautiful sad young woman seemed only to get stronger, but she was certainly difficult to figure out. Something about her kept him interested in making the effort. He'd also gone to the library to find out more about the Hasidic sect she'd come from—Satmars they were called. "Are you worried it's not kosher?" He bent his head to the side, put his hand on his hip.

She shrugged. "No, not really. I'm not going to have any meat."

"Because we could go somewhere like my shop that's kosher?"

Aviva put her elbows on the table and her chin in her hands. Suddenly, she was so exhausted, she wasn't sure she could hold her head up. She wanted to talk to him, wanted to get to know him, wanted to try to trust him, but she realized she had to make an effort to make that happen, not simply act like a lost child.

"I'm sorry, David," she said. "You must think I'm a very strange person. There's just—so much."

He flipped his hand toward her, as if to say, no problem. "Don't worry," he said. "I'll just get us each a bagel. You can eat it or not, and I'll get us coffee."

"I don't have much—I don't have much money," she said.

"This feast is my treat," he said.

"You're always doing that," she sighed.

"All you owe me is to talk to me. Is that fair? I like you, and I really want to get to know you." He turned and walked toward the counter before she could answer.

She wanted to get to know him too. She looked at her left hand, the wedding ring still on her finger. She thought back to the wedding service, when the rabbi had Nachum repeat, "Behold, you are betrothed unto me with this ring, according to the law of Moses and Israel." As Jewish law and tradition dictated, the ring was made of plain smooth gold, no engraving or precious stones, no ornamentation, a simple unbroken circle. Eli had bought it somewhere in the jewelry district and given it to Nachum, who hadn't had any money. Aviva hadn't had the money to buy a ring for Nachum either, which didn't seem to bother him.

At this moment, she looked at the ring on her finger as a representation of Eli. She'd overheard him telling Ilona after the wedding he'd gotten a great deal from this jeweler who owed him a favor—someone had returned it, so it was cut-rate. Cheap, really. The ring suddenly felt hot, too hot to wear. She pulled it off and dropped it on the table, but it clattered to the floor and rolled past toward the front of the store, stopping at David's shoe. She watched it roll but didn't move to pick it up.

"Did you mean to drop this?" David had returned with the food and the coffee. He'd grabbed the ring and stuck it over his pinky. He offered it to Aviva, sticking his hand out to her after he'd put the food on the table.

"I don't want it," she said. "I don't care what you do with it."

"You might change your mind later," David said, slipping it off his finger and into his shirt pocket.

Aviva shook her head firmly. "Go sell it. If you're lucky, it might pay back everything I owe you. But it's probably not worth much." She was glad it was out of sight, even though she knew it was in David's pocket. She never wanted to see it again. "I don't care what the law says. As far as I'm concerned, I'm not married anymore."

David threw back his head and laughed. "But you are!" he said. "In the eyes of the law."

She shrugged.

"You're sure you want to get out of your marriage? You'll have to go to a lawyer."

"I hope they have lawyers for people with no money, because I certainly can't afford to pay one."

"I think they do," David said, "but you just have to make sure this is what you want."

"I've never been more sure of anything in my life."

"Does your husband know?" David took a sip of coffee and made a face. "This coffee isn't very good," he said.

Aviva shook her head. "I don't think he has a clue."

"Don't you think you should tell him?"

Of course she had to tell Nachum. By now, his entire family must be buzzing about the fact that she left town suddenly without letting anyone know. She shuddered to think about the lies they were spreading about her. Ilona would be licking her chops, telling everyone, "I told you so," pointing accusatory fingers at family members who allowed the marriage to happen in the first place.

"I don't want to do it in person."

"I'll go with you if you want."

"No, David. I told you. It's a bad idea for you to go anywhere near them. I have no idea what they will do to you."

"It's so frustrating," he replied. "You seek me out to protect you and seem to appreciate that, but when I make an effort to help you, you reject me. It's hard to understand."

"How much do you know about the Satmars?" She'd raised her eyebrows and was resting her head on her hands. She hadn't touched the coffee or the bagel he'd brought.

"After I met you the first time, I went to the library and read about them," he said. "Library is open for me too, not just you." He laughed, but Aviva thought it was a nervous laugh. "I went online too."

"I don't know how to use a computer," she said. "It's frowned on for women to do that in my world."

"That's ridiculous," he said. "It shouldn't be. I'll teach you."

She shrugged. "So, if you've done the research, you know about how closed our society is, don't you? We are not allowed to have much to do with anyone on the outside, especially women and especially after marriage. There is a group called shomrim who are like a Hasidic police force. They take care of things, and I mean that. If you're within the clan, they come quick, fix problems. And they can also be good to people outside if someone has a problem on our streets. But if you don't follow the rules, or if you appear to be threatening our way of life in any way, they can be cruel. Worse than cruel. There are stories—" Her voice trailed off.

"I read about that," he said. "But can't you call the police then?"

"You don't understand. Shomrim have a close relationship with the police. Police have been known to look the other way when something shady goes on. Shomrim will say you are anti-semitic and need to be stopped. They'll blame you for my lapse. I'm sure of it. Things happen. You just can't go there! Please let me know that you believe me."

David raised his hand and waved it, as if to tell her he would heed her warning. "I have no intention of threatening your people's way of life or putting myself in danger, for that matter. I just want to protect you."

"It doesn't matter. They go on perceptions, not necessarily reality."

"All right, but I think it's important for you to call your husband and let him know your plans. That you're not coming home." He paused. "You're still determined not to go back?"

She nodded in a way she hoped would make him believe there was no way she'd be changing her mind. "But I don't have a phone," she said.

"I do." He pointed to his phone, which was sitting on the table next to his cup of coffee.

"No, I can't use your phone, because they would trace it to you."

"I don't care," he said. "Where I live, I can call the police, and there is no shomrim."

For some reason that she couldn't understand, Aviva suddenly became light-headed. She didn't know what was happening, but she was overtaken by fear. Her breathing became shallow, she felt the blood drain from her face, felt perspiration dripping down her back. She looked down at her hands, both of which were planted on the table, and watched them as they shook but couldn't stop the shaking. Then she found herself gasping for breath. She had an urge to get up and run, but she had no energy.

"Aviva?" David stood up halfway and reached across the table to her. "Are you all right?"

She thought she heard her name, but it sounded otherworldly, as if it was floating in the air from another planet, as if she were planted up on the ceiling looking down at a shell of herself going through some strange motions. She looked up and saw David's lips moving, but now all she could hear or feel was her own, fast heartbeat. She thought she might pass out.

"Aviva what's wrong?" David jumped up and came around the table. He put a hand out to steady her, but she shook his hand off. "Are you all right? Please, talk to me."

And then everything went black. She woke up somewhere, she didn't know where, but it was a very small area and she was lying flat, a needle in her arm, a wet cloth over her head. "Where am I?" she said.

"She's regained consciousness," she heard someone say, a female voice with some kind of accent she couldn't place. "You feel better, honey?" The woman had a uniform on, and she was bending over Aviva. The woman turned her head toward the opening at the front and called out to someone. "You can come up now, hon. She's back with us." Then to Aviva again, "Your name is Aviva, right? Your husband is terribly worried about you. You can let him know you're okay."

"My husband? What is this place?" She started to sit up, the cloth falling lopsided over her eyes, but she felt so dizzy, she just lay back down. The woman reached down and removed the cloth. Aviva looked again at the needle in her arm and saw an IV bag hanging above her to the right of the gurney she was lying on. "What happened to me?"

"Whoa, take it easy," the woman said again. She put a hand on Aviva's shoulder to steady her. "You're in an ambulance. Your husband called for one. He said you passed out. Best to just lie still for a while."

What would she say to Nachum? And how did he know? She was terrified he'd be furious with her. Her mind was a little foggy. She squinted, trying to remember what happened before she got here, and felt the tears welling up in her eyes. She picked up her free hand to wipe her forehead and noticed the wedding ring missing. Her thoughts were so muddled, she couldn't remember why it was gone. She knew she didn't want to talk to Nachum, but the next voice she heard wasn't his. It was a familiar voice, but at first, she couldn't remember whose it was. Her brain still wasn't right.

"Hi, Aviva. I was so worried about you. I'm so glad you're back with us."

Aviva looked up expecting to have to defend herself against Nachum, but she was incredibly relieved to see David's face staring down at her, not Nachum's.

"Do you feel better?" David put his hand out, palm up, but he didn't touch her. It hadn't taken him too long to learn her rules. She wanted badly to grab his hand, but she resisted the urge.

"What happened?" she said. She tried to smile. Everything was becoming clear again. She couldn't believe David was still with her.

"You had some sort of attack, and then you fainted," he said. "I'm so sorry. The EMTs said they think you're just badly dehydrated and maybe had a panic attack. I feel terrible I didn't insist that you have some water. They wanted to take you to the hospital, but I told them we should leave that up to you. The IV is going to help with the dehydration. When is the last time you ate or drank anything?"

"You must think you got yourself into some really crazy situation with me," she said, her voice starting to sound normal again. "Every time you see me, I'm falling apart. I shouldn't be your problem."

"It's okay." David smiled the smile that lit up any place where he happened to be, even this confined, dark ambulance. Aviva remembered that smile as one of the reasons she was so attracted to him. "I think you've had a really hard time." He looked at her face, which had regained some of its natural color, and marveled at how beautiful she was, despite everything she'd been through. She was one of those people who didn't need any makeup. Her green eyes were glistening with the beginning of tears. Her hair out of the wig was a honey blonde color, wavy, thick, but spiky, because it was still short. He had an urge to brush it off her face, to lean down and kiss her on the forehead, but he put his hands behind his back and bit his tongue.

"So," the female EMT called up to them. "We'd like to take you to the hospital to get you checked out. What do you think?"

Aviva tensed. If they did that, they would discover that David wasn't really her husband and insist on calling Nachum. Eli might even come, or Ilona. She couldn't let that happen. She shook her head as strongly as she could. "No hospital," she whispered to David. "Please, don't let them take me."

"You think you're okay?" His brow furrowed, and he wiped his sleeve across his forehead, as if that might help make the decision.

"I will be, as long as I don't have to go to the hospital."

"You promise you will drink water when I ask you to? That you will eat something?"

"I promise," she said. "Please!" she said again.

"She said no hospital," David called out to the woman.

"Well, she has the right to refuse to go," the EMT called back, "but we'd like to give you some instructions about how to make sure she doesn't get dehydrated again. It's been very hot and muggy, you know? Have to keep drinking. Extremely important."

"She promised me she will do what she needs to do," he said. He looked back down at Aviva and put his index finger across his lips as if to tell her not to say anything else, just in case she was tempted to resist. But she smiled. Her first smile since this had happened, whatever it was.

"And if it happens again, sir, promise me you'll bring your wife to the ER right away."

"I promise," David said, his eyes crinkling up into the crows' feet wrinkles Aviva loved so much. He put his finger up again.

"She thinks you're my husband," Aviva whispered.

David nodded and smiled. "Our little secret," he said, winking.

"Thank you so much. I would have killed myself if you had let them call Nachum."

The smile disappeared, and David's eyes widened. Aviva laughed a little. "I was kidding," she said. "I wouldn't have killed myself—I think."

David smiled again. "I'm just glad there's nothing terribly wrong with you," he said. "That EMT read me the riot act about letting you get dehydrated. Irresponsible thing for a husband to do, she said. Told me I should be ashamed of myself."

Aviva laughed again. "How long does this thing have to stay in?" She looked up at the IV bag.

"I think it's almost done," he said. After it was, he knew he had to figure out what to do with her next. He was trying not to think too far ahead, but that was almost impossible.

CHAPTER THIRTEEN

David and Aviva

They rode without speaking on the 7 train to Queens. Aviva still looked a little pale to him, but at least she was smiling and drinking the bottle of water he'd bought, taking little bites out of the bagel. Her hands weren't shaking anymore either. When they were close to the stop, he spoke up.

"So, I want to apologize in advance for my place," he said, his chin in his hand.

"Why?" she asked.

"It's pretty small. I can't afford a big place. And it's pretty crowded with all my drums."

"Oh, you're a drummer?"

He nodded.

"Don't worry, I will clean your place for you."

David laughed. "It's clean," he said. "Just small."

"Laughter makes a small space seem much larger," she said, moving her chin up and down as if to emphasize her point.

"So, I befriended a philosopher, did I?" he said. Joking around was fine, he knew. But the serious business in front of them was the "elephant in the room"— Aviva's husband, her in-laws, her community. But he was positive telling them had to be one of the next orders of business, before there was some sort of explosion. If Aviva had been honest with him, he realized it was not going to be a pleasant piece of news to deliver.

Aviva laughed. "But seriously, you don't mind my staying with you? I—um—I don't have anywhere else to go." She took in a breath. "You don't have—don't have a girlfriend, do you? I don't want to make anyone angry."

David shook his head. "No girlfriend," he said. "I don't mind having you if you don't mind staying in a postage-stamp-sized apartment."

"I don't take up much room," she said, pulling her body tight around her middle, tucking her head. "See?"

He chuckled and shrugged. "Yes, you are very tiny and invisible."

"But," she said, her face moving from the bright smile to a serious look, her mouth turning down a little, "I will have to get a job. I'm not sure how I will do that. No way I'm willing to make you pay for me."

"I'm pretty sure they've been looking for help at the shop. I could ask if they'd consider hiring you. Would that work?"

Her face brightened almost immediately. "Oh my God, that would be amazing. I have experience," she said, "in the bakery. And I'm really good with math. I don't let anyone get away with anything."

"You are a tough cookie," he said, laughing. "I don't want to get on your wrong side."

Aviva made a face. "You better remember that," she said.

"Okay, that's settled. I'll ask. They like me, so cross your fingers they say yes."

The small one-bedroom apartment had a tiny kitchen, which Aviva noticed was spotless. There was a pass-through opening in one of the kitchen walls, with a counter and two stools mounted on the living room side. The living room was rectangular, with one wall of exposed brick and a window on the far end. There was a futon against the brick wall, and a floor lamp next to that. David had put up shelves along the opposite wall, where he had a television, a stereo, many books, and a great deal of drum equipment. His drum set sat beside the window. She was fascinated with all of its parts and wondered how loud it would sound when he played. Other than that, the walls were mostly bare, except for some colorful hangings and some photos of some of his performances he'd put up. The bedroom was so small, his bed took up most of the space, except for a small bureau in the corner. But she couldn't help thinking that the place, as small as it was, was so much more cheerful than her apartment in Brooklyn, it made her heart feel warm. She felt instantly safe here.

"Would you like some more water?" he said, moving around the kitchen, taking a glass out of the cabinet.

"Do I have to? I feel as if I'm overflowing with water now, after that IV and the bottle of water you made me drink on the way home. When I move, I can feel it sloshing in my stomach."

"I guess you don't have to," he said, "but in a couple of hours, I'm going to make you drink another glass. And what would you like to eat?"

Aviva still didn't feel very hungry. "I feel bad that you're waiting on me," she said. "Besides, I have a stomach ache."

"No, I'm doing my penance for being a bad husband," he said. "That ambulance woman said I was." He smiled at her. He'd sliced up a tomato and a hard-boiled egg and put them on some lettuce, brought them out of the kitchen.

"Here." He put the food down on the small counter attached to the half opening between the kitchen and the living room. "Come on. I promised that EMT, and I think she'll come and find me and give me a harsh talking-to if I don't make you eat." He patted the stool that he pulled out from under the counter.

"You cook, too?" Aviva sighed, but she couldn't deny that although she'd been here less than an hour, it was already fun playing house with this man—this stranger who seemed less like a stranger than people she'd known all her life. The thought of Nahum making food for her was impossible to comprehend.

"I wouldn't exactly call this cooking," he laughed. "But I'm pretty good at it."

She walked over to the counter and sat down on the stool. "Thank you," she said.

"Would you like some coffee?"

Aviva laughed. "You're really trying to force fluids into me, aren't you?"

David shrugged. "Just doing what I'm told." He stood over her as she ate the food, which tasted much better than she thought it would. She finished it all and pushed the plate away.

"Are you happy now?" she said, looking up at him. "Thank you. It was really good. I guess I was hungry after all. My stomach feels better."

He took her plate to the sink and washed it, putting it in a dish drainer afterward. "Now, we have to talk seriously," he said.

"I know. I'm worried," Aviva answered.

"There's no way you can stay here without letting your husband know," he said.

"He won't be home now. He'll be studying."

"Anyone else you could call?"

Aviva thought about her sister-in-law and shuddered. "No. There is no one else I care to talk to," she said.

"Well why don't you call and leave a message? Then he can call back on my phone. Maybe that will give him some time to get used to the idea? You know, a little warning."

"I don't know what to say," she said. "I know he'll be furious."

"Does he have a bad temper?"

Aviva shook her head. "Not really. He doesn't usually show much of any emotion," she said. "But I'm afraid that might change when I tell him I'm not coming home."

"So, if he doesn't have a bad temper, and he doesn't show much emotion, I have a question." David put his finger up to his chin, and his eyes narrowed, the smile disappearing.

"What?"

"What is so bad that you refuse to go back there, refuse to talk to him face-to-face? Maybe you could work things out?"

"Are you trying to get rid of me?"

"No, no," David said. "It's not that. I'm just trying to understand. I feel as if there's something you're not telling me."

Aviva gasped. "Why would you say that?"

"No reason," he said, dismissing it with the wave of a hand. "I didn't want to upset you. But tell me there's nothing else—" He raised his eyebrows. "Can you?"

Aviva didn't answer. "I should call," she said. "I'm worried about your phone, though."

David brushed it off with a wave of his hand. He pushed his phone over to her, and when she took it from him, his hand brushed against hers. This time he didn't pull it away. Aviva felt an electric charge go through her body, from her hand up to her shoulder, and then down to her toes. She'd never felt anything like it before. She let her hand linger there for a few seconds, and then she moved it away, but slowly. When she stole a glance at him, his lips were turned up slightly and his eyes twinkling. She knew she wanted more of that feeling. But for her own sanity, she was going to have to ease into it slowly, and she was grateful he seemed to understand that as well.

Aviva felt her voice shaking as she spoke to the answering machine. She couldn't remember ever having felt this nervous, not even their marriage night, when she'd had no idea what to expect. As it turned out, the wedding night shouldn't have worried her. Nachum had begged off doing anything—too tired, he told her, too much dancing and drinking. He'd gotten into bed with most of his clothes still on, turned on his side with his back to her, and gone to sleep. She'd been so relieved, it gave her a burst of adrenaline that kept her awake for hours. She wondered whether he would try something later, after he woke up, but he never did. In fact, for the first two weeks, he never even touched her. It was only after she saw Ilona having a serious discussion with him that he tried to consummate the marriage. But all these months later, there had been no consummation, for which she was positive Ilona would blame her. She shuddered as she held the phone.

"Hello, Nachum." She cleared her throat. "This is Aviva." She paused and looked up at David, who made a circle with his thumb and index finger, nodded his head. As hard as it was doing this, it was somehow easier with David giving her moral support. "I am not coming home. I am done with the marriage." She emphasized the word "done," extending it to two syllables. At this point, Aviva started to cry. David came close.

"May I put an arm around your shoulder?" he said softly. "Maybe I can give you some strength. It makes me sad to see you suffering like this."

Her first instinct was to recoil in terror, but she somehow managed to convince herself that David was not Eli—not a threat. He'd met her at the bus station, called an ambulance when he could have left her unconscious in that restaurant. He had fed her and offered her space in his small apartment. He seemed truly concerned. And he had not overstepped any of the bounds she'd insisted on. She nodded, and he touched her gently on the back. But she squirmed, so he took his hand away.

"I don't know what happened to you," he said, "but I promise I will never hurt you."

Those words helped Aviva calm down a little. She wanted desperately to trust David. "Please call me back at this number," she said, speaking the number carefully into the phone. "But I won't be coming back. That's final." She handed the phone back to David, and he pressed the off button.

"You're shaking," he said. She was really trembling now, more than she had been during the phone call. She dropped onto the futon and put her head in her hands. "Do you think he'll call back?"

Aviva looked up, nodded.

"Are you afraid of your husband, because if he did anything to you—" David was flexing his fists without realizing it.

Aviva looked up, raised her hand. "No, no. It wasn't him," she said. "He didn't do anything. That was part of the problem."

"Then who?"

She waved her hand again. "I can't—" She shook her head. "I'm sorry, I just can't talk about it."

"I can't help you if you won't tell me what's wrong," David said. He thought he'd shown her unequivocally that he wasn't going to hurt her, was on her side, so it was frustrating that she still refused to trust him. He turned and walked into the small kitchen, took a bottle of water out of the refrigerator, and poured half of it into a glass. He realized he hadn't drunk anything in hours either.

"I'm sorry," she said again. "It's not you. You saved my life. Again." She sighed.

"Okay, well, I can't force you to talk to me," he said, coming back into the room where she sat. "But when you're ready, I'm ready."

"Thank you," she said. "I do feel safe with you."

Before David could answer her, his phone rang, and Aviva stiffened, all the blood draining from her face. Her muscles became so taut, it felt as if they might snap if she moved. She gripped the arm of the futon with one hand until her knuckles were white. David glanced down at her, and then he walked into the kitchen and turned his back on her. He was talking softly, so it was impossible to hear what he was saying. She had mental scenarios of what was going on in that phone call, that it would be Nachum yelling or Eli yelling or Ilona yelling. But the phone call took quite a long time, and David was speaking in Spanish. Nevertheless, she let her imagination take her to terrible places. By the time he got back, she felt faint, as if she might lose consciousness again.

"Wow," he said, before he really got a good look at her. "I can't believe what just happened."

Aviva jumped. She looked straight at David, but he was smiling broadly, the crows' feet firmly in place, his eyes shining. It had obviously been a positive conversation.

"What's going on? Was that—?"

"Oh, no," he threw his hand up to the side of his head. "No, that was not anyone calling for you."

"Oh, thank heaven," she said, feeling the color returning to her face. "Was it good news? You look so happy."

"Yeah, the most incredible thing just happened. I've been wanting to play a gig with this guy, this amazing bass player, for a long time—years maybe. I've met him in passing, but honestly, I didn't think he knew I existed." David laughed, wiped some perspiration off his brow with his sleeve. "That was my friend Carlos on the phone! He plays with the guy all the time, but their regular drummer got appendicitis, so he can't do this show tomorrow night, and he called to ask if I would sit in."

"Oh," she said. The relief she felt was like a breath of fresh air. "That's wonderful for you. I'm happy for you too."

David's gaze darkened. "Oops," he said. "The gig isn't here. It's in Boston. I have to go there, like right now."

Aviva gasped, not even realizing she had. Where would she go if David was going to Boston? Why did everything have to be so complicated?

"Oh, right, we have to figure out what to do with Miss Aviva," he said, laughing. "You don't have to be so dramatic."

"I don't think it's very funny," she said.

"It's no problem," he said. "You have two options—stay here. There's food in the fridge, water, a sort of comfortable futon to sleep on. And you'll be safe. No one but me knows you're here."

Aviva must have lost color again, because David bent down toward her, although he kept his hands in his pockets. "I'm worried they'll trace your phone and come here to grab me," she said. "I'd be afraid to stay here alone."

"That's understandable," he said. "But I told you there are two options."

"What's the second?" she said.

"You come with me. I'll be staying with my friend Carlos and his wife in Boston. You can stay in the room with me—don't worry," he added quickly. "I will be a gentleman. If there's only one bed in the room, I'll sleep on the floor. Is that all right?"

"Boston?" she said.

He nodded.

"You don't mind?"

He shook his head.

"What will I do when you are playing your show?"

"You can come and hear me!" he said. "Unless," he said, his smile fading, "you don't want to?"

"No, I want to," she said. "I'm not sure what to do at a show, though."

David laughed. "You either sit or you stand, and you listen, and if you like the music, you clap, and you can dance all you want."

"Will there be a lot of other people there?"

"I sure hope so," he said. "Working with these guys is really good for my career. So, the more the merrier." He stared at her face, the mouth drawn, the eyes narrowed, the pallor of her skin noticeable. "I think you might have a nice time?"

"I've never been to Boston," she said. She couldn't think of anything else to say, although the thought of going with this man to a different city had suddenly scared her. What was she doing?

"Are you having second thoughts?" he said, tilting his head to the side, as if that might enable him to read her mind more easily.

"Second thoughts?"

"About leaving your husband—your people? It's probably not too late to go back." In his mind, David juggled the pros and the cons. He knew he was incredibly attracted to Aviva. She was beautiful, she was smart, and sometimes when she forgot herself, she was funny. And she would laugh at his jokes, which was endearing. And he enjoyed the fact that he could guide her, help her. It made him feel powerful in a good way.

On the other hand, there was no doubt she'd been damaged terribly by something or many things in her life. From what he'd read in the library, her sect was extremely exacting, harsh, unforgiving. One had to do exactly what one's sex and station demanded, and the rules were especially strict for women. But then, Aviva had been different. She'd been sticking one toe in the water, so to speak, for years. She'd spent hours at the library, had learned to be proficient in English and math and history and many other things her peers had never learned, mostly because she hadn't had parents to guide her on the path of righteousness, at least according to the sect. And she'd read everything she could get her hands on, which was another thing her peers were discouraged from—actually forbidden from—doing. So despite her fearfulness, there was something about her that made him believe she was a risk-taker against all odds, which to him was more than attractive—it was incredibly sexy.

"I cannot go back," she whispered.

"So, two options, then," he said, trying to get out of his own head, lifting two fingers in the air. She had to make a decision, because he had to leave for Boston almost immediately. "Which do you choose?"

"There's only one possible choice," she said. "I have to go with you."

CHAPTER FOURTEEN

David and Aviva

It wasn't as if they were taking a trip to Zanzibar or somewhere terribly romantic, but despite the fact that they were driving on I95 only from New York to Boston in a clunky old car David had bought from a friend, Aviva was so excited, she felt as if she might jump out of her skin.

"Tell me again," she said. "what are we going to do when we get there?"

David laughed. The radio was tuned to an "oldies" station, and he was tapping his fingers on the steering wheel in time to the Beatles' "Lovely Rita Meter Maid." He'd been astounded when Aviva said she'd never heard the song, indeed only vaguely knew who the Beatles were.

"I already told you twice," he said.

"Yes, but I'm so keyed up, I just keep forgetting everything you tell me. So, tell me again."

"You don't have to be keyed up," he said, starting to hum along with the song. "We're staying with Carlos and Sylvia. They're some of my best friends. Everything will be fine. They will love you."

"What are you going to tell them about me?"

"What do you want me to tell them about you?" he said.

"Do you know this? I don't like it when you answer a question with a question," she replied, pouting. Then she burst into giggles.

"Why?" he said, and then he laughed again. "Okay, so we get into Boston, and then we go to Carlos's house. They have a spare bedroom. We can stay overnight at his place, so I can get a little bit of rehearsal time in tonight with him. I'm sure you and Sylvia will find something to do."

"The same room?" She frowned.

"I told you, if you want me to sleep on the floor or in a chair, I will."

"Okay, but who do they think I am?"

"A friend?" He glanced over at her to see the expression on her face before turning back to the road.

"There are a lot of big trucks on this highway," she said.

"Yup, that's how they move all the stuff around the country."

"Stuff?"

"For someone who's kept her nose in a book all her life, you really don't know anything about anything, do you?"

"Are you making fun of me?" she said.

"No, I'm sorry, I didn't mean to. Just kidding around." He wanted to touch her, put a reassuring tap on her leg or on her shoulder, something he would normally do with anyone, but he kept both his hands firmly on the steering wheel. He was amazed at what she did and didn't know, but he realized she was so sensitive about something he couldn't put his finger on, he tried to force himself to take a step back from his normal wisecracking. Otherwise, he ran the risk of making her feel so self-conscious about it that she would feel attacked. "Stick with me, and I'll give you an education, okay?"

"I feel as if I've had an education already, all the hours I've spent at the library."

"True," he said, "but I'm not talking about book learning. I'm talking about what goes on in the world learning."

Aviva looked out the window and sighed. Despite the fact that in one sense she found this adventure thrilling, something she could neither ignore nor explain was sadness about leaving her apartment, her job, and the community she'd always been a part of. She couldn't figure out why she should feel that way, when she'd been so unhappy there, so she was annoyed with herself. But she thought about the little alarm clock that had been her father's, her mother's dressing table, the blue wooden stepstool—now with paint peeling off—that had been hers as a child, which she had placed in the kitchen where she could use it to reach high cabinets. And there was a pretty necklace, costume jewelry, her father had given her mother. She wondered whether she'd ever see those things again.

Superficially, it didn't make sense. They were just things. Replaceable. Her life had been one series of painful incidents after another, culminating in the assaults by her husband's uncle and her resignation to the fact that she had to give up hoping her mother would ever be a mother to her. For the first time in a long time, she felt exhilarated about possibilities and safer than she had for weeks. But this new experience, whatever it was, was such an unknown, the farther away they got from New York, the more unnerved she became. What if David wasn't what he seemed on the outside? What if at some point he changed and hurt her the way Eli had hurt her? What would she do? She had no money, no way to get back home, nowhere else to go.

She chided herself. Even though she'd been told—lectured to her entire life—that she was not to have any dealings with, not to trust anyone outside their own community, every intuition screamed out that David was a *mensch*.[7] Everything he had done since they met had supported that. He even seemed to understand her aversion to being touched. But in addition to her upbringing, after what had happened with Eli, it was hard to trust any man, and she'd known David for only a very short time.

"Are you all right, Aviva?" he said.

"Are you reading my mind?" she replied.

"No, of course not," he said, laughing. "But you sighed, and then you got very quiet and turned away from me. I figured you were thinking about something bad."

"Not exactly bad," she said.

"But?"

She turned toward him. "Why do you care about me? I'm moody, I'm always crying, I don't know anything about the world, I have no money. Why do you care?"

That struck a nerve with him. He admitted to himself he'd thought about that very question, and he knew his friends would likely question him about it too—question his motives, even his sanity. He was a musician working in a bagel shop to make ends meet, someone who didn't need or really want any permanent ties right now. He'd had a couple of fairly long-term relationships, but those all fizzled out in the end, and he'd come to the conclusion it wasn't time to settle down yet, at least not until he established himself in the music world. But here she was. He was silent for a moment, but she stared at him, her eyes making an attempt, unsuccessful, to burn into his soul.

---

7   A fine person possessed of high integrity and honor.

Finally, he responded. "I—I'm not exactly sure," he said. "I have to be honest with you. Whatever it is that we are doing together doesn't make too much sense. But something about you makes me want to know more about you, a whole lot more. I want to be with you, and I have this feeling that I want to protect you. I hope that's not insulting?" He glanced over at her, taking his eyes off the road for a moment.

Aviva smiled. "Maybe I should be insulted," she said, "but I don't think anyone has ever wanted to protect me before, at least since my father died. It kind of feels good. Should I be angry at you for caring?"

"I'd like you not to be," he said. "I enjoy your company. You seem very open to learning about everything, and that's fun. What you don't know, you pick up so quickly. And I admire you for taking a risk and going on this adventure, for coming along with me."

"I was thinking the same thing," she said, "although truthfully, I felt it would be riskier for me not to come." She sighed, clasping her hands in her lap. She didn't want them to start shaking again.

"I know you don't like me to get too close to you," he said, "but I have the greatest urge just to touch your hand. Would it be all right?"

Now she couldn't hide the trembling in her hands, but she decided she had to force herself to get over her aversion to being touched. Nachum hardly touched her at all, and Eli had touched her in such a barbaric way, just the thought of it made her stomach churn. But David was neither Nachum nor Eli, and she couldn't convince herself she was not very attracted to him. She nodded and moved one hand closer to him. He reached over and lay his hand lightly on top of hers.

"Your skin is so soft," he said, rubbing her index finger lightly with his. His hand was warm. She felt the same thrill she'd felt the last time their hands touched. For a moment she couldn't speak.

"Aviva? You all right? Want me to stop?"

She shook her head, but she felt the blush creeping up quickly from below her neck to her forehead. Nothing had ever felt this good, and he was just touching her finger.

"You sure? I don't want to push you."

"I'm sure," she said, but her voice cracked as she said it. "I've never had the feeling I'm feeling right now, with your hand on mine."

"I hope sometime you can tell me what happened to you," he said. It was a recurring theme. From time to time, he would remind her that he wanted to know why she was so skittish.

"You know that in my religion, once you're married you never touch a person of the opposite sex, except your spouse," she said.

"You told me that," he said, "but you have been insisting that you don't want to be married anymore, that you don't feel married. Doesn't that give you permission to touch and be touched?"

"You just need to give me time."

"And I said I would. But you like this, don't you?" He gave her hand a little squeeze.

"I like it," she said softly, not looking at him. He smiled. "But if I'm being completely honest with you, I also have to admit I've been having some feelings of loss. Homesick feelings. I can't stop thinking about my apartment and about my friend at the bakery."

David stopped smiling. "Do you want to go home? I could take you to the train station."

"No, you know I don't—even if I wanted to, I can't."

"Well then," he said, "let's just try to have a nice time, all right? Let's say we're good friends, and we enjoy each other's company, and we're going a couple hundred miles away from home, so we can pretend we're two different people in a different place and forget about our troubles."

"You have troubles too?" She felt the frown lines jumping up at the bridge of her nose. "All I talk about is myself. I feel bad about that. I never even ask how you are."

"It's okay," he said. "Even though I don't know exactly what your problems are, they are obviously more serious right now than mine. So, it's fine to concentrate on yours—on getting you better. All right?"

"Thank you, David. I don't know what I did to deserve you."

David laughed. "You're so pretty," he said. "Especially when you smile, which isn't that often."

"There are a lot of pretty girls," she said, not smiling. "Why me?"

David shrugged. "Not sure. But I'd like to find out."

CHAPTER FIFTEEN

David and Aviva

Aviva was feeling like a little child being taken to the city for the first time. As they approached Boston, it seemed to have appeared out of some kind of mystical cloud. She thought she might be dreaming, because until this moment, she could never have imagined being in another city that was not New York. She looked around as they drove through the streets of buildings that looked like nothing she had ever seen, except possibly in a picture book about London in the library.

David glanced over at her and laughed. "Your eyes are so wide," he said.

Aviva felt a little embarrassed. "I'm sorry," she said. "This is a very new experience. This city is—well, it doesn't look anything like Brooklyn. And I keep thinking I should pinch myself to make sure I'm not dreaming right now."

"Do you like it? Do you think it's interesting?" he said.

"Everything seems so much smaller than it is in New York," she said, "and the buildings look older. Except for some of them." She pointed to a glass and steel skyscraper that seemed to impose itself on the Victorian skyline. "There are surprises everywhere."

"I lived here when I went to college, so it looks perfectly normal to me," he said, "but I see what you mean. It is very different from New York."

They were driving around what looked like a large lake. "What is that?" she said, pointing.

"Oh, that's Jamaica Pond," he said. "We're almost at Carlos's house."

"That is a very large pond," she said.

"I suppose it is," he agreed. "Being with you makes me feel as if I'm looking at everything with brand new eyes."

"This is part of the city?" She watched as they drove by old homes, some low brick buildings, many trees, no skyscrapers at all.

"Yes, it's called Jamaica Plain," he said. "We're here." He turned right and made a few other turns, and then pulled into a parking place on a street of attached houses. "Let's go."

Suddenly Aviva felt very shy, as if she wanted to curl up and stay in the car. "You're sure it's all right that I'm here?" she said.

"It's fine. I already talked to Carlos and Sylvia, and they said you will be very welcome here. Don't worry. You will like them. They're great people." He opened his door but looked over at her. "You okay? Remember, we are in a different city, so we can pretend to be different people."

"I did agree to that," Aviva said. She stepped out of the car and looked up the street at the houses. It was a normal day. No one was running out of their homes pointing at her. People on the sidewalk didn't give them a second glance. She took a deep breath. "I'll try."

"Hey, you two!" Sylvia had stepped outside the door of one of the houses and was waving. Aviva thought she was very attractive, very stylish. She looked down at her clothes and felt insecure. "Hi, David. This must be Aviva?"

David slipped an arm lightly around Aviva's waist, and then looked over at her, his eyebrows raised, as if to ask her permission. She nodded.

"We made it," he said.

"Well come on in. You need Carlos to come out and help you with the drums?"

"Nah, I'm fine." David waved the offer away with his hand as he unloaded his things.

"You want some coffee? Are you hungry?" As David made his way up the front steps with Aviva behind, Sylvia held the door opened wide. When he put the cases down, she pulled him away and enveloped him in a huge clinch, which he returned. They kissed on both cheeks. "You're a sight for sore eyes," she said to him. "It's been too long."

"We'd love some coffee," David said. "Right?" He looked at Aviva. She nodded. Coffee seemed to be a sort of common denominator. If they were all sitting around a table raising their cups together, it somehow made everything feel right.

"Great." She looked over David's shoulder at Aviva. "She need help with bags or anything?"

With some embarrassment, Aviva realized she really didn't have anything to bring in. She'd run from her apartment with nothing much but the clothes on her back. She felt like some sort of refugee, hugged herself, her arms tightly around. David hoisted his backpack on his back and carried in his snare drum and cymbals. "*She* is Aviva, and she speaks English," David said, pulling out of the hug and slipping his arm through Aviva's elbow. "This is Sylvia," he said. Then, "We're good."

Fighting back the urge to run, Aviva let him shepherd her through the narrow vestibule. Sylvia had put her hands on her hips and was leaning backward, looking Aviva up and down. "You are beautiful!" she said.

Aviva looked at the other woman's olive skin and shiny long black hair. "So are you," she said. She hoped the ice was broken.

"Come on into the kitchen, so you can meet my husband Carlos. I think the boys want to rehearse, so you and I can do some girl talk." She raised an eyebrow. "That okay?"

"It's fine," Aviva said, hoping it would be. David walked ahead to greet his friend. He and Carlos were in the hallway, slapping each other on the back and giving each other a huge bear hug.

"Too long, bro," Carlos said. "We should do this more often."

"I know," David said. "I've missed you too. So happy to be here. And this is Aviva." As if Carlos had been warned, he didn't try to hug her but stood about a foot away, smiling and reaching out his hand. Aviva didn't reach back, but she smiled and nodded.

"Nice to meet you," she said.

"Well come on and take a load off. Sylvia has the coffee on already. Really, the coffee is on all the time," he said, laughing. "You guys hungry?"

"Thanks so much," David said. "We had a bite on the way, so I thought that after we played for a while, I would take Aviva into the city and show her around. Grab some food. This is her first time in Boston."

"That right, Aviva? You're gonna have fun. It's supposed to rain though, do you guys mind?"

Aviva looked up at David. She didn't mind some summer rain, but she didn't know how he felt. She was still trying to learn everything she could about him. "What's wrong with a little rain?" he said. "Maybe it will clear out this muggy air." He paused. "Unless you mind?" he said to her.

She shook her head. "I like rain," she said. "It feels good on a day like this, and it smells good."

"It's settled then," David said. "So, let's have that coffee, and then Carlos and I will rehearse for tomorrow's show, and then Aviva and I will have our little adventure."

"David and Aviva's excellent adventure," Carlos said.

The coffee was delicious, but Aviva felt a little shy again when David got up to go into the other room with Carlos. She hoped she could talk to Sylvia without getting tongue-tied. Sylvia didn't leave much time for discomfort.

"All right, my dear, tell me everything about yourself."

Aviva smiled. "I'm not sure how much time you have," she said.

"David told me a little, but only a little. You are Jewish?"

Aviva nodded. She wondered whether Sylvia knew about the Satmars or, if she did, how she felt about them. She decided it was better not to get into it. "Have you been to New York?"

"Oh yes," Sylvia said, "many times. Carlos and I met in college. I was a singer in his band. We've performed all over the place—in New York City many times. Somehow, we just became close as performers, and then we became good friends, and then we fell in love, and, well, the rest is history. How did you and David meet?"

For some reason, the other woman's invitation broke some sort of barrier in Aviva. She began talking and told Sylvia most of her personal history—with the exception of Eli's assaults. It was easy to talk to Sylvia. It felt as if the woman was curious about everything. She reached across the table and put her hand on Aviva's. "You've been through quite a lot for someone so young," she said.

Aviva shrugged. "We play the cards we're given," she said.

"But your face is sad," said Sylvia. "Beautiful but hauntingly sad. Your eyes. Is there something you haven't told me? I see you smile sometimes, but mostly I feel a great sadness."

Aviva wasn't ready to share what Eli had done. "My—my community," she said, trying not to stumble over the words, trying not to cry, "is very strong, very isolated. It is not encouraged, no it is forbidden for us to deal with the outside world in any serious way."

"I'm not sure I understand," Sylvia said. "I don't know whether I want to ask you why or how. You live in Brooklyn, David said. Is that right?"

Aviva nodded. *At least, I did*, she thought. *I'm not sure where I live now.*

"So that's in the middle of New York City. How can you possibly be isolated? You're in one of the biggest cities in the world."

"That's true," Aviva agreed. "But everything we need to live is in our little corner of that city, and we are not supposed to learn much about the outside world. The rules are very strict."

"Why?" Sylvia said, raising her eyebrows.

Aviva sighed. "So, during World War II, Hitler decimated the Jewish population of Europe." She looked up to see what Sylvia's reaction was, but Sylvia was nodding. She continued. "Millions of our people were killed."

"Yes, that is a terrible history," Sylvia said. "It's in everyone's history book."

"So," Aviva continued, "the Satmars were a highly orthodox Jewish sect that started in 1905 in Hungary."

"Yes, but that was well before World War II."

"I know. We were allowed to live our lives as we wished, practicing the most orthodox religion we wished to. But when Germany occupied Hungary in 1944, they began deporting our people to concentration camps, where most were slaughtered."

Sylvia put her hand up to her mouth. This was well known, but hearing someone so close to it talking about it made it more real than it ever had been. She took a deep breath.

Aviva continued. "The people managed to save the chief rabbi by secreting him on a train to Switzerland and out of the hands of the German invaders. He emigrated from there to Palestine, but Satmars are against the state of Israel."

"Another why?" Sylvia said.

"It's complicated. The ultra-orthodox feel that there should be no forced return to the holy land," Aviva said. "They feel that the Messiah has not yet come, but it is only the Messiah who can mandate the formation of a Jewish state, not the government of any country."

Sylvia's mouth flew open. "I had no idea about any of this," she said. "But why did the rabbi refuse to let people assimilate with the rest of the population?"

"In 1946, Rabbi Teitelbaum left Israel and emigrated to the United States, where he settled in a small area of Williamsburg in Brooklyn. The entire sect that had remained in Europe was wiped out by the Holocaust, so the goal was then to repopulate to make up for all of the millions killed during the War, and not to allow any migration to Israel. And because the United States Constitution mandates the separation of church and state, we were able to maintain ourselves as a separate religious community without any regulation by the government."

"He thought that keeping people isolated and not speaking English would guarantee the survival of the sect?"

Aviva nodded again.

"But your English is very good," she said.

"Yes, as I mentioned, I had a rather unconventional childhood," Aviva said. "I spent a lot of time as a child sneaking off to the library and learning everything I could."

"But David said you're married? And I can see just by looking how young you are."

"I really had no choice. My grandmother was getting old, and she really wanted me out of her hair. My mother was and continues to be severely mentally ill. So, I agreed to the marriage, but it was never happy." She hung her head.

"That still doesn't explain why you ran away," Sylvia said, resting her hand on her chin and looking straight into Aviva's eyes. "Lots of people have unhappy marriages, but they don't all run away with someone they just met."

Despite her best efforts, the last sentence, especially the words "someone they just met," brought up all the emotions of the past weeks. She began to cry, and the crying turned to sobbing. David and Carlos were in the next room making beautiful music. Aviva was grateful it was loud enough to prevent David from hearing her.

"I'm sorry," Sylvia said. "I didn't want to upset you. Honestly, I was only trying to understand what you were doing and why you needed to run."

Aviva wasn't sure what to make of the other woman. Sylvia wasn't more than ten years older than she, but Aviva felt almost a motherly vibe coming from her. She desperately wanted to trust Sylvia, and for some reason, her resolve to keep everything to herself slipped away. "I need to tell you something," she said.

"You can tell me anything," Sylvia said. "I want to get to know you."

It all came pouring out. How Nachum and his family had been so unloving, how there had been no consummation of the marriage and thus how she hadn't gotten pregnant, and finally how Eli had committed the assaults that finally triggered Aviva's determination to flee.

Sylvia stayed silent and still for several moments, saying nothing.

Aviva continued to cry softly. "Do you hate me now?" She managed to get out between gasps of air. She felt as if she'd removed a great weight from her shoulders. Now it was up to Sylvia. She could tell David he should get rid of Aviva right away, or she could be compassionate. Either way, the words could not be taken back.

"I certainly don't hate you," Sylvia said. "Why would I hate you? You've been to hell and back. No wonder you don't smile much. Does David know all this?"

"Most of it," Aviva said, "but not the part about Eli. I was embarrassed to tell him about that. And I was worried if I did, he would reject me, like everyone else."

Sylvia cleared her throat. "David has spoken to me about you," she said.

Aviva felt her face begin to flush. Her eyes widened. "He did?" she sighed.

"Yes, my dear. That man is completely smitten by you. He has decided to take it upon himself to protect you as long as you need protection. But I do think you owe him the full story about Eli. He will never be able to understand everything until you tell him."

"You don't think he'll be so repulsed by me then that he will tell me to get out of his life?"

"Why on earth would he be repulsed by you? What happened with your husband's uncle was not your fault."

"I can't help thinking maybe I did something to deserve that."

"You can't think that way, Aviva. No woman deserves to be assaulted like that. No woman. I don't care who she is or what she's done. No man has the right to violate a woman that way. Do you understand what I'm saying?"

Aviva nodded.

"I will repeat that to you over and over until I think you believe it," she continued. "Do you promise to try to tell David? I think you like him as much as he likes you."

"I'll try," Aviva said, nodding. "He is one of the few friends I've ever had—certainly the best one. I feel very—very close to him. I don't think I've ever had this feeling before." Something stopped Aviva from telling Sylvia she was in love with David. She didn't know whether she could trust the feeling.

"Well, here." She handed Aviva a tissue. "Wipe your eyes. You've told me, and I didn't kick you out." She laughed a little. "And David won't either. But it's impossible to have a true friendship without trust."

Aviva shrugged.

"Perhaps I shouldn't tell you this," Sylvia said. "But David went through a terrible breakup a year and a half ago. It devastated him. He thought he'd found the love of his life, but it just didn't work out. He'd been with that girl for four years, and he was terribly hurt. So, when he called and told me about you, with all the hope and excitement in his voice, I felt very worried and protective."

Aviva looked up the other woman, her eyes wide. She prayed Sylvia would encourage David not to let her go, especially after everything she'd said.

"So, I made it my quest to make sure you aren't going to

hurt him too," she said, shaking her head. "I never want to see him suffer like that again."

"I will never hurt him," Aviva said, wondering whether it was even possible to promise such a thing. She wanted to believe it. She cared so much about him, she didn't want to endanger the relationship the two of them had forged.

"I hope you're being sincere," Sylvia said. I can see what has attracted David to you, over and above how pretty you are. I think someone who has suffered such hurt can empathize with someone else who has suffered hurt as well. And you have certainly suffered hurt."

"But I don't want that to guide my life," Aviva said. "I want to get beyond that, I really do."

"I feel that," Sylvia said, tapping her index finger on the table. "And, if we make some progress right now, I was thinking, looking at what you're wearing, maybe we can go up to my bedroom and pick out a different outfit for you. How about it? I think you might feel better if you looked a little more like most of the other people around."

Aviva glanced down at the shapeless black skirt that reached almost to her ankles, the black oxford shoes, the heavy hose underneath, the dark maroon oversized sweater and the shapeless black wool jacket that went down below her hips. It was August, and it was hot, but Aviva had always accepted the required mode of dress before, although removing the hot wig had been a welcome revelation, just as she thought it would.

"You would do that for me?"

"Absolutely. We look about the same size, although you might be a little smaller. But until you can get some new clothes, let's get you out of this getup and put you into something fashionable. At least more comfortable. Come on, let's do it before the guys finish playing. David will be so surprised." She smiled and stood up, reaching her hand out to Aviva, who took it readily. The more time that went by, the more she realized she wanted to look nice for him.

"You think so?"

"I know he will."

"Okay," Aviva said, standing. "Thank you."

"Good. We'll go up and go shopping in my closet. And maybe you'd like to take a quick shower too?"

CHAPTER SIXTEEN

Aviva and David

"Wow!" The low whistle resonated through the room. "You look great!" Aviva and Sylvia had come down the stairs at the same time David and Carlos had finished rehearsing and were on the way to find them. Aviva felt herself blush. After she showered, she'd picked out a pair of tight jeans—Sylvia said she'd gained a few pounds, so she couldn't fit into them anymore—and a V-neck, stretch cotton tank top in light turquoise that skimmed over her curves and was slightly low cut. When she'd put it on, she kept yanking the neck up, but Sylvia had laughed and told her just to leave it, that it was sexy. Then Sylvia had styled Aviva's short hair and let her borrow some lipstick.

Carlos was nodding his head, and David was flashing that bright, hundred-watt smile that Aviva loved.

Sylvia put her arm on Aviva's back, pushing her slightly toward David. She'd insisted that Aviva take off the heavy shoes, because one pair of silver sandals seemed to fit her okay, although they were probably half a size too big. She'd even loaned Aviva a pair of black lace bikini panties, which had made Aviva laugh when she held them up. "It's good to feel sexy," Sylvia had said, "even if no one can see what's making you feel that way."

"If you say so," Aviva had said.

"You like it? Doesn't she look adorable? No one could tell she had boobs before. But she's got 'em." Sylvia winked.

"Sylvia!" Aviva put her arm up across her face, as if that would keep the men from looking.

"You look beautiful, Aviva," David said, walking closer. Aviva crossed her arms over her chest. "Don't worry, just looking," he said, as if he could read her mind.

"Yeah, now she can go out and enjoy the warm summer air without feeling as if she's dressed for a snowstorm." Sylvia laughed.

"So, we're done for now," David said, waving toward Carlos. "We'll rehearse again tomorrow for the gig tomorrow night. So, you ready to go paint the town red?" He raised his eyebrows, looked straight at Aviva.

"Yeah," Carlos said, "you're gonna feel like a native Bostonian when David gets done with you."

Aviva laughed. "I hope so."

"So, let's go. We'll get some food and we'll have some fun," David said. "I'm starving, and I'd love a beer right about now." He beckoned to Aviva, and she walked toward him.

"Thank you so much, Sylvia," she said. "I hope I can get used to these clothes. Do you think people will look at me and think I look weird?"

They all laughed but Aviva. "You don't look weird at all," Carlos said. "No one will look at you, except to notice how pretty you are."

David reached out for her hand, but Aviva pretended not to notice and put her hands behind her back. She followed him out the door, and he opened the car door for her.

"So, do you have any idea where you would like to go?" he said, after he'd gotten behind the wheel.

Aviva shrugged. "No, I don't know anything about this place," she said. "I read about Boston's history at the library—one if by land, two if by sea, right?"

He smiled.

"But that happened in the seventeen-hundreds," she said. "The only thing I'm sure of now is how charming this city looks, how different from New York."

"Okay, I have an idea," he said, slapping the side of his head. "I should have thought of this. Let's go to Fenway Park. There's a bar there that's right under the stands. You can see right out to the field."

"Stands? What is Fenway Park?"

David smiled. "Right," he said. "It's the place where the Boston Red Sox play baseball. Ever been to a baseball game?"

She shook her head.

"Not even on TV?"

"We don't have a television," she said. Then she corrected herself, "Um, I meant, I didn't have a television."

"But—" She stopped, as if she couldn't think of what to say.

"What?"

"I'm only nineteen."

"It's a restaurant too. I'll order you a Coke, okay?"

Aviva smiled. "I'm kind of excited." Then she frowned. "Will they let me in—like this?" She made a gesture with her hand to demonstrate that she was talking about her clothing.

"Of course they will let you in. You look amazing. Try not to think about what you're wearing."

"I can't help it," she said. "I've never—it's never—I just don't know what to think."

"I'm with you, so you don't have to worry."

"Then, as if she'd had an epiphany, she put her head in her hands. David worried she might be about to cry again.

"Aviva? Something wrong?"

"I thought of something," she said. "Is this restaurant—does this restaurant have—is it kosher?"

David gasped a little. She'd been so willing to change her clothing, get rid of the wig, be open to a trip outside the state, be with him—he felt guilty for not even considering her food requirements. "No. Does that mean you can't eat anything there?"

"Do you think they have salad in different containers than what they keep their meat in?"

"I don't know," he said, "but we'll ask. If not, I'm sure we can find a kosher restaurant in the city. Anyway, being vegetarian, that question is important to me too. We can find out together. Is that all right?"

"I think so," she said. She felt a little better that David had similar concerns to her own, despite the fact that it was for a different reason.

"So, this is Fenway," he said after they'd found a parking spot pretty close to the ballpark. He pointed up at the green walls.

"It's—it's big," she said.

"Actually, a very small ballpark," he said. "Old. It's such an institution in this city that whenever someone suggests tearing it down and building a new, bigger one, everyone screams and yells bloody murder, so it never happens."

Aviva laughed. "Boston versus progress," she said. "Kind of like the Satmars versus the modern world."

He smiled. "You hungry? Or you want to walk around the outside of the park for a little while?"

"Let's walk," she said. "If that's okay with you?"

He nodded. "I can deal with my hunger for a little while longer," he said.

It was cloudy and threatening rain, but they were able to make a big circle around the perimeter of the stadium, walking across Brookline Avenue, taking a left on Jersey Street on one side, another left onto Van Ness Street, and finally a sharp left onto Lansdowne.

"Hungry yet?" he said.

"Sounds like you are," she laughed.

"Here's the place I was telling you about. It's actually built right under the stadium." He looked at her with wide eyes before he put a hand on her arm to guide her toward the door. She surprised herself by letting him do it. It actually felt good to be connected to another human being in this way. She couldn't remember the last time she'd had that kind of feeling. Maybe it was when she was a very small girl, and her father hoisted her up on his shoulders and held on to her legs. That sweet memory wafted into her consciousness.

As they stood in front of the hostess station, he slid his fingers down and picked up her hand, held it gently. The electricity happened again, and she felt as if she might faint, but she didn't let on. She was worrying there would be nothing here that she could eat. But she held on to his hand, which felt warm and exciting. And as if he'd gotten a shot of courage because she hadn't pushed him away, he intertwined his fingers with hers and gave a little squeeze. She squeezed back. She wondered whether anything could feel better than this.

"Right this way, folks." The hostess grabbed two menus and led them to a booth toward the front. Instead of sitting across from Aviva, David slid in beside her, grabbing her hand again.

"No game tonight?" he asked the hostess.

The woman shook her head. "They're out of town," she said. "I think Toronto. But we'll have it showing up there." She made a move with her chin toward some big TV screens behind the bar. Then she walked back to her station.

"See out there?" He pointed with his free hand straight ahead toward the window.

"Yes," she said.

"That's actually the field. That's where they play baseball."

"Right there?" Aviva said.

"Yeah," he said. "It's so cool when there's a game on."

Despite the gray sky and the sun starting to set, it was still possible to see the emerald green grass, neatly mowed in stripes. She was starting to enjoy this entire thing, when it suddenly occurred to her that she didn't have enough money to pay for anything on the menu. She pulled her hand out of his and rested her elbow on the table.

"You okay?" he said. "Did I do something?"

"I—um I'm not—not sure how to say this," she stammered. "I don't have enough money. I'm sorry. This place is too expensive."

"I'm getting really good pay for my gig tomorrow," he said. "Don't worry about it. My treat."

"You keep taking care of me. Why?"

David pulled her hand out from under her chin and laid it down on the table. Then he put his on top of it. "Because I like you," he said.

"Why? I seem like a giant burden." She started feeling weepy, but he refused to liberate her hand.

"You are beautiful, you are sweet, you are mysterious, and you need a real friend," he said, "somebody who has your back." Then he paused. "I'm so attracted to you. I want to know everything about you."

"I am mysterious?" She smiled. "I don't feel mysterious." His eyes crinkled into the smile she loved. "Do you trust me?"

"I do trust you," she said. "I think."

"Do you trust me enough to tell me what happened to you?"

"Why do you think something happened to me?"

"I know something happened to you," he said. "It took two days for you to let me hold your hand."

"Well, our culture—"

"I know about your culture," he said. "You told me about that. But you said you don't want to go back there, you're wearing Sylvia's clothes, and you're here with me. There is something making you very sad, and you sometimes go into a kind of trance, someplace where I can't follow. When that happens, your face looks tortured, even when you try to hide it. Then I have to joke you out of it. If you really trust me, you will tell me what happened to you."

"If I tell you, you won't like me anymore," she said. She tried to pull her hand out from under his again, but he held tight.

"That is impossible," he said. "Did you kill someone?"

"No," she said.

"Did you rob a bank?"

The smile turned into a little like giggle. "No, silly."

"Kidnap a baby? Overthrow the government?"

This time she just laughed.

"Then I will still like you after you tell me. I promise."

"You guys want a little more time to look at the menu?" A waitress had approached the booth. "Something to drink?"

"I'd love whatever IPA you have on draft," David said. "A tall one." The waitress nodded and then looked over at Aviva as if she was about to ask for ID. "And the lady will have a Coke." The waitress smiled.

"Great. I'll bring those over and then take your order." She walked off toward the bar.

"We'd better figure out what we're eating," he said.

Aviva looked at the menu in earnest and decided to order a salad after the waitress told them the place used different utensils and bowls for non-meat dishes. "Lots of our patrons are vegetarians," she said, "and lots of vegans." David ordered a veggie burger and French fries. As they ate, the skies opened up and there was a rather fierce but fast moving thunderstorm. The lightning was so close, it illuminated the entire field. The rain followed, but then after a few minutes it stopped and everything was peaceful again, the field alive in a bright green.

"That was a sign," David said, "that we should be together here." Aviva raised her eyebrows and shook her head. She pointed her index finger, about to shake it at him, but he grabbed it and kissed it. "Tastes like salad," he said.

Aviva laughed. She couldn't remember the last time she'd laughed so much. After David paid the check, Aviva felt as if she wanted to walk hand-in-hand with him all night. "Where to now?" she said. They had continued up Lansdowne Street, and David noticed a gate that seemed to be unlocked, ajar. He led her up to it and peered around it toward the ballpark.

"You know, it looks like someone left this gate open, and there's an open door down there. Want to go see the field?"

"Are we allowed to?"

"The gate is open," he said, shrugging. "Let's!" Before she could protest, he had put his arm around her waist and was ushering her through the gate. "No one is around," he said. "See? It's really meant to be."

CHAPTER SEVENTEEN

David and Aviva

Although she'd begun to trust David, Aviva felt a bit of the old fear creeping back in. They were trespassing in Fenway Park. It was getting darker by the minute, and although it had stopped raining, the air was so heavy with moisture it felt as if there might be a downpour again at any moment. It was hard to see the green anymore, because the darkness colored everything in shades of gray to black. And they were completely alone, in a huge open space, vulnerable to anything from above or around them. What if David began to act like—Eli. Her hand began to shake, but David gripped it harder.

"You okay?" he said, half pulling, half pushing her toward the middle of the field. "You worried?"

"I don't know," she said. "I don't think we're supposed to be here. Are we going to get in trouble?" She didn't want to voice her fear about him and what he might do to her. She tried to wipe those thoughts from her mind. Everything she knew about him so far told her she was safe with him. The residual rain and wind made her shiver in the light clothing she wasn't used to. The dampness had found its way through the fabric to her skin, and she felt gooseflesh starting up on her legs. She wished she were wearing her old outfit. "I'm kind of cold."

"I can warm you up." David pulled her a little closer, as if he were going to envelop her in a hug, but she resisted, found the strength from somewhere to break free of his grasp. Then she crossed her arms over her chest, as if it would warm her up and protect her at the same time, and she started running away from him across the wet field. She inhaled deeply, trying to gain strength, until the smell of wet, newly mown grass infused itself into her consciousness. It smelled wonderful, gave her a sense of peace in a crazy situation. She threw her head back and inhaled hard—trying to smell it more.

She'd gotten a head start on David, but his long strides brought him to her quickly, and he reached out to touch her back. Then, as if it had been scripted, his shoes took a skid on the wet surface, and before he could right himself, he had slid fast, on his back, feet-first onto the field. As he passed her, to slow himself down, he reached out and grabbed her ankle, causing her to lose her balance. She felt herself falling, and although time stopped for a moment, within seconds she'd landed on top of David, who was now splayed out in the wet grass, laughing so hard he thought he might start hyperventilating.

"Oh my god," she said, as she touched down, landing neatly on him, on her stomach, their faces less than an inch apart. He reached both hands around her waist, but her body became rigid. The two of them were so slippery, she was able to wriggle free of his grip. She pulled herself off him and stood up, bending over at the waist, trying to catch her breath. David was still laughing, and despite her anxiety, Aviva started laughing too. *If I read this in a book,* she thought, *I would never believe it.*

As she tried to regain her composure, David popped up, shook the water off himself and approached her, throwing his arms around her. The one thing he was sure of was that he wanted her badly, but he knew he was walking a fine line. However, she'd been laughing as much as he was, so he decided to take that as encouragement. He pressed her to him, lifting her feet off the ground, and, before she could escape again, he leaned down and kissed her lips—softly at first, as if he were trying to gauge her reaction, to reassure her that his intentions were not salacious. When she blessedly stopped resisting, he kissed her harder. He let her down slowly, never pulling his face away from hers, until she landed on her feet.

Aviva was shocked at herself that she was not trying to get away. As his hungry lips devoured hers, his tongue avidly exploring every corner of her mouth, the feeling she'd had when he first touched her hand returned, ten times as intense as it had been. His mouth on hers was deliciously sweet—she wasn't sure whether she wanted to absorb him, or whether she wanted him to absorb her. Her body was almost vibrating with excitement. The kiss lasted a long time, and she didn't want it to end. All she wanted was more. For a moment, she felt as if she were somewhere above, looking down on a stranger who looked just like her but acted like someone else. Could this really be happening to Aviva Stern, born and raised in the Satmar community of Williamsburg?

When he finally loosened his hold, she kept her arms around him, laying her head on his chest. She was still breathing hard, inhaling his smell of grass and sweat and soap, which made the feelings even more intense.

"Are you all right?" he managed to gasp. "I'm sorry, I just—I couldn't stand it anymore. I had to kiss you."

Aviva didn't lift her head. She simply nodded. She didn't know how or why it was all right, but she knew she would want more from him, that she never had felt this way before. She held on tight. "I liked it," she said.

"Me too." He squeezed her, pressing her breasts to his chest. He never wanted to let go.

David was feeling great. He still had no idea why Aviva had been so fearful, so untrusting. It was obvious something terrible had happened to her, but now that he'd been able to break through to the next level with her, he would insist she tell him. If he could lay her down on the wet grass now and make love to her right here, he would do it in a heartbeat, but that was obviously impossible, as deliciously tempting as it was.

But, standing there, in the middle of the soaked, dark stadium, he tried to figure out how he would convince her to have sex with him. If he could get her to trust him enough to tell him what had happened, what had caused her to run away from her life and her home, he hoped he could be so supportive and trustworthy that she would want to sleep with him as much as he wanted her to. Right now, he was pretty sure he had a good chance. He fantasized about what it would be like with her. He admitted to himself that no one had ever made him feel quite this way before, even in his serious relationships. He felt a bit selfish, but didn't want to wait. For a few moments, they didn't say a word. He was leaning down to kiss her again, when a voice rang out from the far end of the field.

"Hey! What the hell you people think yah doin'?" David and Aviva sprang apart. David's eyes had become used to the dark, and he watched as a large, lumbering figure started to move closer. The person was wielding a strong flashlight, which he pointed at the two of them. He was limping a little, slow. David had an urge to grab Aviva's hand and run for it, but the man was between them and the gate where they'd come in. David put an arm tightly around Aviva's waist and stood, his other hand on his hip, waiting. It took a good ten minutes for the man to cross the field. David felt sweat mingling with the rainwater.

"How'd you get in hee-yuh?" The man was out of breath, almost gasping, as he finally closed in on them. He was obviously out of shape. David wondered what was wrong with his leg. "No one's allowed in hee-yuh now." He shined the flashlight directly in David's eyes. David's free hand flew across his face. He felt Aviva gasp and tightened his grasp around her waist even more.

"Um," he said, "sorry. The gate over there—" He pointed across the field to where they'd entered. "It was open. We didn't mean—"

"Who the hell ah you, and what ah yah doin' hee-yuh?"

"Do you mind not shining that light in my face, sir?" David tried to be as respectful as he could. The guy was not a cop—no badge, no uniform, no gun. He looked like some sort of groundskeeper, and he held a phone in his free hand. Although it was dark, David felt he was middle-aged, and obviously quite overweight. He wore coveralls, and as the light beam went downward, David saw "Maintenance Crew" embroidered on the bib. David knew he could easily take the guy, but the last thing he wanted to do was to cause trouble. Also, the guy could call nine-one-one easily. Even though the light was dim, there were probably all kinds of powerful surveillance cameras pointed at the field.

"You people got ID? What's yah names?"

"Um, John Smith," David said. The minute he said it, he knew it was ridiculous. He bit his lip, trying not to laugh.

"With that accent?" the maintenance guy said, spitting on the ground. "I don't think yah name's John Smith. What about you?" He pointed the light at Aviva.

"Aviva Stern," she said. David flinched when she used her real name.

"Whey-uh you people from?" he said.

"I'm from Williamsburg," Aviva answered.

"Whey-uh the hell's that?" The man wasn't going to let up.

"Brooklyn," she said. Her voice was a hoarse whisper. She wasn't sure whether her heart was beating fast because of the kiss or the fear of what would happen to them now.

"Jesus, you're not even from around hee-yuh? What the hell?"

"I went to school here," David said. "I was just showing her around, sorry. She's never been to Boston before."

The man snorted. "Didn't look much like you was showin' her around, sonny," he said. "Looks more t'me like you were tryin' to get some." The man tilted his head and made a clicking sound with his tongue and his teeth.

"So, sir," David said, turning his head away from Aviva as if he might be able to extract some understanding from another man, "yeah, I guess so, you know?" He winked at the man, didn't know whether the man had seen it, but the flashlight was strong. "That's all. I didn't mean anything. The gate was open—"

"I should call the cops," the man said. "Specially since you didn't even give me yah real name."

"If you just let us go, I promise we'll never do it again." David shrugged. "I was just—we were just—please let us go. That's *her* real name, and she's really scared. She had nothing to do with it. This is all my fault."

Aviva had gone silent. He just kept squeezing her hand,

which was shaking, as if that would let him soak up some of her fear.

"You should be happy I'm in a good mood," the guy finally said. "I could call the cops and they'd throw the book at yah. You got no right to trespass in hee-yuh."

David crossed his fingers he'd gotten through to the guy. Another man, pleasant memories of youthful indiscretions, whatever. He held his breath for a moment.

"Okay, get the hell outta hee-yuh," the man said, pushing some hair off his face and then pointing a finger toward the gate. "*Now*, before I change my mind. And don't nevah do that again."

"Yes, sir. Thank you very much. Fenway's a beautiful ball park!" David pulled on Aviva, who seemed to be riveted in place. "Come on, honey," he whispered. "Let's go." Finally she snapped-to, and the two of them ran toward the gate, hand-in-hand. Aviva was slower than David, feeling especially tentative about losing her balance again on the wet grass. David was tempted to pick her up and carry her. She was light as a feather. He was worried that by the time they got to the other end of the field, the maintenance man would have dialed nine-one-one. But they made it. As they rushed out the gate where they'd come in, David looked back across the field, and he could just barely make out the man still standing there in the same place.

"Thank heavens," he said, breathless, as they made their way back up the street toward where he'd parked the car. "We dodged a bullet."

"John Smith?" she said.

Then he began to laugh, and somehow Aviva did as well. It felt as if they might never stop. As they got into the car, still wet, with wet grass sticking to their clothes, they were both laughing as if the world was the funniest place they'd ever seen. For the rest of the ride back to Carlos's house, they didn't speak. Aviva couldn't get the kiss out of her mind. It had been so romantic. The way his lips had felt on hers, the sweetness of his taste, the touch of his hand, the feeling that maybe, for the first time, someone really cared for her and wanted her. She closed her eyes and relived it over and over. She had no idea whether it would be repeated, or even if she could bear to let him do it again. She just didn't know. What she did know was that she felt a certain contentment she hadn't realized was even possible. And the experience with David was so distinct from what she'd gone through with Eli that she was hopeful she might be able to get over that, even though when she wasn't paying attention, it always managed to creep back into her mind.

David turned the radio to a soft-rock station and unconsciously tapped his fingers on the steering wheel in time to the music. The only thing he could think of was having sex with this girl. She'd opened a door. The tantalizing appetizer, as strange as the location had been, had whetted his appetite for her even more. He wondered whether Carlos's house was soundproof, whether the guest room was far enough away from the master bedroom that they could engage in some energetic lovemaking without being obtrusive. He didn't want to offend his hosts. But even though he was nailing her a hundred ways in his head, he couldn't stop the nagging thought that something terrible was going on with her, and he needed to get to the bottom of it before he pushed her to have sex. He made a promise to himself that before he'd start anything tonight, he would try to get her to come clean with him, to let him know why she was so closed off.

CHAPTER EIGHTEEN

Aviva and David

"Jesus Christ, what happened to the two of you?" Sylvia had been watching out the window as they pulled up in the car. "You guys are like two drowned rats," she said, after they stamped their wet feet on the doormat.

"We kind of got caught in the rain storm," David said as he and Aviva walked into the house. "Sort of forgot to bring umbrellas."

"I didn't realize it was that heavy a rain," Sylvia said, putting her hand up to stop them as they walked into the foyer. David and Aviva cast what they thought were furtive glances at one another. "Please, remove your shoes. They are making wet squeaky noises. I don't want you tracking water and whatever else through the house."

Aviva and David did as they were told.

"Looks like I'm going to have to find some more clothes for you, Aviva. Let's go." She pointed to the staircase.

"Sorry," Aviva said, shrugging. "We—um, we got kind of wet."

"That's pretty obvious," Sylvia said. She wasn't smiling. "How'd you get that grass on you?"

"I'm going to change clothes too," David said. "Do you

mind putting my wet things in your drier?" He walked behind the two women, putting a hand on Aviva's rear as they all ascended the stairs. She shook his hand off, shot a glance behind her, wrinkling up her nose.

Aviva followed Sylvia into the master bedroom, while David disappeared into the guest room.

"Where in the world did you two go?" Sylvia said to Aviva, after she closed the bedroom door.

"We went to Fenway Park," Aviva said, trying to sound as nonchalant as she could.

"There was a baseball game today?" Sylvia said, raising one eyebrow.

"Uh-uh. We just kind of went over there."

"How'd you get so drenched?"

Aviva was trying to think of what to say, wondering whether David would tell Carlos what actually happened. They should have gotten their stories straight when they were alone in the car, but it didn't occur to her that they'd be given the third degree.

Sylvia was rummaging through the drawers in her bureau. "Okay, young lady, get out of those clothes." She threw a towel over to Aviva, who started to peel off the wet clothing that was sticking to her body, giving her goose bumps. Sylvia came up with another tank top, this one white, a pair of white lace panties, and black jeans. "I hope these fit. You are really tiny."

"I can't wear this bra until it gets dry," Aviva said, standing naked with the towel wrapped around her.

"That's okay. Just go without. I'll throw everything into the drier after we go downstairs."

Aviva started to get dressed.

"So, what's the deal, Aviva?"

Aviva bristled. She had no idea whether Sylvia was asking her to talk about this evening's adventure, or just about herself. "What do you mean?"

"So, you told me everything. Have you told David yet? About what happened to you?"

Aviva pulled the tank top on. She shook her head.

"Don't you think he has the right to know? It looks like he likes you a lot. I told you before, he is very special to me. You know you might be hurting him if you don't tell him everything?"

It began to feel like a cross examination, and Aviva's "up" mood had suddenly been pulled way "down."

"I feel as if you're very naïve about a lot of things. Very young. You know David's a lot older, right?"

She nodded. Then she said, "He doesn't feel that much older to me." She admitted to herself she was becoming defensive. "We get along fine. Anyway, I had to grow up fast where I lived."

Sylvia looked her up and down. "Yes, I'm sure he gets along fine with you," she said. "You are quite beautiful. Obviously, you would turn most men's heads."

"I'm not sure what you mean by that?" Aviva said, her voice rising. She was questioning her decision to get rid of the wig.

"Well, just that, you know, men are attracted to pretty, sexy girls. What if you decide to go back to your husband? Where does that leave David?"

Aviva felt the blood run out of her face. She sat down on the edge of Sylvia's bed. "I am not going back to my husband."

"That's what you say now," she said. "But you told me about your community and how strong the pull is. It must be very difficult to leave this way."

"The community is very strong," Aviva said. "But I am an individual, and I know what I need."

"Don't you think you should grow up a little more and put some space between you and your bad marriage before you go after another man?"

Aviva turned red, as if she'd been slapped in the face. Sylvia had seemed so warm before, she'd felt almost comfortable telling her everything that had happened. Now it was as if Sylvia had taken that information and turned it against her. "I didn't go after him," she said. The good mood was entirely gone. She looked down at her feet.

"He doesn't have a lot of money, you know. I hope you don't think he can take care of you. He's a struggling musician."

After what had gone on at Fenway Park, Aviva felt a little confused. "Why are you saying all this to me? Did David tell you to say these things?"

Sylvia shook her head. "No. I just care about him a great deal. It would kill me to see him hurt by you."

Aviva was tempted to tell Sylvia that she cared for him a great deal too, but she wasn't in the mood to be chastised and mistrusted anymore by someone who didn't understand anything. "I don't need anyone to take care of me," she said. "I'll leave right now if David doesn't want me to stay."

Sylvia shook her head. "David has been Carlos's best friend for years, and he's one of my best friends too. I just want to make sure he's not taken advantage of by—"

A loud knock at the door stopped the conversation in its tracks. Aviva closed her eyes and gave a silent thank you. "Hey, you girls still in there? What are you doing? How long does it take to put on dry clothes?"

Aviva didn't know whether to be happy or worried that David was looking for her. She shot a glance toward Sylvia,

EDUCATING AVIVA

who had gone to open the door. "Just having some girl talk," Sylvia said, letting David in. He sat down on the bed next to Aviva, started to put his hand on her knee. She moved away from him.

"What's up with you?" he said, his smile disintegrating into a frown. Sylvia was still holding on to the doorknob. Aviva looked at her, and then back at David. "Is everything okay in here? Did I interrupt something?" he said.

Aviva didn't speak. "You two need some time to talk." Sylvia said, staring into David's eyes. "Go right ahead. I'll be downstairs. Come on down for a beer or something after." And she was gone, closing the bedroom door behind her.

For a few moments, Aviva continued to be silent. David sat, without touching her, a foot or so away on the edge of the bed. Then he stood, took her hand, and led her into the guest room, which was pretty empty except for a bureau against the wall and a big bed in the middle. He patted the edge of the bed, and she sat down. Then he stood and looked down at her, his eyes wide. Finally, he broke the silence. "Tell me, please, what is going on?" he said. "You're scaring me a little."

Aviva sighed again. "She hates me," she said.

"Who hates you?"

"Sylvia."

"No way." He slapped the bed with his hand. "Impossible. She doesn't even know you."

"When we first met, I thought she really liked me. She seemed so friendly. But she thinks I'm after your money. She gave me a lecture about not going after you," Aviva said, her voice almost a whisper. "I didn't think that's what I was doing," she continued. "If that's the way you feel, just tell me. I'll leave, go somewhere else, won't bother you anymore."

David sat down, very close to her. "Oh Jesus," he said, running his hand through his hair. "She thinks she's my mother. She had no right to say those things to you."

"I was worried you told her you felt that way."

"God, no," he said. "Did what happened at Fenway make you think I felt that way? Shit, I wanted to make love to you! I still do." It was out, despite his resolution to talk to her first about the issues that were obviously troubling her. He put his head in his hands.

Aviva blushed, from her toes up to her forehead. "I think that was part of Sylvia's point. She said it was easy for a man to be attracted to a pretty girl, but that the girl shouldn't take advantage of that."

"Are you taking advantage of me?" He had a wry smile now, one side of his mouth higher than the other, as if he had thought of something very humorous but very ironic.

"Are you serious?"

"No, silly, I'm not serious. Don't you see? She's just being overprotective of me. She doesn't hate you. She just thinks I've gone a little bonkers."

"Have you gone bonkers?"

"Probably. Over you."

"But you don't really know anything about me," Aviva said. "She said it's just because of physical attraction—chemistry."

He shook his head. "Nothing wrong with a little physical attraction, is there?"

Aviva sighed. She couldn't deny she was incredibly attracted to him.

"You sound exasperated," he said. "This was supposed to be a fun trip, wasn't it? I thought we were having fun. You didn't tell me to stop back at Fenway when we were—"

"I'm a little confused," Aviva said, interrupting. "Please, you have to understand this is so new for me. What we did at Fenway—it felt incredible. It made me happy. It's just that—I've never—I don't know how to do—" She wanted to tell him Nahum had never consummated the marriage, that she was a virgin, but she felt ashamed, as if it was her fault.

"Are you telling me you have never had sex?" He put his hand on her thigh, above her knee, and she moved closer to him, put her hand on top of his. "Oh sweetheart, no wonder you were unhappy in the marriage."

"I kept thinking I must have been doing something wrong."

"Wow," he said, "believe me, *you* weren't doing anything wrong. I'm just so surprised—you were married for two years."

She shrugged. "He just—he just couldn't."

"Well, that explains a few things," he said. "I guess that makes you a terrible person." He winked and gave her a hug.

"Everything's a joke with you, isn't it?"

David shrugged. "Sometimes joking is the best way to get someone like you out of a bad mood."

"I was in a wonderful mood when we got home. And then Sylvia—"

"Shhh." David leaned down and put his finger across her lips. Then he kissed her, the same way he'd kissed her before. This time the two of them were warm and dry, and she felt her entire body respond. She kissed him back, this time putting her tongue into his mouth, exploring his the way he'd explored hers. He pulled her back gently on the bed, and then he began to run his hands up her shirt, lifting it up. "You're so beautiful," he said. "So sexy. No fair not wearing a bra. I can't resist you."

He leaned down and kissed one of her breasts, sucking it into his mouth and running his tongue around the nipple. She wanted so badly for him to keep doing this, but as she looked up at David, an image of Eli flashed before her eyes.

"No!" she screamed, pushing him off.

"What did I do?" he said. He pulled his hands back. "Please, Aviva, I need to know what's wrong. Is it me? Did I do something? I thought I was being gentle. I promise I won't hurt you."

"No, she said, the tears welling up and running down the sides of her cheeks. "No, it's not you. You have been nothing but sweet and kind and wonderful with me, from the moment we first met. You make me feel like I've never felt before, inside and out. Make me feel cared for. I—" She turned her head to the pillow and sobbed.

"It's not fair to me, not to know your whole story. You've told me some, but I know there's more. I want to have this— this joy with you, but you won't let me. If you keep doing this—" He moved away from her. "You're making me crazy." He turned his back on her.

Aviva looked over at him, her brow contracting. She'd never given it a thought about how her problems might affect him. She felt guilty.

"I'm so sorry. I never wanted to hurt you. I didn't want to lead you on."

"Then please tell me how I can make you feel better," he said. "Just talk to me, tell me what you're worrying about."

"I'm afraid when I tell you, you'll hate me just like Sylvia does," she said. "You won't want me anymore."

"We've been through this, Aviva," he said. "I do not make judgments about people. Whatever awful thing you went through, I am sure it happened *to* you. I don't think you made it happen in any way. I haven't known you for very long, but every instinct I have tells me you are a very good person, not a liar. He turned back toward her and stretched his arm out across the pillow. "Come on. Please? Lean on me and tell me. I promise I'll behave," he said. "I won't touch you until you tell me it's all right."

The issue was, Aviva knew she was starting to crave his touch. It was just that every time he touched her, the memories of Eli got the better of her. She sighed. "All right. But if you hate me for this, just let me know. I'll be devastated, but I'll go away."

He shook his head. "I won't hate you, and I don't want you to go away."

It took a long time for her to tell him everything. She started from the beginning again—her strange childhood in a stranger community, how she was virtually on her own after her father died and her mother became mentally ill, because her grandmother was not really healthy or strong enough to raise a small child. She told him again about her thirst for knowledge, about her fascination with the outside world that most of the other Satmar children had no idea about. Told him how her marriage had been arranged quickly, because her grandmother was sinking into the throes of late stage dementia, and how despite the fact that Aviva felt she was too young, she had been betrothed to Nachum, who had some physical disabilities and wasn't sought after by any of the daughters of the more desirable families.

After offering each new piece of information, she looked over at David's face, tried to gauge his reaction. When she got to the part about Eli, she felt her hands start to tremble. He seemed to notice, and grabbed her hands in his, steadying them. She spoke slowly, almost as if she were in a trance, because she worried she would lose her nerve and run out of the room, out of his life, if she tried to tell the story normally.

David never changed his expression, which made her wonder whether he was gearing up to tell her he didn't want her anymore. But as she gave him—in a quivering voice—all the details, David pulled her closer to him. She was crying as she finished, and when she looked over at him, so was he. And she noticed that his entire body had tensed up. She tried to sit up, but he held her tight.

"Please stay," he said. "I need to hold you." She relaxed a little. "I want to kill him. Want to take that knife you were using to slice that chicken and stick it in him until he screams in pain. Want to watch him bleed."

For some reason, that made Aviva giggle, and she wiped the tears from her eyes. "So, you don't blame me?"

"If I'm telling you I want to kill him, why would you think I blame *you*?" he said. "You didn't ask for it, you told him no, but then he even tried to do it again. What kind of a disgusting human being is he? It just makes me furious." He clenched his fists.

"Me too," she said. All of a sudden, she felt exhausted, as if she'd been through not only an emotional trial but severe physical exertion. She wanted to roll over and go to sleep, snuggled in his arms.

"Should you call the police?" he said, finally, after they'd been silent for a few minutes.

"No. The police won't do anything, and besides, I don't want to have anything more to do with him, ever. I never want to see his face again."

"People like that shouldn't be allowed to get away with it. Who knows how many others—"

"Honestly, no one would believe me, and you can be sure he would deny it, tell them I am a mental case like my mother. His word against mine. You still want to be with me?" She lifted herself up on one elbow, studied his face.

"Yes, I still want to be with you," he said. "I only hope you're able to put your thoughts of it out of your mind. I will never *ever* hurt you like that. Never."

"Thank you," she said. Then she settled back down on the pillow. David leaned over and kissed her softly on the lips. Then, almost instantly, she drifted off into a deep dreamless sleep. He pulled the quilt up over her shoulders and got out of bed. He stood looking at her for a moment. Asleep, without the worry that seemed to swirl around her most of the time, her features were relaxed and even more beautiful than they were when she was awake. He sighed. Then he tiptoed out of the room and down the steps.

CHAPTER NINETEEN

David

"Everything okay up there?" Carlos met David at the bottom of the staircase. "You guys were behind closed doors for a long time. What were you doing?" Carlos smiled and slapped David on the back. "She's pretty cute," he said. "Way hot if you ask me. You get lucky?"

"Nothing like that," David said. "We were just talking."

Carlos raised his eyebrows, but David brushed him off with a wave of the hand. "Really. We have a lot to talk about."

"Hey, you want some wine or a beer?" Sylvia was calling out from the kitchen. "Come on, I haven't even had a chance to spend time with you—alone."

Carlos hooked his arm in David's and pulled him toward the kitchen. Sylvia had poured a glass of red wine and was reaching it out to him as he walked in. "Thanks, this hits the spot," he said.

She pushed a plate of cheese and crackers closer to him. "Where's your—friend?" she asked, craning her neck to see if Aviva was following. "She decide to go back to New York?"

"She's taking a nap," he said. "It was kind of an exhausting evening we had."

"Inquiring minds want to know," Carlos said. "Don't leave anything out."

After David finished telling them about the wet baseball field and the forgiving maintenance man, Carlos was convulsed in laughter. "I don't believe you had the balls to do that, man," he said, slapping David on the back again. "Didn't know you had it in you."

"Seriously, David?" Sylvia's face had contorted into a dark frown, lines forming where there were normally none. "Are you crazy? You could have gone to jail. We might have had to bail you out. What the hell were you thinking? And that girl went along with it? Wait—was it her idea?" She had moved close to David, her face only inches from his. He leaned away.

"'That girl' has a name. It's Aviva," he said, putting down his wine glass a little too hard. Some of the wine splashed on the counter, and Sylvia walked around to the sink to get a rag to clean it. "I'm not getting this attitude, Sylvia. What's your deal? She had nothing to do with it. It was all my idea." He took a large sip of the wine. "What do you have against her, anyway?" He felt his skin turning hot. "She thinks you hate her."

"Come, let's sit," Sylvia said, pointing to one of the bar stools around their kitchen island. "I don't hate her." She patted the stool, and David sat down.

"What's with the hostility then? Never seen you like this. You don't even know her."

"Isn't that the point, honey?" she said. "Neither do you. What the hell are you thinking, anyway?"

"You keep saying that. I don't get it."

"Convince me," she said. "I'm all ears."

"For the past five years, since I was—what?—twenty-four or so, you've been urging me—nagging me—to grow up and find a life partner," David said, in between sips of wine and bites of cheese. "You were almost as brokenhearted as I was when I broke up with Daniella."

Sylvia shrugged.

David continued. "Don't you agree you keep saying it's time for me to settle down? That I'm gonna get set in my ways if I don't find a girl soon?"

"Yeah, that's true," Sylvia said. She'd taken the stool next to David and had her hand on his knee. "I just worry about you. You live alone long enough, and you won't be willing to open up your life to anyone."

"What are you? Thirty-three?"

"Thirty-one and a half," she said, slapping David's knee. "That's bad enough—don't make it worse."

"Right. So, you're like three years older than me," he said. "And what? You're looking for a kid to scold? If you want a kid, have a goddamn kid."

Carlos groaned.

"I don't need to be lectured," David continued. "I'm almost as old as you."

"Yeah, old enough to know better. But don't you dare change the subject. Tell me everything about this girl. First of all, she's so young. Wouldn't you rather have someone closer to your own age? Someone who's a little more mature?"

Carlos shook his head and laughed into his hand. He and David exchanged a glance. David ran his hand through his hair. "If you'd been through in your thirty-one and a half years anything like what Aviva has lived through in her nineteen, you would be an old gray-haired lady," he said. "Very mature."

"I know enough about those people to understand that they close themselves off from the rest of society, live in some sort of cocoon that keeps them from interacting with the world around them. They make their kids stop going to school after like the eighth grade, and they marry off the girls as teenagers so they can stay home and have baby after baby. Did you see those clothes she was wearing?"

David shrugged.

"Is that what you're looking for in a wife?" Her words were loud and staccato.

"Who the hell said anything about marriage?" David said, pushing Sylvia's hand off his leg. "Jeeze, back off! We just met."

"Well, the way she looks at you," Sylvia said, rolling her eyes and flipping her hair so close it almost whipped him in the face, "I'd watch myself. Whatever you do, don't get her pregnant, or you'll be stuck for life."

"Sylvia," Carlos hissed, putting his index finger across his lips. "Come on. Enough. You're not being fair. You don't even know anything about how David feels. Don't jeopardize our friendship by acting like a bitch."

"A *bitch*?" she said. "I'm just trying to protect him from something I know he'll regret. And you should put your eyes back in your head and stop salivating over her and back me up on this."

"Whew, well, I think we *should* change the subject," Carlos said. "How's New York treating you? I keep thinking maybe we should move there too. Lots more opportunity."

"Not so fast," Sylvia said. "I'm not done. I'd like to hear about this rough life you say she's had. Did she tell you everything?" She raised her eyebrows and stuck her thumb up and pointed it toward the staircase. "And I'd really like to know what you find so damn intriguing about her."

Carlos and David exchanged more looks. "Well, since you told me my eyes were unhinged from my head since I noticed how gorgeous she is, I'm thinking you noticed too, honey, right? Or you wouldn't be this worked up about it." Carlos started drumming his fingers on the counter. The crackers jumped on their plate.

"Yeah, I hope you can put them back in the sockets," she said, turning her nose up at her husband. "But seriously, gorgeous gets boring after a while," she said. "There has to be more than gorgeous. Gorgeous is not a reason to give up your freedom for—for someone from a cult."

"If I didn't know better, I'd think maybe you are a little bit jealous of David? Maybe you won't be the only woman in his life anymore." Carlos said. "Someone else may be stepping into your shoes."

"Oh get real," she said. "Why would I be jealous of David? I'm just a good friend who doesn't want him to make a huge mistake."

"Wait a minute here," David said. "Last time I checked, I was in the room. Maybe not talk about me like I'm not here?"

"I'm really sorry," Carlos said. "Sylvia, I don't think this is a good conversation. Time to put it to bed."

Sylvia shot him a glance, one eye squinting. She pointed at David. "This is really for your own good. You are too old to be fooled by beauty or sexiness or whatever the hell she has. Step back and think about what you're doing. Those people—" She flipped her hair again. "You should stick with your own kind—not someone like that." Then she got up and walked out of the room.

David put his head in his hands. "I've never seen her like that," he said, "in all the years we've been friends. What's with her?"

"I don't know, amigo," Carlos said. "I don't know. She wants you to be happy, I'm sure of that."

"Well, she has a strange way of showing it. She's got to trust my judgment. Acting this way isn't going to do a lot to cement the friendship."

Carlos put his arms out to the sides and shrugged. "I will talk to her, but you know Sylvia. Once she's got something in her head, it's hard for her to let go of it."

"Maybe we shouldn't stay here? Maybe she'd feel better if I took Aviva and we spent the night at a hotel? Then we'll leave right after the gig tomorrow. I'm not sure what else to do."

"No way, man," Carlos said. "You were my friend before I even knew Sylvia, and this is my place too. I would feel terrible if you left."

"Okay," David said, "but please tell her not to attack Aviva. Aviva didn't do anything to deserve it."

"I'll try. Here," he got up and went to the refrigerator, "have a beer. I think we need something a little stronger than pinot noir." He poured the beer into glasses and pushed one over to David.

The two men drank in silence. Sylvia never returned to the kitchen, leaving her half-drunk glass of wine on the counter. When David finished, he put his glass and hers in the sink. "Thanks, that was good. I'm pretending that conversation with Sylvia never happened."

"Don't worry too much about it," Carlos said. "She'll get used to the idea of you and Aviva. Just try to ignore her for now."

"Yeah, try to ignore the pink elephants dancing around the room," David said, laughing a little. "Try that too."

Carlos shrugged. "Another beer?"

"Nope, I'm kind of bushed. I'm going to turn in," he said.

"Okay then," Carlos said. "Rehearse a little more tomorrow? With the bass player?"

"Sounds good," David said. "Looking forward to making music with you, bro."

"Yeah, sometimes it really beats talking." The two men did a high five, and David headed for the stairs, hoping he wouldn't run into Sylvia, but she never re-emerged from wherever she'd gone. He opened the guest room door quietly, but when he walked in, Aviva was sitting up in the bed, smiling at him.

"Hi. How long have you been up?"

"Oh, a while," she said. "Did I hear raised voices down there?"

"Nah, must have been your imagination," David said, sitting down on the edge of the bed and taking her hand in his. He bent down and kissed her hand, and then smiled at her. "You look so pretty just sitting there," he said.

"You are so full of compliments," she said. "It's a little embarrassing. I'm not used to it."

"Well, get used to it."

"You're not too hard on the eyes yourself," she said, laughing.

"Is it okay if I kiss you?" He had moved over toward her, leaning his face close to hers. "I don't want to do anything you don't want to do." He hoped she believed him. but if he were actually being truthful, he knew he just wanted to move in and make love to her without another word. He gave her a small kiss on the cheek and was happy she didn't pull away.

"Being around you is probably the nicest thing that's happened to me in the past two years," she said. "Maybe ever."

"Wow, that's a long time," he said. Then he leaned down and kissed her again, on the lips, first tenderly, but when she began to respond, more hungrily. They kissed for a while, his arms tight around her. When he pulled away, she sighed. "You okay?"

"Oh, much better than okay," she said.

"Do you want me to sleep in that chair over there? Or on the floor? I don't mind, if it would make you feel more comfortable."

She leaned back against the pillows. "I want you to sleep right here." She patted the bed next to her.

David gave a silent prayer of thanks. "Okay, but I don't want you to be afraid."

"I'm not afraid of you."

"Good," he said, sitting on the edge of the bed. "You don't have to be, ever."

"Do you want to turn out the light?" she said.

"You're so beautiful, I'd rather leave it on so I can look at you," he said. "If that's all right?" He didn't wait for an answer but leaned in again, this time not stopping at kissing. To his relief, she didn't resist. He removed her clothing, and then his own, and then he pulled back the covers and got under them with her. He loved watching her body, was happy to see the joy on her face as he kissed her all over, starting with the neck and making his way down.

"Still okay?" he managed to say, finally coming up for air.

"Oh God, don't stop," she sighed. She tried hard not to make noise, feeling uncomfortable knowing Sylvia and Carlos were right next-door, but it was impossible to stay silent, and she moaned as she came. Then, kissing her lips, he entered her and took his time finishing. When he was done, he lay on top of her, not wanting to uncouple. He tried to lift his body so he wouldn't suffocate her, but she wasn't protesting.

"That was incredible," he finally managed to say. "Was it—did you like it?"

"Didn't you hear how much I liked it?" she said. "I can hardly believe—" It even surprised her that she didn't mind lying there naked, with him looking straight at her.

"Good," he said. "That makes me happy. I was worried I might be making you sad, making you—scared." Pushing himself up on the bed with both hands, he finally sat up, stretching. "Wow," he said. "You're amazing."

"No, you are the amazing one." Aviva watched him as he sat there. His body was taut, well muscled. She loved his face, his smell, the sound of his voice, the strength but gentleness with which he approached her, his warmth—how what he did to her made her feel. She had never felt any of this before. She would have been happy to make love all over again, but she was even more exhausted now, and David looked as if he were ready to crawl under the sheets and sleep for hours. Nevertheless, she stared at this man she'd known only a couple of weeks, and wondered whether what she was feeling was love—whether it was possible to fall in love with someone that quickly. She'd never thought about love before. If this wasn't love, she didn't know what it was. She had a fleeting thought of Nachum and what physical contact had been like with him. It almost made her sad for him, certainly made her a little guilty that she was experiencing this kind of joy when he would possibly never do the same. But Nachum left her thoughts almost as soon as he had drifted in.

"Whatcha looking at?" David said, his lips turning up in a half smile. "I look okay?"

"You look amazing," she said. "But you look tired. Shall we turn off the light and go to sleep now?"

CHAPTER TWENTY

Aviva

Before she gave it some thought, Aviva didn't know why she was feeling so anxious, almost sad. She and David were in the car on their way back to New York. The gig had gone great—an outdoor venue, beautiful weather, and hundreds if not thousands showing up to enjoy the music on the Charles River esplanade. Many people danced, and Aviva hadn't been able to take her eyes off David as he played his drums, which was obviously what he loved to do more than anything else. His joy transferred to her soul and made her feel happier than she ever had. She was beginning to wonder how she'd ever lived without him.

David was in such a good mood, he'd been whistling since they hit the road. Sylvia hadn't been exactly friendly to Aviva, but at least she'd been polite, and she also let Aviva keep on the outfit she'd loaned her the day before. "Just send it back to me whenever," she had told Aviva. Now that Aviva had had the experience of wearing light, comfortable clothing, she didn't want to go back to her old, heavy, ankle-to-neck-covering getups. She'd rolled up her old clothes and shoved them to the bottom of her bag. But as they drove down the Massachusetts Turnpike toward Connecticut and then toward home, Aviva's mood got darker and darker.

"You're not talking much, honey," David said to her. "What's wrong? I thought the show was great. I love it when everything comes together like that. Everyone was smiling, dancing, having a fantastic time. And the weather cooperated. Perfect day."

Aviva nodded.

"Did you enjoy the music?"

She nodded again.

"Come on, what's wrong? Did I do something to make you upset?" He reached over and ruffled her hair. "Talk to me."

"No, no, it's nothing," she said. But it obviously was something.

David was on such a high, he chose to take her at her word, at least at first. Halfway home, he pulled into a rest area. "Gotta go," he said. "You?"

"Sure," she said, unbuckling her seatbelt. Afterward, he asked if she was hungry. "I'm gonna get some food," he said. "You want something?"

She shook her head.

"Okay, that's it," he said. "Sit down here." He pointed to one of the picnic tables outside the snack bar. "Wait here, I'll be right back. We're gonna talk. Enough of this, something is really bothering the crap out of you."

He returned with two cups of coffee and a few snacks, which he proudly showed her had little Ks in a circle on the package. That, she had explained to him, meant they were kosher. She smiled but turned her head away from him, trying to hide the fact that she'd been crying.

"What's up?" he said, handing her a napkin.

She wiped her eyes, took a deep breath. "I think it's just that when we were in Boston, I could forget about Williamsburg, about Nachum and his sister and their—uncle. It was like being in a sweet dream. You and me. I never knew I could be so happy."

"So, what's the problem? It's still you and me."

"Now we're on our way back home, and there are a lot of things I'm going to have to deal with right away. Nachum has probably figured out I really meant it when I said I was leaving, so I'm sure he is very worried about it and very angry at me. Ilona detested me from the start, but she's probably called my aunt in Kiryas Joel to complain about what a horrible wife I am, and that puts my aunt in a terrible position. She knows what happened, but I asked her not to talk to Nachum's family about it. My aunt has her own problems."

He handed her his phone. "Call her. Tell her you're all right and have a place to live."

After Aviva finished explaining her situation to her aunt, she told David she was relieved, at least a little bit. "I was right. They've been hounding her. She was very worried about me. I asked her not to give them any information, and she said she wouldn't. I know she doesn't completely approve of what I'm doing, but at least she understands my reasons why. And now she has the phone number, so she can get in touch."

"I'm glad you spoke with her," he said. "One day I'd like to meet her and thank her."

Aviva shrugged. "I'm not sure we'll be able to," she said. "But who knows? I can't keep thinking about it all, because it makes me feel very alone."

"The difference is, you have me now," he said, sitting down next to her on the bench, slinging his arm around her shoulder. "I will be with you. I'll help you through all of it. You're not alone."

"Thanks," she said.

"And besides, why do you always think everyone hates you? You're so sweet. Definitely not a despicable person." He laughed a little.

She waved her hand in front of her face. "You don't understand."

"I'm trying," he said. "I can't unless you explain."

"I can't stop worrying about you, too," she said.

"Why?"

"They'll either completely ignore you, pretend you don't exist, or—"

"Or what?"

"I'm worried about what they will do to you."

"They can't do anything to me," he said. "I'm not afraid of them."

"They don't like it when someone leaves."

"Leaves?"

"Goes away from the—tribe." She cleared her throat.

"We'll deal with it together. I promise. Trust me."

"I want to so badly," she said.

David gave her a little squeeze, and she lay her head on his shoulder. She wondered whether the electricity she felt every time he touched her would last forever, or whether she'd get used to it. She hoped she wouldn't get used to it. "Well then just do."

"But I don't think you understand how angry they will be."

"They'll get over it. They'll see it's better for everyone if you get out of there."

"They don't care about that," she said. "It will make them look bad, my running away—people will talk. And they will be completely furious about that. At me."

"From what you told me, your husband wasn't that happy with the marriage anyway, was he?"

"I don't think so," she said. "It's hard to tell. I didn't really see him that much. He was always out studying. It wasn't a pleasant relationship, at least not for me, and he hardly ever smiled." She thought about David's smile and how much she loved it. "You and I have talked more in the time we've been together than Nachum and I talked in two years."

"What do you think he'll do?"

"I hope he comes to his senses and gives me a get," she said.

"A *what*?"

Aviva smiled for the first time. "A get."

"I don't know what that is."

"I thought you told me you went to the library and studied about us," she said. She reached up and squeezed his hand.

"I did, but—"

"It's a divorce document. Recognized by Jewish law. You can't get married again if you don't have one."

"So how do you get one of those—gets?" he said.

"Nachum has to give it to me, and if he doesn't want to, I'm still married to him."

"Why wouldn't he want to?"

"It will make his life harder. He'll be embarrassed, lose face. He'll have to find another wife."

"So, we'll just call a lawyer. Go to court. Get it done that way."

She waved her hand in front of his face. "No, you don't understand," she said. "It has to do with Jewish law. For all I know, I'm not really married in the eyes of the court."

"What do you mean?"

"I never signed any marriage license or anything."

David's mouth flew open. "You mean, seriously, you're not legally married?"

She shrugged. "I don't think so."

"Well if that's true, it's even better," he said. "Then you don't have to worry about anything else."

"But I do. Because without the get, he won't be able to remarry in the community, and his family will be shamed, and he won't have kids, and they won't leave me alone until I come back."

"But you're not going back, right?"

She nodded. "Never."

"So, then it will be to his advantage to give you the get, won't it? It makes sense to me he'd want it. But it doesn't really affect you at all, since you're not going back there."

"I know this sounds crazy, but that is a little scary to me too. Damn. I'm so confused."

"Aviva, you really—" He paused. "You really like me, don't you? You said so. And after what happened last night—"

She pushed harder into him, felt his body against hers, thought about how amazing the sex had been, looked down at her hands. "No, of course you're right. Last night was heaven. But that's a little scary too."

He laughed. "I think we should make the decision to take everything one day at a time," he said. "Don't keep thinking about what will happen tomorrow or next week or next month. We'll deal with it all. I really want you in my life. Do you believe me?"

"I think so," she said.

"I will prove it to you, I promise. Besides, you're breathtakingly beautiful and you like my music." He laughed again. "So, you're perfect." He turned her toward him and kissed her deeply. She wished she could just disappear into his body, his soul— wished things could be as easy as their beautiful kisses.

She tried to feel lighthearted. She knew he was right. She'd made her choice. Every time she started to feel a pang of homesickness, she thought of Ilona and Nachum and especially Eli. Then she was sure she was doing the right thing now—the only thing. And she knew that no matter how it turned out, she'd been so lucky to find this man who was willing not only to make love to her, but to agree to help her deal with her problems head-on, to protect her. If she'd run away without anyone to go to, it would be a thousand times worse, likely almost impossible.

"I'm still worried about Nachum."

"Is he your age?"

"Just a few months older," she said. "His family is pressuring him to have kids."

"So, it's to his benefit to give you the get so that he can remarry, right?"

"Yes, if you look at it all logically," she said. "I just worry about them trying to punish me because their pride is hurt."

"But that seems so backwards," he said. "Lots of marriages don't work."

"I know, but that's the way it is with us—um—them. And this is going to sound ridiculous, but all of this makes me anxious, the thought of being set free, even though I know I don't want to be married to him anymore. I've never known anything else but my life there. It's frightening to be alone without any safety net."

David smiled and pointed his index finger toward his head. "Here's your safety net," he said, smiling broadly.

"But—"

"But what?"

"What if you get tired of me?" she said. "If you start thinking I'm a freak? That I'm not worth all the trouble. Then what?"

"I guess there are no guarantees in life," he agreed. "But right now, I can't imagine getting tired of you. After last night, it's—well it's not gonna happen." He smiled broadly and brushed her lips with his finger.

Aviva sighed. "I so want to believe that," she said. "I promise I will improve myself continuously so you don't get tired of me. I will take care of you. I will massage your back and rub your feet. Scrub your clothes, shine your shoes. I will do whatever you want." She sighed again. But he laughed so hard, there were tears in his eyes.

"You are not signing up to be my slave," he said, wiping his eyes with his sleeve. "Just help me with the dishes and take out the recycle once in a while. Pay half the electric bill. That's all I ask."

"I can cook," she said, leaning her head closer to him, her eyes wide. "You just have to tell me what you like to eat." Then she moved away, rubbing her forehead with her free hand. "And I am going to have a hard time figuring out how not to be kosher."

"We'll live on vegetables and fruits and eggs, how's that? That's all kosher, right?"

For the first time, Aviva smiled a little. "Can I tell you something?"

He nodded.

"You have to promise not to laugh."

"Cross my heart," he said, making an X symbol across his chest.

"I think I may be—probably am—falling in love with you." It was out, but she couldn't look in his eyes now, and she felt herself blushing.

"Whew," David said, "I wasn't expecting that. But I don't think it's funny."

"I'm sorry," she said.

"No, that's very flattering," he said. But if he were being honest, he couldn't tell her the same thing. He was utterly enchanted by many things about her—her beauty and her sweetness and in a way, her neediness. It made him feel like a big important man to be able to take care of her. But was that love? Probably not quite. And as much as he didn't want them to, Sylvia's warnings cycled through his brain. Perhaps what he felt for her might develop into love. But at this moment, he couldn't say those words back. He just wasn't sure how to respond.

"I shouldn't have said anything. I didn't mean to make you feel uncomfortable."

"It's okay," he said.

"Forget I said it," she said.

They drove for several miles in silence. Then he squeezed her hand. "Don't you feel a little better now that we've talked?"

"I don't know. I think I just put my foot in my mouth." She cleared her throat.

"Don't worry about that," he said. "Really, I'm flattered."

"I just want to be honest with you, but I understand it's not going to be as easy as you think," she said, "for either of us. I wouldn't blame you if you decided not to be with me. Especially now when you know how I feel."

"Stop saying that, Aviva," he said. "I want to be with you."

She had to admit she had felt a oneness about the two of them she'd never experienced before with anyone. She nodded.

"Well?"

She turned her head back toward him. "Last night was amazing," she said. "I had no idea I could feel like that."

"Well, if I didn't want to be with you, I don't think it would have been so amazing," he said.

"Thank you for being here for me," she said.

"Thank you for being here for me, and for scrubbing my clothes."

CHAPTER TWENTY-ONE

Aviva and David

They made a pact not to get bogged down in serious discussions for the rest of the trip, and for the most part, Aviva was able to abide by the rules. They talked about their favorite colors, their favorite books, their favorite music, their favorite foods. She told him that in her trips to the library she'd become fascinated with medieval history and art. He said he wanted to get a dog. She said she'd never been allowed to have a pet but would be willing to try it.

"I love learning about you," she said.

"Me too," he admitted. He promised to take her to the movies, because she'd never been. "Really? Never been to the movies?" he said, his eyes wide.

"No."

"Wow," he said. Then, "Oops, I promised no judgments. We will go. I'll take you to a funny one. I know you're gonna love it."

"What about the job?" she said, as if it had suddenly occurred to her. "I really need that."

"We'll go tomorrow," he said. "I know they'll love you. They'll realize you're very smart, and you will improve the look of that store a hundred percent." He laughed.

"I need clothes," she said.

"There's a second-hand store a few blocks away from my house," he said. "I'll take you there. You can buy some nice things there for very little money." He glanced over at her to see if she was okay with that. "You will make any clothes look better," he added, as if he didn't want to offend her.

"Oh, no, that's a relief," she said. "That's good. At least until I have some money saved from the job. That is, if I get the job."

"You worry too much," he said.

"I can't help it," she said.

"We have to work on that," he said.

Her eyelids were feeling heavy, but she didn't realize she'd dozed off until he tapped her lightly on the shoulder. "Aviva? We're home," he said.

At first, she thought it was a dream. She had a sudden fright that he meant they were at her house in Williamsburg, and she started, making a little noise. She felt dizzy.

"What's wrong, honey?" he said. "You fell asleep. It's okay. We're in Queens, at my place."

"Oh," she said, "thank heavens. How long was I asleep?"

"For a while," he said. "You looked very peaceful so I didn't want to disturb you."

"My neck's a little stiff," she said, rubbing it. It occurred to her she'd have to start calling this her place too. At least for the near future.

He leaned over and kissed her neck, rubbing her shoulders. "I shouldn't start anything here," he said, laughing. "Let's get the stuff out of the car and go inside."

"Yeah, I could use the bathroom," she said. "And a shower."

She couldn't wait to explore his things more carefully, see what he loved and what he kept around him. The place smelled a little like him—a smell she had come to love—and she breathed deeply. "Feel free to go first," he said, pointing toward the bathroom. "Here's a towel for you."

"Thank you, I will." Once in the small room, she stripped her clothing off. She felt free as she got under the shower. She stood under it and closed her eyes, letting the water massage her sore neck. At first, she didn't notice that David had walked in and was standing on the other side of the shower curtain.

"Hey, can I come in too?" he said.

"Oh, I guess so," she agreed. But when he stepped in, although they had shared the greatest of intimacy the night before, she suddenly felt shy, trying to cover herself with her arms.

"Does my looking at you like this make you nervous?" he said. "I'm sorry, but you are so beautiful, I love looking." Then he put his arms around her and pulled her toward him. Their wet bodies bonded, and Aviva felt him get hard.

"I don't know. It's just—"

"I don't want you to worry. If you don't want me in here—" he said.

"No, stay. I want you. When you're beside me, I feel stronger, as if I have the strength of both of us combined and then some. I just have to get used to—"

He held her for a few moments. "If it's less stressful for you, turn around with your back toward me," he said. "I know all of this is very new to you. I don't want to make you move faster than you're comfortable with."

She did as he asked, and he held his arms around her waist, fitting the shape of her body into the shape of his.

"Thank you," she said.

"I want you right here," he said. But he let go of her and washed himself quickly, stepping out of the tub.

"I don't have anything else to wear," she called out to him.

"I've got something," he said, bringing in a large button-down shirt and hanging it over the doorknob.

She finished in the shower, dried herself off, and put on his shirt. It came halfway down her thighs. It smelled good, clean, like laundry detergent. She breathed in the smell. She felt renewed. When she walked into the bedroom he was standing there, still naked.

"You are very sexy in my shirt," he said.

"Really?" she laughed. "I wouldn't say this shirt is sexy."

"Not until it's on you." He beckoned for her, his arms and hands extended. "I need a big hug," he said.

Aviva giggled as she walked slowly toward him. Her skin was hot, and she realized it wasn't just from the shower water.

"Come on, you've been married for a while, haven't you? This can't be completely new to you." He pointed down at his nude body, his erection pointing toward the ceiling.

"I'm telling you," she said, arriving at his embrace, "we were never naked together. At least not outside the covers. Hardly even under them. Until you, I wasn't entirely sure what a naked man looked like."

"Then, I guess now I'm still educating Aviva, aren't I?" He held her in a strong embrace, leaning down to kiss her neck. "Do you want a little more education?"

"I love being educated by you," she said, giggling again.

He led her to the bed, and they fell back onto the coverlet as if they were one person. He removed the shirt in one motion, over her head, and she lay with her arms up, her eyes closed, her mouth slightly open, her body tingling. His bed was a little softer than the bed at Carlos's house, and Aviva felt as if she was getting lost in it and lost in the lovemaking, which was even more exquisite this time than it had been the night before.

"Please always tell me what you like," he managed to say in between kisses.

"Whatever you're doing is what I like," she said. "I like it all. You make me feel better than I ever thought possible."

"Good. If I ever do anything you don't like, please let me know."

"I can't imagine it," she said.

"So, may I tell you what I like?" He raised his head a little, looking at her face.

"I'm a little nervous," she said. "I feel so inexperienced. I will try to do whatever you like. Just guide me."

"I will," he said.

Afterward, completely spent, David fell asleep on his stomach, his arm loosely draped over her breasts. She lay there, watching his body move up and down, listening to his calm breath, snuggling into his warmth, inhaling and exhaling as he did, until she felt goose bumps forming on her skin. Then she pulled the covers over both of them and fell into a deep sleep.

Aviva felt disoriented when she awoke to the sound of David's voice, loud and angry. At first, she couldn't remember where she was. It was still dark out, but she had no idea whether that meant it was sometime in the wee hours of the morning, or sometime just before dawn.

She shook herself a little, and then she sat up in the bed. David was in the other room, his voice louder than she'd ever heard it. When she was finally awake enough to focus, she suspected he was talking either to Nachum or Eli, although it was impossible to tell which one. She felt her body begin to shake, her mouth become dry. She wanted to hide, to disappear, but she was well aware this was the beginning of a new phase in her new life—one that would be very difficult.

She groped around on the floor next to the bed, picked up David's shirt, slipped it on, and got out of bed, bracing herself against the wall for support. There was one small light on in the living room, and David was pacing back and forth, one arm on his hip, yelling into the phone. The last thing she heard him say was, "You have no right to say that about me. I love her." She burst into tears. Then, after a short pause, she heard him say, "You *do*? You have an odd way of showing it."

"What time is it? Who are you talking to?" Her voice came out as a hoarse whisper. She cleared her throat. David saw her, picked up his hand, and made a signal to her that she shouldn't come closer. He continued arguing with whoever was on the phone.

He finally took a breath and put his hand over the phone. "It's not even six o'clock," he said.

"I never heard the phone ring. Let me talk," she said. Her voice was stronger, and she felt wide awake now, but scared. "Is it Nachum?"

Finally, David came close and handed her the phone. He nodded. "It's your husband," he said. Aviva shuddered.

"Hello?" she said. Then the storm exploded. Nachum was yelling at her in Yiddish, and she lapsed into the language of her youth as well, trying to get a word in edgewise. He called her names, called her a disgusting slut and a whore, yelled that she was going to hell, that she should be punished. He screamed that David was a home wrecker and should be beaten up. Finally, trembling, she took the phone away from her ear and stood there, her eyes wide, tears streaming down her cheeks.

"Do you want me to talk to him again? Want me to tell him to hang up unless he calms down? He has no right to upset you like this." David was close to her now, an arm around her waist. She shook free of him, shook her head.

"I have to do this," she said, trying to get control of the shaking. She put the phone back up to her ear and continued to speak in Yiddish. David had no idea what she was saying, but he did hear her say the name Eli several times. He hoped she was telling her husband about his uncle's assault, hoped that would make Nachum back off.

"No, I am not lying," she said, very loudly, in English. "If you won't believe me, that's not my problem. You tell me today for the first time that you love me, and yet you don't believe me? Call me terrible names? Your honored uncle did this, and I will never come back there. Nothing you say can change my mind. I want a get, and I never want to see any of you again." There was a pause, and she said something else in Yiddish. Then, slumping onto the couch, she clicked the phone off and handed it back to David, who sat down beside her.

"He get my number from your aunt?" David said.

She nodded. "I told her not to tell anyone, but—"

"Oh. Well, I guess it had to happen sometime."

"Yes. At least I don't have to be in fear of the first conversation anymore. But I'm scared to death they'll try to grab me away from here. And that they'll—that they'll hurt you."

"We need to get you a phone," he said.

"I know, but every time it rings, I'll have a panic attack."

"If they try anything, we call the police," David said. "The police here do their job. We'll get you a restraining order."

Aviva put her head in her hands. "I really messed up my life, didn't I?"

"I was thinking you improved it a lot," he said. He put his arm around her shoulder.

"Did you mean what you said?" she whispered, after a few moments of silence.

"What? I can't hear you," David said.

She looked up. "Did you mean that? What you told Nachum?"

David tilted his head. "What did I say?"

"You told him you love me. Did you mean that?"

"I wouldn't have said it," he replied, "if I didn't mean it. He was screaming all kinds of horrible things about you, and I realized at that moment you are more important to me than anything else in the world. More than I was willing to admit to myself until I got on the phone with—him. Aviva Stern, I love you. I do." He bent over and kissed the top of her head. "Something bigger than both of us threw us together, and here you go. I love you." He threw his hands up. "Go figure." He looked at her for a reaction.

Aviva pulled away. "He yelled at me that you only want me so you can get your citizenship," she said. "That's not true, is it? He said as soon as you don't need me anymore you will throw me out."

"Aviva!" David slapped the side of his head. "I just told you I love you."

"I know, but I can't help hearing his words, over and over again, playing like a recording in my brain."

"He called you very bad names?"

She nodded, the tears starting to flow again.

"Do you believe what he said?" He pulled his hands into his lap.

"I'm trying not to believe it," she said. "When you're told something over and over, you start thinking it's true."

"Have I done anything to make you think I'm going to throw you out?" Now he turned and looked directly into her eyes. "Seriously. I'm not joking. Have I?"

"Of course not," she said, wiping the tears away.

"Did what happened between us over the past few days feel as if I don't want you? That this is just a trick to get my citizenship?" He pulled her gently toward him.

"Of course not," she said again.

"I love you. That's all I can say."

Aviva laughed. She had no idea why she was laughing, but she laughed. "How can I cry and laugh at the same time?" she said. "I love you too. Are we Romeo and Juliet?"

Now David started laughing. "Yes, but we're going to live in the end," he said. "We are going to live and love and have the life we are meant to have. Not fair to go through all this for nothing."

"I want to believe you so badly," she said. "I can't stop worrying about what they're going to do next. Nachum is the least scary of all of them, but he scared the hell out of me just now. I never heard him like that. And I'm not only scared for me—I'm scared for both of us."

"First you *have* to believe me. I love you and want you. Then understand we will fight it together. I'm here for you, no matter what." He leaned over and kissed her tenderly. She responded, putting her arms around him.

"It's not going to be easy," she said, resting her head on his shoulder.

"Maybe a little time will help. Maybe they just have to get used to it."

"Maybe, but I'm just not sure time is enough."

CHAPTER TWENTY-TWO

Aviva and David

The next few days were starting to seem almost normal. Aviva had started working at the bagel shop, and she was doing well there, stepping up to train some of the other counter help in more efficient ways to do their job.

"Thanks for bringing her," David's boss said to him when they were both on a break. "She's fantastic—smart. If she keeps this up, someday she might be a manager."

David and Aviva had had a long conversation the night before about her ambitions, and she had firmly told him her goal was to get her GED and then go to college, then graduate school, possibly to be a history professor. She wasn't sure. She'd also thought about accounting. Or maybe law school. "There is so much out there to learn," she'd said with a sigh.

David laughed when his boss mentioned the possibility of her aspiring to be a manager at the bagel shop. "Yeah," he said, "I think she can probably be whatever she wants to be. You're right—she's smart. But also ambitious." He'd requested they have the same schedules, and although the boss hadn't been keen on this at first, now that he saw Aviva was going to be an asset, he agreed to it. That way, she and David were relieved she wouldn't have to be alone in the apartment.

About four weeks after she'd started the job, they headed back to Queens together at the end of the day, laughing about celebrating her one-month anniversary with a bottle of wine. They climbed the stairs to the second floor, Aviva first and David behind her.

"Oh my God," she gasped as they pushed open the door from the landing.

David eased by her. "What are you doing here?" he said. "Who are you?"

"It's Nachum," Aviva said. Nachum had posted himself in front of their apartment door. He was sitting on the floor, his arms around his knees, his head down. He was crying. The side curls bobbed up and down as he bawled, wiping his eyes from time to time on the sleeve of his long black coat. He was wearing a tall round fur hat. Aviva's first reaction was to laugh, but not because she thought he was funny. Her hand flew up to her mouth.

"How did you get in here?"

Nahum was silent.

"Get up off the floor," she barked at Nachum in a voice David had never heard. "You're getting filthy."

"What are you wearing?" Nachum said, as he pushed himself up against the door frame. "You look like a slut."

David looked at Aviva, who was wearing a short-sleeved white tee shirt and white cropped jeans with sneakers. There was no uniform at the bagel shop, as long as the clothes were neat and laundered and didn't have holes in them. And everyone wore an apron, a clean one every day.

"She doesn't look anything like a slut," David hissed. "What's wrong with you?"

"Shhh, honey." Aviva put her finger up to her lips. "Let me talk to him."

David threw up his hands, but posted himself between Aviva and Nachum, his arms crossed over his chest. David was at least four inches taller, but Nachum's hat seemed to make them look almost equal in height.

"Did you bring the get?" she said, one hand on her hip. It hadn't been that long since they'd been living together, but Aviva had become much surer of herself.

Nachum shook his head. He wouldn't look her in the eye.

"What are you waiting for?"

"Please, Aviva," he said, casting a sidelong glance at David. "Can we talk?"

"Talk," she said. "I'm all ears."

"Yeah, but I don't think I want to talk in front of—him." He pointed at David.

"I'm not leaving her alone with you," David said. "Anything you can say to her, you can say to me."

"It's okay, sweetheart," Aviva said, putting a hand on David's arm. "I'm not afraid of him."

"But—"

"He is your sweetheart?" Nachum said. "I am your husband."

"Was," she said.

"I know we can work it all out," Nachum continued. "We need to." He gasped, as if he'd been crying for some time. "I'm sure of it. Just come home, and everything will be different." He bowed his head, refusing to look at David, who scowled, his eyes turning into slits, his mouth pulled into an angry line.

"Let's go inside and talk," Nachum, Aviva said. "It's not comfortable out here in the hallway."

David raised his eyebrows. "What about me?" he said.

"Would you mind just waiting out here? Just for a little while?" she said, putting both hands on his bent elbows.

"Please?" She tilted her head, looked up at him. He was annoyed with himself, because she was being a little flirty, and he knew he was a sucker for it.

"I'm worried about you in there alone with him," David said.

Nachum cleared his throat, glaring at David.

"Don't worry, it will be all right. Maybe you should go down and have a cup of coffee somewhere?"

"I'm not moving from here," David said, his chin jutting out as if he were a recalcitrant child.

She shrugged. "Okay, then. We'll be out soon." She opened the door and made a gesture with her hand. Nachum walked in first. She turned her head back to look at David, closing her eyes and smiling. "Really," she said. She kissed the air.

David didn't know whether he was angrier or more worried. This man who'd been her husband should give up whatever crazy act he was putting on. David paced back and forth in front of the door. At first, he heard nothing, which made him furious. If he had to be out here, at least he should be able to hear the conversation. Soon, however, the voices became louder, angrier, but although David could now hear, he realized Aviva and Nachum were speaking only in Yiddish. That was even more frustrating. Then it became very quiet again. Although it had probably been about fifteen minutes, David felt as if they'd been in the apartment for an hour. Finally, he couldn't stand it anymore, and he threw open the door and barged in.

"What is going on here?" Aviva and Nachum were standing close together, face to face. Aviva had her arms around him and was cradling him, back and forth. Nachum was crying softly. She made no move to loosen her grip on him.

"I told you I'd be out in a few minutes," she said softly, turning her head toward David. He tried to figure out whether she was angry, but he didn't sense anger—at least not at him. Perhaps a little frustration. But he was frustrated too.

"I don't understand," he said. He didn't know whether he should run out of the room, yell at Nachum, sit down, or simply stand there and demand answers. "What are you doing?"

"I am trying to comfort him," she replied. "He's very upset."

I'm very upset too, David thought. *This is really not fair.* But he decided it would be best not to say that right now. "Will you be done soon? I'd like to be able to sit down in my own apartment."

"Almost," she said. "Would you just give us a few more minutes?" There was very little emotion in her voice.

David tried hard to interpret from her behavior whether he should be worried. Would this other man's breakdown—whether it was real or feigned—turn her head? Convince her she'd made a mistake? She'd been doing so much better—with the job, with the new customs and clothes, with him. They'd been talking about plans and the future and what life might look like from now on. But seeing her with her husband made him realize nothing was going to be as easy as he'd hoped it would be. He was scared to lose her after finding her and falling in love with her, scared that the sweet new relationship they'd been nurturing might evaporate, because she had some sort of misguided loyalty to a husband she'd never loved and who had never loved her, to a life that had scarred her terribly.

"I'll be in the bedroom," he said, finally, after he realized she wasn't going to back down. He walked in, closed the door convincingly without slamming it, and sat down on the edge of the bed, his head in his hands. He began to feel a little nauseated, but it wasn't from anything he'd eaten. He tried to hear what was going on in the living room, but the voices were too quiet.

It felt as if hours passed. He lay down and tried to sleep, thinking that would at least relieve him from his thoughts, but sleep didn't come. Finally, the door opened with a slight creak, and he sat up too quickly, almost hitting his head on the headboard.

"What?" he said. She walked in and sat down on the edge of the bed.

"He's gone," she said.

"For good?"

"This is not easy for me, you have to understand," she said. "I left more than a man. I left a life."

"And do you miss it?"

She shook her head and lay back, her head on his lap. He reached down and brushed away some strands of hair that had fallen over her forehead. The tear stains on her cheeks were prominent, even in the low light. "It's more complicated than saying do I miss it or do I not miss it. I love you. I love my life with you. I've been completely honest with you about that."

"Then what's the problem?" he said, feeling the sour tasting impatience rise in his throat.

She sighed. "Nothing is black and white, sweetheart. But you don't have to worry. I'm not going back with him."

David felt his entire body relax. If he could be sure of this, it would make all the difference. He still felt the entire thing was too raw to have complete faith in her statement, although he knew she'd been up front with him about everything.

"Do you want to talk about it?"

She sat up again, leaning back and resting against his chest. He turned slightly, putting his arms around her waist.

He lowered his face to her hair, breathing in the sweet smell. She put her hands on his hands. "I've tried so hard to fit in here," she said.

He tensed again, feeling his arms get rigid. "I thought that was happening." It was starting to feel like a roller coaster ride. "But?"

"No—no but. It's just that Nachum's life has been thrown into a terrible tailspin, and I'm worried about him."

He sighed. "I don't think you should take this all on yourself. You are not the one responsible for breaking up your marriage. And it seems Nachum cares about Nachum and not much else." He wanted to say, "What about me"? But he held his tongue.

"I know that," she said, trying to turn her head to look at him. He leaned down and kissed her on the cheek. "He kept saying you would get tired of me and then I'd have nothing. He said we have absolutely nothing in common."

"How many times can we go over this, Aviva? I'm not going to get tired of you. I love you. You're different from anyone else I've ever known. You challenge me, which is exciting. I'm not sure how else to say it. All life is a risk, isn't it? We don't have guarantees of anything. Maybe *you'll* get tired of me. But I can't live my life worrying about that. It's not productive. Anyway, look at the two of us. He says we have nothing in common? How about the fact that I left my life and my country to come here and struggle? Do you think that was easy?"

A pang of guilt struck her once again. She had never considered the fact that David had come to a completely foreign place, just as she had. With him, though, it was a five-hour plane ride away. With her, a half-hour subway ride. "I don't suppose it was easy."

"Well, you're right. And you'll say it's different, because my parents and my family are still alive. But they are not here with me. I miss them terribly. And I rarely get to see them. Did you ever think of that?"

Aviva squeezed him, kissed him on the cheek. "I'm so sorry, my love. It never occurred to me. I'm a terrible person."

"No, you're not a terrible person. But I just want you to understand that we have more in common than you or your ex-husband realize. Do you understand that I empathize with what you're going through? Because I went though it myself—still am."

For some reason, her skin felt a little tingly. It was as if she'd had an epiphany. "How on earth would I ever get tired of you? You are really the first person since my father died to bring joy into my life, no matter what the obstacles. I will be grateful to you for all time."

"But don't you see you've brought great joy into my life too? I thought everything was just fine just the way it was. I had no desire to get involved in a serious relationship. My life is unsure. You know that. I live from gig to gig with a stupid part-time job I need to help pay the bills."

"What's your point?"

"I never would have chosen to bring another person into my life, not at this point when my career is uncertain, when I can't even promise to be able to take care of someone else. But then there was you. And everything changed."

"But why?"

"I don't know. How can we ever explain love? I can tell you superficial things. You are so beautiful. You are so sweet. You love my music. You can cook. You laugh at my jokes. You are smart and challenge my thinking. I love making love to you. We have something in common that binds us.

But all of that doesn't really explain love, does it?"

"I don't know either," she said. "I've never felt what I feel for you—I had no idea I could even have these feelings."

"So, there it is. We love each other. Don't we owe it to each other and to ourselves to go on exploring each other, letting our relationship develop, seeing where it can lead? Figuring out how to meld two very different cultures? Growing old together?"

"Are you asking me to marry you? Because I don't—"

He laughed, but she could tell it was a nervous laugh. "No, not exactly. I don't think we have to talk about marriage. But I thought we'd decided we wanted to make a commitment to each other. Was I mistaken?"

"No." She shook her head.

"But sometimes it seems as if you're having second thoughts." He stared into her eyes. "I wish I could look into your mind—your heart—and know everything that's in there."

"I'm just having trouble explaining myself. I'm not having second thoughts. But—"

"It hurts me there's a 'but.'"

"No, it's just that it's not black and white. Nachum says my leaving means I'm a terrible failure."

"You can't really believe that? After what his uncle—"

"And my happiness has made Nachum very unhappy."

"So first he tears you down, calls you a slut and a failure, informs you I am going to get tired of you and kick you out. On top of that, he has no desire for you to have a happy life—but he begs you to go back with him? Does that make any sense? Why would someone who has that little respect for you want you back? Did he tell you he loved you?"

EDUCATING AVIVA

She shrugged. "He doesn't believe me about his uncle."

"So, you're a failure, but his uncle can get away with—" He slapped the side of his head. "You think it's right for you to be miserable so he can be happy? Does that make any sense?"

"His family took me in when I had no one."

"Oh, you're really frustrating me, Aviva," he said, trying not to flex his fists but doing it anyway. "Scaring me, really." He pulled his arms away and ran his fingers through his hair. "The world wasn't created to make you feel obligated to be unhappy. You've had enough—what do you call it in Yiddish? *Tsuris*?[8] For about two lifetimes."

She laughed.

He continued. "You've shared all your beautiful hopes and dreams with me, and I'll be your cheerleader all the way. It would kill me to see you abandon all those hopes and dreams because you feel guilty about leaving a man who doesn't love you, doesn't believe you, doesn't protect you, insults you to the core, and is not man enough to wish you the best life you can possibly have."

"You're right," she said. Then she went silent.

"I know I'm right," he responded, "but I'm worried you will forget that again if your ex-husband comes back to the door crying his eyes out. He needs to learn a lesson from this too. That the world doesn't revolve around him, like the sun doesn't revolve around the earth. He needs to grow up."

"I'm sorry to put you through this," she said. "I've really messed up your life. I'm not sure you will ever understand the pull of my old community on me."

"I've repeated this over and over, and I will continue to repeat it. If I didn't want to be with you," he said, "I wouldn't

---

8   Troubles, woes.

be with you. And I will try to understand as long as I am with you. But you have to understand I have feelings too." He shook his head. "I know you feel I'm stronger than he is, but you have to remember I'm only human. If you stick me, it hurts."

She turned and threw her arms around his neck. "I'm sorry," she said. "This is very hard for me."

Then he kissed her, and at least for the moment, she was sure she was in the right place.

CHAPTER TWENTY-THREE

Aviva and David

David had told Aviva to expect he'd be offered a gig out of town from time to time, often without much advance notice. But this time, it was a chance to play with some musicians he admired in Chicago. He didn't want to pass up such a great opportunity. He'd have to leave early, go to the airport and fly to O'Hare, rehearse, play the gig, stay overnight, and then come back the next day. She was almost frantic with worry.

"What if Nachum comes back while you're gone?" she said. "What do I do if you're not here?"

"How will he know I'm gone?" David said. "What would make him come back?"

"I don't know," she said. She felt her hands shaking as she was cooking them dinner. Leaning forward, she laid her hands flat on the counter and pressed hard to make the shaking stop. "I think they have some kind of sixth sense. They seem to know when I'm most vulnerable."

"That's silly," he said, pushing her hair back and dropping a kiss on her neck. "You smell good," he said. "Like flowers and spaghetti sauce."

"You can't make me laugh, baby," she said. "I'm serious.

I'm really worried."

"So just don't let him in. And if he's sitting outside in the hallway, call Miguel. We talked to him about it, and he's willing to step in."

Aviva nodded. "I know. But what if Miguel is out? I don't expect him to sit home and be on guard because I'm having a panic attack."

"Anyway, you can text me any time. I'll keep my phone on, okay? And you can call nine-one-one too. Nachum and Ilona have no right to intrude on your life that way."

Aviva didn't want to admit it, but she felt a little hurt—a little jealous—that he was so excited to leave. They'd been together a little over two months, but she still hadn't gotten the get from Nachum, only some vaguely threatening emails about how she needed to "come home or else."

"It's like waiting for the other shoe to drop," she said. "Every time we get home from work, I expect him to be sitting on the floor in the hallway in front of our door again."

"You can't live the rest of your life worrying that your ex-husband is coming after you," he said.

"Until he gives me the get, I probably will."

They started eating dinner in relative silence. They'd had discussion after discussion about what a future for them might look like. Although she would not go back to her old life, if she was being totally honest, she felt an unmistakable pull backward. At the same time, she'd been looking into classes for high school equivalency and even checking out community colleges in the area. The idea of formal education had become so exciting, so enticing, she couldn't wait to start.

For David, the questions continued as well. He heard regularly from his friends Carlos and Sylvia. In particular, Sylvia asked constantly whether he and Aviva were still together, whether he'd given serious thought to Sylvia's warnings, why he should break it off with her before it was "too late." He never let Aviva in on the fact that Sylvia was still offering her unsolicited opinion that they should separate sooner than later. He wondered what she meant by too late. It annoyed him that his old friend didn't trust his judgment enough to believe in it, but he generally didn't answer Sylvia's questions, simply sent "I'm good, how are you?" messages to her.

"Maybe you could go stay with someone from work while I'm gone?" He looked up from his dinner plate and raised his eyebrows. It wasn't like Aviva to be so quiet. "Would that make you feel safer?"

"I just don't feel as if I'm close enough with anyone at work to ask them," she said. "And there's the food—well, you know what I mean."

"I think at least some of them keep kosher. Anyway, you could bring food from the shop."

She shook her head and bowed it, her fork full of spaghetti hovering between her plate and her mouth.

"Okay, I don't want you to do anything you're uncomfortable with."

"This is still new to me, David. You've made it so—so easy. So much easier than it would have been without you." She glanced up at him. Every time she looked at his face, it made her feel as if she'd made the right decision. His ready smile seemed to surround her like a hug.

"I know, babe. So then just try to be brave. You know help is at the end of the phone, right?"

She nodded. "When are you leaving?"

"It hasn't changed. We've discussed this. Tomorrow morning. And I'll be back the next day. As early as I can."

She sighed. "Okay," she said.

"I still think you should have gotten a restraining order."

"I know you do," she said. "It's just—it's just that I don't hate the—them." She paused. "Well, most of them, anyway. And I don't want to make their lives any worse than I have to because I took off. This is very difficult for them."

"You didn't take off for no good reason," he said, shaking his head. "And you sometimes seem to forget how difficult it was for you to be there." They'd been through this time and time again. He tried to fight his annoyance about how often he had to reassure her. On the other hand, he was so excited about the trip to Chicago, it was hard to put a pall on his good mood.

"I know. I'm sorry. I don't want to make you feel bad. It's just that—"

"Maybe you should call your aunt?"

"I suppose. I don't even know whether she's still speaking to me though. I'm sure Nachum's family has bombarded her with their opinion of me and ordered her to make me go back. And none of this has anything to do with her."

"But she's family. You're so lucky to have family—at least some family—here. I'd feel better if you gave her a call. Just let her know I'm going to be away overnight. Then you'll have two people looking out for you."

"I guess so," she said. "I feel awful putting her through this. She's been very kind to my mother."

He pointed to her new phone. She'd been having a good time with it, like a kid with a new toy—exploring all the apps, playing games on it, learning how to text and make phone calls and listen to music. "Why don't you do it now? Then you won't forget." He knew she wouldn't forget. But he wanted to make sure she made the call, because he was pretty sure that if he didn't press her to do it, it would "slip her mind."

She picked it up and pressed the keys. By the time her aunt answered, she was almost in tears. "Hello? Aunt Rachel?"

David began to clear the table. He wanted to listen to the conversation, but he felt maybe it would be less uncomfortable for Aviva if he weren't hovering. "Tell her hello for me," he said, as he made some noise with the dishes and the pots.

"I'm okay," she said. "David says hi. How are you?"

David hoped Rachel would be supportive. She had been great so far, really going above and beyond what she might have been obligated to do for her niece, given Aviva's defection and the rules of the community. In fact, it wouldn't have been out of the realm of probability for Rachel to disown the rebellious Aviva, but she hadn't done that. Aviva kept telling him they would meet "one of these days," but it hadn't happened yet.

"Yes, he's going overnight, so I was feeling a little nervous being alone."

Each time Aviva spoke, there was a moment of silence, as she waited for Rachel's response.

"Oh, no, I wasn't suggesting you keep me overnight," she said. "I know your situation—the money, my uncle. I don't want to get you in trouble, really. It's fine. I just wanted to talk to a friend." She giggled a bit nervously, David thought. He peered around the door, but he was happy to see that Aviva was completely engaged in the call.

"Really? You would do that? Yes, that would be fun, I'd love to. I do have to work though, so I'll just take the bus after work if that's okay? Thank you so much."

Another pause.

"I love you too, Aunt Rachel. See you tomorrow. I'll call you to give you my arrival time."

Aviva got up and brought the rest of the dishes and the leftover food into the kitchen. She put her arms around David from the back and rested her head just below his shoulder. He turned and enveloped her in a tight hug. "I love you," she said. "Thank you for suggesting I call Rachel."

"So, what's happening?" he said.

"She invited me to dinner tomorrow night. There's a kosher diner in the next town over from Kyrias Joel. She'll meet me there. I get off at three o'clock tomorrow, so it will all work out."

"How will you get there?" He leaned down and kissed her on the lips.

"We have to clean up the kitchen first," she said, kissing him back. "If we start this now—"

But it was too late. He scooped her up and carried her to the bedroom. "Sweetie, what about the food out there?"

"It'll keep," he said, pulling her down onto the bed and then pushing her shirt up over her head and fiddling with her bra.

"Wait, let me. You'll rip it, silly." She reached back and removed her clothes. She had gotten to the point—with David's encouragement—where she was completely unselfconscious about removing his, which she then did. It was still incredible to her how much she loved making love with him. GED, college, and career notwithstanding, she felt he had taught her an entire degree program in love and life in the short months they'd been together. She had much more to learn, and she appreciated the fact that he was a sweet, generous lover, but their lovemaking was also strenuous and often exhausting. Nevertheless, she loved every second of it—couldn't resist him.

After they were done, she lay back on the pillows, still naked, still reveling in the feeling of being so completely merged with, subsumed by another person. He turned on his side and looked at her, his head propped up on his elbow.

"How did I get so lucky?" he said.

"No, I'm the lucky one," she said, tracing his lips with her index finger. "Never in my wildest dreams—" She closed her eyes and sighed. Her hair was growing in fast, and he brushed it off her face.

"You are so beautiful," he said, leaning over and kissing her deeply, cupping her breast with his hand. "I want to be with you like this forever."

"What about when I'm old and fat and wrinkled, so you can't stand looking at me?" she said. "Then you'll send me back to Nachum and go snatch another pretty young girl for yourself."

"No, because I'll be old and fat and wrinkled too," he said, laughing. "And I won't have the strength to do the snatching."

"I will love you no matter how old and fat and wrinkled you get," she said. "And I'll love looking at you too."

"Well I feel the same way," he said, kissing her again.

"I think I should go finish cleaning the kitchen," she said. "Before we end up doing this again. Then I won't have the energy to do anything besides go unconscious."

"Will you walk into the kitchen slowly, and do it naked? So I can watch you as you go? Please?"

She gave him a little slap on the shoulder. "You have a dirty mind," she said.

"Yup, I do," he said.

She climbed over him and stood up by the side of the bed. He reached up to grab her rear end, but she jerked away. "No touch until the dishes are done," she said.

He laughed.

She picked up his shirt from the floor and slipped it over her head, tying the ends into a loose knot.

"You're even beautiful wrapped up in my sweaty work shirt," he said.

"I love it because it smells like you," she said.

"That's true love if you still love my smell after I've been working in a hot bagel shop all day." He reached under the shirt and ran his hand up her side, stopping at her breast. She squealed.

"You're a bad boy," she said. "Let me go finish, and then I'll give you your punishment." Then she made a little curtsey, turned, and walked to the kitchen. He was tempted to go after her, but he lay there, knowing that if he did, they'd probably end up making love on the living room floor, and the dishes might never get done.

CHAPTER TWENTY-FOUR

Aviva

The next morning, David had insisted on accompanying her to the bagel shop, although she reassured him she was capable of going by herself.

"No," he said, "what if they're lurking nearby. I want to make sure you get there okay. Inside the door. And for God's sake, take an Uber to the bus terminal afterward. I'll text you every couple hours."

"Don't worry about doing that while I'm here," she'd said. "The boss won't be too thrilled if I'm leaning down to text you back when there's a line of hungry customers."

"Okay, but after three o'clock, you're getting a bunch of texts." He paused. "Except when I'm playing, of course." Then he'd hugged and kissed her goodbye and left her at the door to the shop, quite happily going off on his adventure to Chicago. She was annoyed with herself, but as she watched him walk up the street whistling, a wave of emotion caught her, and she felt tears welling up. Not only was it the first time they'd be apart overnight since the day she'd moved into his apartment, but Carlos was meeting him in Chicago. What if Carlos convinced him that she wasn't a suitable girlfriend? What if Sylvia was still campaigning against her? She wiped her eyes on her sleeve and walked into the store. She realized she depended on David to feel safe, but she hadn't realized how much his absence would affect her.

But the day was ordinary, although she looked out the front windows quite often, hoping she didn't see anyone she knew from Williamsburg, as absurd as that even seemed. As the day progressed, she began to feel a little less anxious. Everything seemed entirely normal.

"I'm leaving," she called to the boss after her shift was over. She dropped her apron into the dirty clothes bin and waved.

"Okay, Aviva. See you tomorrow."

Tomorrow she would have to navigate here by herself, but that really wasn't a problem. As she crossed York Avenue, still trying to look around at a three-hundred-sixty degree angle whenever she could, she saw a bus approaching from uptown. *Perfect timing, not necessary to waste the money on an Uber*, she thought. She decided to take that as a good omen, because sometimes they had to wait up to twenty minutes for a bus. This way, she could spend the money she saved on something they needed for the house. She stepped on the bus, smiled at the driver, who smiled back, and then she sat down. It had a been a busy day in the shop. She was tired and wanted to close her eyes, but she was still being hyper-vigilant, just in case Nachum or Ilona or Eli might have been watching her, so she stayed alert.

At the big bus terminal, she boarded the next bus, which was waiting, and settled into an aisle seat. Finally, she allowed herself to relax a bit, hoping no one would sit next to her. She didn't feel like having a conversation with anyone. The anxiety and paranoia had crept in again—what if Nachum had hired someone to follow her, and they cornered her in her seat. *Stupid idea*, she thought. *They have no way of knowing I'm even going somewhere, so how could that happen? I have to pull myself together.* But she kept the aisle seat anyway, in case she had to make a quick escape. Just as the bus closed its doors and began to make its way out of the terminal, a young woman tapped her on the shoulder. Aviva jumped.

"Oh, sorry, didn't mean to startle you. This taken?" the woman asked, pointing to the window seat. Aviva glanced around the bus, but it was full. She shook her head. The woman climbed over her carefully and sighed as she leaned back onto the headrest. "Oh man, what a day," she said.

Aviva didn't respond, but tried to keep her eyes closed, hoping her seatmate would leave her alone.

"I have such mother issues," the woman said. "My name's Melissa."

Aviva almost laughed. She almost wished she had some "mother issues." Or that she really had a mother at all. "Aviva," she said, not opening her eyes.

"Never heard that name before," Melissa said. "It's pretty."

"Thank you."

"Where you going?"

Aviva gave up trying to pretend to sleep. She hoped the young woman would do all the talking and not be too curious about her. "I'm meeting my aunt at a diner." That seemed innocuous enough.

"Oh, I'm going to Woodbury Common. Gotta do some retail therapy," she said. "My mom drives me crazy. Other than weed, it's the only way I can chillax." She laughed.

Aviva had never heard of Woodbury Common. She found herself curious, despite her original plan not to talk to anyone. "What is Woodbury Common?" she said.

Melissa laughed. "You kidding? You never been there?"

Aviva shook her head.

"Wow, you've been missing out. It's this huge outlet mall. I can't believe you've never been. They have everything there, and I mean everything. You could spend your whole paycheck in one afternoon, easy."

Aviva smiled. Maybe one day she'd take an excursion to a huge outlet mall and spend all her money.

"You from this country?" Melissa said.

Aviva wheeled around toward the girl. "Yes. Why would you ask that?"

"You have a little accent," she said. "I can't figure it out."

"Oh, probably my Brooklyn accent," Aviva said. She hoped that would satisfy Melissa's curiosity. It seemed to.

"So, you like your aunt?"

"Yes, she's really nice."

"Well, my mom is a pain in the ass," Melissa said. "I started dating this guy, his name is Craig, and she hates him. She detests him. And he's the greatest guy. But she thinks she can forbid me to see him, and I'm not gonna listen to her. So, we had a huge fight. I hate when she treats me like a child. I'm eighteen, and I should have the right to decide who to date." She cleared her throat. "One of these days I'm moving into my own place, and then she won't be able to say a word."

Maybe if she didn't spend her money at the mall, she'd be able to move into her own place, Aviva thought. "Why does your mother hate him?" she said.

"He's half black, half white," Melissa said. "So my mom says, no dating black guys. But I said to her, if he's half white, how come he's black? Why can't we call him white?" She made a kind of rough sound with her throat that turned into a laugh. "That's why I'm going to the mall. If I feel like it, I'll get her some stupid little gift, and maybe she'll back off. She likes Coach, so hopefully they have a big sale going on. I'll say whatever it is, he bought it for her. Then, maybe?" She looked over at Aviva, widening her eyes. "How old are you?"

"Nineteen," Aviva said.

"Does your mom get all in your business like mine does?" she said. "Does she let you date who you want?"

Aviva sighed. If Melissa only knew her story—but of course, she never would. She shook her head. "It's different. I live with someone."

"Oh, that's cool. And your parents are okay with it?"

"I guess so," she said. *If it were only that easy. What would Melissa say if she knew about Nachum and Eli and marriage at seventeen?* "You know, I'm sorry Melissa, but I'm really exhausted. I worked all day before I got on the bus, and I feel like I need to take a little nap."

Melissa's screwed her face into a half-frown. "Oh, okay," she said. "You work?"

Aviva nodded.

"Me too. I got out of high school, and my parents wanted me to go to college, but I'm done with school. D—O—N—E. I got a job at this car dealership. I'm the one who says hi to people when they come in, you know? Gotta look cute and friendly so the guys who come in get in the mood to buy. Red lipstick. Short skirt almost up to my ass. Low cut blouse." She pointed toward her chest. "But the deal is, after I'm there one year I can get a great deal on a car. I can't wait."

"That's nice," Aviva said, not paying much attention, hoping Melissa would stop talking. She turned her head away and closed her eyes for real. She drifted into a light sleep and dreamed of a time when she was a very little girl and both her parents were alive. It was a happy dream, but the bus went over a bump, and she was jostled awake. She glanced over at Melissa, who was listening to music on her phone, swaying in time to it, so she turned away again. She thought about the dream and wondered, had her father not died and her mother not gotten so sick, whether she would still be in Williamsburg and married to Nachum or to someone else like him. She wondered whether her father would have protected her from Eli, or perhaps whether Eli wouldn't have assaulted her if her father were in the picture. The entire thing made her angry and sad, so she tried to blot it out of her mind.

"Woodbury Commons!" the bus driver called back, pulling over the bus to a jerky stop.

"Nice meeting you, Evita," Melissa said chirpily as she climbed back over Aviva. Aviva opened her mouth to correct the mistake, but then changed her mind. It didn't matter. She gave a little wave to the girl, who, she thought, had no clue what it meant to have real problems. Several people got off the bus, and then it edged back onto the road.

THE LAST STOP WAS HERS. STEPPING OFF THE BUS, AVIVA saw the diner perched on a small hill about five hundred feet away. She felt excited. It occurred to her that she was looking forward to seeing her aunt more than she'd even realized. She was relieved her aunt had agreed to meet her here. She had no desire to elicit the stares and disapproval of the citizens of Kiryas Joel, but neither would she even entertain the thought of putting on the Hasidic costume she'd repudiated to go back there. She saw her aunt immediately as she entered the front door of the restaurant.

"Yes, miss?"

"I see my aunt over there." She pointed toward the back of the diner."

"Okay. Waitress will bring you a menu."

Rachel stood up to greet her, and Aviva couldn't help gawking at the wig and hairband, the long skirt that glanced the tops of her aunt's ankles, the plain shoes and heavy opaque stockings, the blouse buttoned up to the neck. "Honey, I'm so glad to see you." Rachel enveloped her niece in a hug, and then put her hands on Aviva's shoulders and pushed her away gently. "Wow, it's a good thing I know your face, or I wouldn't have recognized you."

Aviva felt the blush creep up her neck to her cheeks. She wasn't sure what to say, so she just slid into the booth.

"Oh, I didn't mean to embarrass you. It's just that—"

"My life is very different now," Aviva said.

"You're also way too skinny. Doesn't this boy feed you?"

Aviva laughed. "He's not a boy, and we feed each other."

"Well eat more, then. It's not healthy, how skinny you are."

Aviva thought about all the times she couldn't touch a bite of food because of anxiety or fear or depression. Eating wasn't as important to her as it was to Rachel.

"Are you happy?"

Aviva didn't detect any malice or mocking in the question. It was just a question, just meant to gather information. "Happier, Aunt Rachel."

"I know you weren't happy before, darling," the older woman said. "But I always thought, maybe, if you could have gotten over the Eli thing—"

Rachel raised her hand as if to say, "Stop!" and pushed it toward her aunt, across the booth. "The point is, I never could have gotten over the Eli thing, Aunt Rachel—I never will, completely. And anyway, I wanted more. I needed more."

"I love you, but I'm still not a hundred percent sure why you felt you had to do this. I'm trying not to judge you, because I know you've had a hard go of it. You are older than your years—always have been."

Aviva shrugged.

"You said you really needed to talk to me?"

"Yes, a few things. How is my mother?"

"Just the same, I'm afraid. I don't think that will ever change. At least she is living a calmer life with the medication. But the longer it goes, the surer I am that she will never be able to function normally again." Rachel made a noise like a stifled sob.

Aviva hung her head. "I wish there were something I could do for her."

Rachel shook her head, waved her hand as if to dismiss Aviva's thought. "There's nothing any of us can do, really. You should try hard not to feel bad, because none of it is your fault. If I thought it would help her to have you visit, I'd tell you—but I'm afraid she doesn't even recognize me. But what else did you want to talk to me about?"

"So, I did want to tell you I'd like you to meet David." She looked up at her aunt, narrowing her eyes, trying to gauge the woman's reaction. "He would like very much to meet you. He feels strongly about family—he's so far away from his own family." She paused. "If that would be all right with you?"

"Where did you say his family is from?"

"Colombia. Bogotá."

Rachel shook her head slowly from side to side. "Catholic?"

"Yes, but he doesn't go to church." Aviva looked up at her aunt, trying to gauge her reaction. "And he respects my traditions."

"Seriously?" Rachel said, raising one eyebrow. "What about when he realizes you are completely different from him? You have a different religion, different background, different language—what happens when he gets tired of working so hard to make this all work? It's so much easier to be with someone—one of your own kind. You have to agree."

"One of my own kind? Like Eli? Like Ilona, who judged me for every breath I took? Like Nachum, who really didn't care whether I was there or not, as long as his dinner was on the table in time."

"I understand you had a difficult situation, Aviva. But after the excitement wears off, what if this David decides he wants someone Catholic? Or someone from his own country? What if his parents want him to marry a girl from Colombia? Not some girl from the Hasidic community who eats different food and speaks Yiddish."

"We're not getting married, and anyway, that's not what I wanted to talk to you about," Aviva said, trying to force back the tears.

Rachel wiped her forehead with the back of her hand. "I just have to ask you. This—relationship—is something you feel serious about?"

"I found out what love is, Aunt Rachel. I found out what it's like to really love and be loved by a man—to *be* in love. David makes me very happy."

"And what about Nachum? You don't love him?"

Aviva tried not to laugh. She choked.

Rachel didn't pursue it. "Did he give you the get?"

"Well, that's one of the things I wanted to discuss with you. He hasn't, and in fact, he appeared at my doorstep weeping. It made me feel terrible."

"But not terrible enough to try the marriage again?"

"No, I have thought about it a great deal, believe me. But even if David were not in my life, there is no way I could ever go back to Nachum and my old community again. I could never feel safe there. And I want to go to college, want to have a career. I want to experience all of life, not just what happens in a few cloistered blocks in Brooklyn."

"Perhaps if you were my child, I'd be giving you different advice, Aviva. Perhaps I'd be horrified if you were my daughter, but somehow being your aunt gives me a little distance, a little perspective. You are so smart, so sure of what you want—as much as your leaving the community pains me, I can't tell you not to. Even if I did, I don't think you'd listen. The only thing you have to remember is, if you have second thoughts and want to come back, that probably will be impossible. Have you given that any consideration?"

"Yes, of course I have," Aviva said. "I've thought of almost nothing else, except what I am doing with my life and how irrevocable it is. Other than David, I have no one to talk to about that, except you. And he is a wonderful support, but he doesn't really understand the full extent of what I am doing."

"How could he?"

"Except that he too left his country and his family for a different life, and I know he misses them terribly."

"But nothing is keeping him from going back to his country if he wants to—correct? He always has that option."

Aviva nodded. Her phone beeped, and she looked down. It was a text from David. *Everything all right?* it said, with a red heart at the end of the message and a little emoji face puckered up with a kiss.

"He just texted me," she said. She clicked a little red heart on his message and replied with, *Everything good,* and *Love you.* She felt a little guilty, because she hadn't even thought to ask him how the trip to Chicago was going.

Rachel put her elbows on the table and rested her head on her hands. She stared at her niece for several moments. "I'm sorry to say this, Aviva, but what if this boy decides it's too hard to be with you?"

"This again?"

Rachel sighed. "You have to understand that your relationship is going to require a great deal of care and work. I know you're young, but I also know you should be aware of that."

"I am aware of it. Of course I'm aware of it," Aviva said.

"What if he meets some girl, more like himself, and decides he doesn't want to be with you anymore? That it's just too difficult? What if he stops loving you?"

Aviva sighed. "David and I have talked about this until we're blue in the face. Life doesn't provide guarantees for anyone, does it? Anyone who thinks it does is very misguided. We are committed to doing everything to keep our relationship loving and successful. I think it has to be one day at a time. You said it yourself. I've been through a great deal. I don't think I'm naïve."

Rachel sighed, wiped her forehead again. She opened her mouth, paused, and then started to talk. "Do you know about Footsteps? They are a group that gives support and counseling to people who have left the Hasidic community. Perhaps? It might help?"

"Yes, I've heard of it. I haven't reached out yet, because I wasn't sure whether they would try to urge me not to do what every cell in my soul is telling me to do. I couldn't stand it if they tried to convince me to go back. I'm just not sure."

"I don't think they're there to try to convince people to go back."

Aviva felt her eyes widen. She'd been putting off contacting them. It was just another thing to think about. There had been so much.

"Well, perhaps you should give them a call. I believe they do good work. If, God forbid, anything happens with this David, they can provide support. I can only help you by telling you I love you, you are my beautiful niece. But I obviously have no experience with what you are doing, and I would be lying if I said I wasn't worried for you. And further, my friends and relatives would be very angry with me for even coming out here to talk to you."

Aviva put her hand up to her mouth. "I never wanted to get you into any sort of trouble."

"No, don't worry. That's the beauty of meeting here. Not too many of us venture out to have dinner in a diner," she said. "We're lucky there's a kosher one so close-by."

The waitress approached their table. "Are you ready?" she said.

After they had ordered, Aviva reached her hand across the table and patted her aunt's. "I have one huge favor to ask you, Aunt Rachel." She looked at her aunt's face and noticed it sagging a little. "Don't worry—nothing much, but something that will make me feel much better—give me some relief." Rachel seemed to perk up.

"What is it, honey?"

"Sometimes when David goes on one of his gigs outside the city, I may be a little nervous being alone in the apartment. It's going to take me some time to get over my fear of Eli—even my concern about being ambushed by Nachum, although it's only been the one time. At least until I have the get."

"Yes?"

"May I just call you if I have an emergency? If I'm afraid?"

"Of course, but I'm so far away. I don't know what I could do to help," she said, her forehead contracting into a sea of horizontal wrinkles.

"Just having your voice there on the other end of the phone would help me a lot," Aviva said. "I know I'll get better about this, but until I do—?"

"You can call me any time. If that will help you, it's the least I can do. But—"

"But?"

"You shouldn't hesitate to dial nine-one-one if you're really afraid or in danger. Please, let me know you are willing to do that."

Aviva nodded. "David said the same thing."

"Well, David and I are in agreement about that. And yes, I will be willing to meet him sometime, if he wants to meet me. You let me know when the time is right, and we can meet in this same place again. Is that all right?"

Aviva broke into a wide smile. Just knowing her aunt was—even though she didn't completely approve—not going to abandon her was a huge relief. "Thank you, Aunt Rachel. I love you."

"I love you too, sweetheart. And you deserve some true happiness. I just hope this new life doesn't disappoint you. Things are not always what they seem. Now please eat the food that's sitting in front of you. I can't leave here until I know you've had a decent meal."

CHAPTER TWENTY-FIVE

David

David was excited to be going to a new city to perform. He'd been to many cities, but somehow never Chicago. And he was also excited that he'd be sharing a room and playing with Carlos. The music would be outstanding, and the company would be just as good. He got off the plane and headed for the el stop. That was another cool thing about Chicago he'd been looking forward to, the iconic elevated train. The trip to the hotel was uneventful, and when he got to the registration desk, he was told that his friend had already checked in.

"Oh man, I'm so happy to see you!" Carlos met David at the door to their room. They clinched in a tight bear hug. "Come on in. I took the bed closer to the window. That okay?"

"Sure," David laughed, "finders keepers." David threw down his bag and his drum equipment. "We got time to rehearse?"

"Yeah, of course," Carlos said. "Don't you want to chill a bit first? Are you hungry?"

"I could eat," David said. "The peanuts on the plane didn't quite do it."

"Let's go get a Chicago pizza and catch up," Carlos said, slapping his friend on the back. "So happy to see you, bro. This is twice, in what? Three months? We gotta keep this going."

"Sounds good to me," David said. "A beer would go down great too. You know this city, I don't. So, lead the way."

The two men left the hotel, Carlos pointing David in the direction of a small pizza shop. "I love the pizza here," he said.

Over their meal, the friends chatted about everyday things, until Carlos brought up Aviva. About to take a bite, David put his slice of pizza down and frowned.

"So, the elephant in the room, huh?" Carlos laughed. He wouldn't look David in the eye.

"Not sure I know what you mean, amigo." Of course he did, but he wanted to force Carlos to clear the air. He felt his muscles tense, waiting for whatever Carlos had to say.

"Sure, you know. What's up with her? You still together?" Carlos leaned down to take a big bite of pizza, and then looked up, his forehead furrowed into wrinkles. David took a sip of beer, wiped his mouth on the napkin, and leaned back in the booth.

"So, that took at least ten minutes for you to bring up," he said.

"Why? What's up? Trouble in paradise?"

"Did Sylvia tell you to say that?" David said, shaking his head and trying to ignore Carlos's snarky comment. "Why would you even think that?"

"I didn't mean anything, bro," Carlos said. "You have to admit, it's not exactly a normal relationship."

"What's a normal relationship?" David really didn't want to fight with his best friend, but he was feeling attacked, whether Carlos meant it that way or not, and he felt his hackles going up.

"Oh, come on man, don't get so defensive. You know I'm your best friend here, don't you? I always got your back."

"If you've got my back, then you support my choices," David said. "I feel like you're making it necessary for me to defend myself."

"Jeeze, I'm just asking," Carlos said, his usually calm face tensing into a frown. "I don't mean anything by it. You don't have to go off on me."

"Who's going off on who?" David said, shaking his head.

Carlos took a bite of pizza and wiped his mouth on a napkin.

"The relationship is going great," David said, taking another sip and another bite. "This pizza is really delicious. Wish we could just talk about the food."

"She's good to you?"

"*Good* to me? What does that mean?"

"You know, she gives as much as she takes? Not high maintenance?"

"Get to the point, man," David said. "What do you really want to know?"

"Look, I know she's gorgeous. That's obvious. And she's young. And hot. And all that. But she comes from that—that place, you know? That—those people. It's gotta be hard for the both of you, especially her. I get the attraction to a sexy girl, but what's underneath? And what happens when she decides to ditch you and go back where she came from? You know, she has a heart-to-heart with the rabbi or whoever, and she feels bad that you took her away from everything she ever knew. That's all Sylvia's worried about."

"I figured it was Sylvia who made you promise to grill me. You never used to be like this."

"You never hooked up with one of those people before."

"*Those* people are people," David said, separating the words so that they came out staccato. "Just like us, they have feelings, they have thoughts, they are human, some of them are creeps, some of them are great. Just like other people. It's really a pain in the ass that my best friends can't understand that."

"We just care a lot about you. We don't want to see you get hurt. She moved in with you so quick, like no one even had time to think about it."

"She had nowhere else to go."

"Oh, so you're just roommates?" Carlos wasn't smiling.

"You know, Carlos, I love you like a brother. But if you're gonna do this whenever we talk, I'm gonna have to say sayonara. I can't handle it. When you and Sylvia got together, did I try to talk you out of it? Or did I accept her like a sister?"

"Yeah, but that was different. You have to admit. You and I and Sylvia all come from the same country, we're the same religion, we understand each other. It's just not the same."

"I don't admit a goddamn thing. And by the way, I didn't take her away from anywhere. She came into this with her eyes open. I love her like I've never loved anyone before, and she loves me back the same way. We love each other. We're smart enough to know that we're taking on a complex set of problems. But we don't only love each other—we like each other too. We listen to each other. We both have dreams, and we both respect each other's dreams. We want to make this work, and we *will* make it work. I don't know what else to say to you. You going to back off? I want her in my life, and I want you in my life too. But if you keep on my case and make me choose, I'm warning you now, I'll choose her. Please treat me like an adult and trust me."

"Whew, that speech just sounded like you were running for office," Carlos said, slapping himself on the side of the head and laughing.

"It's not funny. You're not making it funny. I'm not joking."

"Okay, okay. Actually, Aviva's really sweet. I liked her right away. I really did, and not because she's pretty. Sylvia has been putting a bunch of shit in my ear, right from the beginning. And she's my wife, man."

"So?"

"So, happy wife, happy life."

"So, what you're saying is you have no right to tell Sylvia how you feel? Even if she's being unreasonable? That's stupid, bro."

"You don't know Sylvia."

"Yes I do. And I know she's stubborn. But I also know she loves you, and you have a right to stand up for what you think is right. You've been my friend a long time. You've seen me go through crappy relationships, mostly with girls who were what Sylvia would call more suitable, right?"

Carlos nodded.

"I'm telling you, I'm determined to make this one work, and so is Aviva."

"So that's what? An ultimatum? Like her or lose me?"

"I don't want to lose you."

"Okay, I'll try my best," Carlos said. "And I'm sorry for all the lecturing. I know you're a grownup. We just want what's best for you."

"Well then please have faith in my judgment. I don't know how many times I can say that."

David's phone beeped with a text, and he raised his hand to Carlos to let him know he was going to look. It was a text from Aviva. *Had a nice time with Rachel*, it said. *I think she's going to be supportive. Love you.* David texted back a happy face and a red heart.

"I'll try."

"If you want to look out for me, be my friends, not my frenemies."

The two finished their meal in silence. Finally, Carlos spoke.

"You want to go to the place and rehearse? We have a couple hours tonight if we want it."

"Yeah," David said, "I could use a little drum therapy right about now."

CHAPTER TWENTY-SIX

Aviva and David

Aviva couldn't wait to get home after work, even though she knew David wasn't expected until after seven o'clock. She paced around the apartment, cleaning, sweeping, smoothing out the bed, scrubbing the toilet. She hadn't been able to fall asleep the night before, so when David had texted her around one in the morning that the gig was a great success, she was wide awake and answered his message. They continued back and forth for close to an hour, David asking about her day and making sure she was okay, that she hadn't heard from anyone she didn't want to hear from.

> *Sorry if I woke u*, he'd texted.
> *I was up, so happy to hear from u.* Just seeing his words made her feel somehow safer.
> *Don't u have work in the a.m.?*
> *Yes, but I had trouble relaxing without u.*
> *U double-locked the door?*
> *Yes.*
> *U should be fine then.*
> *I miss u. The bed feels empty without u.*
> *Miss u too. I'm kissing you, can u feel it?*

Kissing u back. Love kissing u.
Can't wait till I'm holding u.
Me too.

Finally, he called it quits. *Sorry, baby, I'm bone tired. Gotta catch some shut-eye.* She felt a little guilty for keeping him up so late. *I'm sorry*, she texted. *Go to bed. Miss u. Kisses.* She put a red heart after the message.

U go to sleep too. You have to get up early for work!

Somehow, she did manage to sleep for a few hours. Now, though, after having worked all day and cleaning the apartment several times over, she was feeling a little exhausted. But when he burst in the door at six thirty, she felt a surge of energy that made her body tingle.

"You're early!" she said, rushing to him, throwing her arms around him.

"Whoa, let me put down my stuff," he said, unemcumbering himself from his heavy backpack, as well as the bulky cases containing cymbals, snare drum, and drumsticks. "I'm really happy to see you too."

"The plane was early?" She'd led him over to the futon, pushed him down by the shoulder, and sat on his lap, straddling him, her arms around his neck.

"I got an earlier flight," he said. "I was lucky."

"I'm the lucky one," she said, peppering his neck and face with kisses. "I missed you so much."

"I think I might do this every week," David laughed, kissing her lips. "I'm a little hungry, but I'm thinking maybe we should start with dessert?"

She leaned backward, holding him at arm's length by the shoulders. She felt him getting hard under her. "You sure?"

"I'm actually more hungry for you than for food," he said. He stood up in one motion, picking her up and carrying her to the bedroom. "How did I live without this for one night?"

Aviva never thought that making love to him could be better and better each time, but every time they did, she was surprised that it was more ecstatic than the time before. She couldn't get enough of him, and he seemed to feel the same way.

"I love you," she breathed into his neck after they'd finished. "You energize me. You make me want to climb mountains."

"I don't know about you," he said, "but you exhaust me!" He laughed. "I can't imagine climbing a mountain right now. I guess that's what I get for falling in love with a teenager." They were both lying on their sides, spooning, David's arm draped loosely around her waist.

"I'm almost not a teenager," she said, pouting, even though she was sure he couldn't see her face. "When I'm twenty, you won't be allowed to say that anymore."

They lay still for a while, but then David pulled her around to face him. "We have to talk," he said.

"Don't ruin the mood," she said.

"I know. But I have to get this off my chest."

Aviva worried. They'd just made delirious love, but something in his voice sounded ominous. "Are you going to kick me out now?"

David laughed hard and long. "Why the hell would you say that? After what just happened in this bed?"

She didn't respond immediately. "I had a long talk with

my aunt Rachel," she said, pausing after saying that. "I'm not sure you're going to be happy with what she said to me."

"Yeah? I thought you said she was on our side?"

"Well, she knows what I've dealt with, and she is making an effort to accept us—to accept the fact that I have chosen to leave the Hasidic life—although it's not easy for her. But she warned me that maybe you will get tired of having to deal with me and all my problems?" Aviva voiced her aunt's concerns as a question, because she couldn't stand the thought it might be a statement of fact, a self fulfilling prophecy. Her voice was so soft, David had to concentrate hard to hear her. "I wouldn't blame you," she said, her voice catching. The tears that came often had begun to well up once again. She cleared her throat.

"What on earth would make you think that? I love you," he said. Then he sighed. "I don't know what I have to do to make you trust me."

"I do believe you love me now. But what if down the road you decide it's just too much trouble to love me? I come with all this baggage, and it's a constant uphill battle, talking about mountains."

"Okay," David said, "I guess it's my turn. So Carlos warned me that one of these days you're likely to decide you don't want *me* anymore, a struggling musician who may never make enough money to support you. You will likely have to work for a long time. He said you could get tired of this life, that you might decide it would be easier to go back to your life in Williamsburg. Then it will be 'adios David,' just like that, and I'll be here nursing a broken heart." He leaned over and kissed her gently on the lips.

She shook her head several times. "I'm tired of this conversation," she said.

"You and me both," he said.

"That is never going to happen. I'm never saying, 'Adios, David.'"

"So maybe we should have Carlos get together with Rachel? And they can argue it out? What do you think?" He winked at her. "Meantime we can stay here and make love while they're convincing each other our relationship is doomed." He gave her a little nudge in the shoulder. She laughed through the tears. "If we can't laugh about it, I think we're done. And now that we've enjoyed the delicious dessert, what's to eat?"

Over a dinner mostly of leftovers, David grilled Aviva about her alone time. "You were okay? You didn't worry too much?"

"At first, I was pretty anxious," she said. "I couldn't fall asleep, and every single noise made me jump. But after you and I texted for a while, it really calmed me down. And nothing at all bad happened. Just two regular days at work and one night."

"I just wanted to make sure, because I'll get other gigs. I'll have to leave you. The best thing for me is to get to play my music in a lot of different places. That's how people will get to know me. It's really exciting, these opportunities."

"I know," she said. "I'm happy for you. I think after Nachum gives me the get, hopefully I'll lose the anxiety and start feeling normal." She thought about Rachel's words, about the stimulating life David was starting to have, about her own lack of confidence that he would continue to want to be with her.

"Any word about the get?"

"Nothing," she said.

"You think you should call and maybe press him a little?" He couldn't help running Carlos's warning through his head.

What if she didn't really want the divorce? What if she was just trying out this life but keeping her options open.

She shrugged. "I know I should. I will. Meantime, I called about the GED. I think I'm going to sign up to take the test."

"You think you can pass?" he said. "Without any kind of preparation?"

"I know maybe this is a little conceited of me, but I spent so many hours in the library growing up, I'm pretty sure I gave myself my own high school education. Should I worry?"

"I don't know. Are you in a rush?"

She nodded her head strongly, pounding a fist on the table. "I can't wait to go to college. *You* do something you love. *I* want to do something I love too."

David smiled and grabbed her hand across the table. "It's nice to see you so energized and confident," he said. "It's not conceit. You know your capabilities, and you're smart."

"I guess we'll find out how smart, won't we?"

"Can you take it again if you don't pass?"

She nodded. "As many times as you need to," she said. "But my plan is to pass it the first time so I can continue my education formally. I don't want to always feel as if I've missed something."

"I'm with you," he said.

"I love you," she said.

CHAPTER TWENTY-SEVEN

Aviva

The next few days were uneventful. Work was fine. Aviva was continuing to adjust to her new life. She had met many more of David's friends, and they were more accepting of her than Sylvia had been, although David tried to reassure her that Sylvia would come around. The sex was getting better and better, and she was almost managing to get Nachum and his family out of her mind most of the time. She'd told David to stop urging her to press Nachum for the get, because she felt it would be easier to take care of after Nachum's fury at her and his despondence about her leaving had normalized a little. David agreed to abide by her wishes.

Then one night, about two weeks after David's gig in Chicago, they finished dinner and were in their living room, sitting on the couch together. It was around eight thirty, and the late summer days were beginning to darken noticeably earlier. Aviva had books on her lap, studying for her GED exams. David had earphones on and was listening to a new arrangement of a song he was learning. Every so often one of them would tap the other on the shoulder and share some dreams or observations, sometimes just a smile.

"I definitely think I'll get a Ph.D. and be a college professor," Aviva said, looking up and closing her eyes. "Maybe modern European history. Or philosophy."

David nodded. "I definitely think I'll get a Grammy or two. Then I'll be invited to play with my trio on *Saturday Night Live*."

They were giggling together, kissing, enjoying each other's company. He was rubbing her back, rather unconsciously, and she had her hand resting on his leg, as if they had to have physical contact with each other at all times. She was enjoying it, leaning into his touch. She knew that sooner or later they'd be making love, and she always looked forward to that. Deep in a long kiss, they both heard something—then they sprang apart.

"What is that noise?" she said. They both stood up and walked to the window, but their apartment was in the back of the house, and there was nothing visible below except blackness. But the noise was getting louder. It sounded like persistent banging. As they opened their apartment door and listened, it was coming from the front of the building, as if someone was pounding on the front door. But not only was there the sound of something ramming the door, they also heard raised voices, some male and some female.

"Stay here," David barked at her, leading her by the elbow back to the couch. "I'm going to go down and find out."

"No! I want to go with you."

"Stay here for now, please." He put his hands on her shoulders and pulled her close, hugging her. "I'll figure out what's going on, but I'll feel better if you stay here."

"What about you?" A wave of fear passed over her. She held him tightly, wishing they could make everything go away. Her hands were shaking. The only thing she could imagine was that her people had come to demand her return, but she was almost positive they wouldn't hesitate to use whatever they were banging on the door with to hurt David.

"Don't worry about me," he said, sitting down with her on the couch and giving her one last hug. "I'll be fine." Then he jumped up, grabbed his keys, and went back to the door. "I'm locking this door. Do not let anyone in, no matter what," he said. "Do you understand?"

Reluctantly, she agreed, but after he'd gone, it was impossible to sit still. She paced back and forth across the room. Even though she was behind the locked door, it seemed as if the voices were getting louder, more strident, but she wasn't sure whether that was truth or just her imagination running away with her. Twice she put her hand on the deadbolt, wanting to go downstairs and see for herself. But twice she thought better of it, pulling her hand away as if the door were burning hot. Finally, she went to the couch, sat down, put her head in her hands, and began to cry.

Aviva thought about her life now. She thought about their neat although somewhat shabby apartment, furnished with things David had acquired from friends who'd moved away or from resale shops. She thought about the little front yard with its tree and small green lawn, and the planting boxes David had built to grow tomatoes and herbs in the back. She thought about how when she went out to a shop or the library or a movie, no one was watching her and judging her, reporting to her family on her transgressions. She thought about her dreams of college and a career. She thought about how she never wanted to give this up.

She wasn't sure how long she sat there—possibly ten minutes or so—when she heard the key turning in the lock. She wheeled around toward the door, and was horrified to see David leading two people inside. Aviva stood as Ilona pushed in front of him, pulling Nachum along with her by the elbow. Aviva couldn't move.

"Why?" was all she was able to get out. She felt tears welling up. David made a sign for the two of them not to come closer. Then he went to her, linking his arm with hers.

"We need to get this over with, once and for all," he said. Ilona was standing, arms akimbo, her face drawn into a mass of ugly lines, glowering at Aviva through dark eye slits. Nachum wouldn't give her eye contact.

"So, here they are, sweetheart," David said, leaning down and giving her a kiss on the forehead. Then he stared directly at Ilona, as if he wanted to challenge her. "And you won't believe who they brought with them."

"Who?" Aviva's voice was shaky. She wasn't sure she wanted to know, but she had guessed the answer.

"Their uncle Eli," David said, "and he was pretty sure he had the right to come into our home, even if he had to break down the front door."

Aviva began to shake. Her hands shook, her legs shook, her stomach felt as if it were turning inside out. "You didn't—" Aviva's voice was a soft murmur. She craned her neck to look past Ilona and Nachum toward the hallway.

David shook his head. "No, I told him he was never to come anywhere near our home again, or I would call the police. As a matter of fact, I think we have to get a restraining order as soon as possible, because I don't believe he'll behave. We've put it off too long." David looked down at Ilona, matching her scowl.

"Where is he now?" Aviva's voice was shaky.

"As long as he's at least a mile away from here or from anywhere you are, I'll be happy," David said.

"What did he say when you told him to leave?"

"He protested loudly. He was the one making the most noise out there. There were a few more of them too, and they had baseball bats. Baseball bats!"

"What?" Aviva put her hand up to her mouth. "How did you get them to go away?"

"I told everyone what Eli had done to you."

Aviva slipped out of David's grasp and crumpled softly to the floor. Ilona and Nachum didn't move. David knelt down beside her, trying to prop her head up on his bent knee.

Ilona began speaking in Yiddish, as if she didn't want David to know what she was saying. She said, "My uncle would never do such a thing. You are a liar. I knew you were a bad person, and now it's even more clear to me. How dare you try to blaspheme my uncle's name like that?"

But rather than making Aviva cower or back off, Ilona's words had the opposite effect—they motivated her. She reached her arms up to David, who helped her to her feet. Then she walked closer to Ilona and spoke directly to her, in English, enunciating each word clearly. "When you are in my home, you will speak in English. And you should wake up and see what's going on right before your eyes. I tried hard to do everything right, but nothing I ever did was good enough for you. And yes, your dear uncle did exactly what David said. He assaulted me, brutally, in my house, twice."

Nachum began to cry, burying his head in his arm. Ilona threw her arms up and made a noise that sounded like a rusty gate. "Liar!" she screamed in English, her voice breaking.

"Fine," Aviva said, "if I'm such a terrible person, then why won't Nachum give me the get? He should want to be rid of me, shouldn't he? And when Eli goes after one of your daughters, perhaps you'll believe me and apologize for the way you treated me. You should be kissing my feet for not going to the authorities. I just want my freedom. After that, Eli is your problem."

Ilona raised a hand and started bringing it down, as if she was going to slap Aviva hard in the face. But David grabbed her arm in mid-air. "Don't you dare," he said, his voice low but strong.

Nachum hadn't said a word, but now he raised his head and gazed back and forth from David, who was still gripping Ilona's wrist, to Aviva. "But why did you hate *me*, Aviva?"

Aviva slapped the side of her head. "I didn't hate you, Nachum. I still don't hate you. But I need much more than the existence I ever would have had with you. I need someone who appreciates my intellect, gives me support for doing the things I want to do in life—cares for me."

"Take your hands off, you're hurting me," screamed Ilona. David let go, but he stared at her as if to say, "Don't try anything again, or I'll hurt you even worse."

Aviva continued, "I do not want to be a brood cow, bearing multiple children for a man who doesn't even respect me or seem to like me, let alone loving me. And even if you were that man, I could not stay in your family, when you are not willing to believe me and protect me." She sighed. "I still have nightmares about that man. All the time." David put his arm around her shoulders, and she leaned into him.

"*Umfrukhperdik froy*[9]!" Ilona yelled. "I knew Malka was right you were going places on buses, sneaking to this—this man." Ilona yelled, shaking her finger at Aviva. "I knew you were sneaking to the library."

"Yes, like a thief, right?" David said. "Sneaking to the library. What a criminal she is."

---

9   Yiddish for "barren woman"

"You don't understand our ways," Ilona said to David, in English. "You have no right to make judgments." She raised her fists. David reached up to grab her arm again, but she pulled her hands down.

"I do know what is right and what is wrong," David said, "and your uncle should be in jail for what he did. Not going to people's homes with a baseball bat to do—what?"

"That was just for self protection," Ilona huffed.

"Really? My neighbor downstairs said he was banging it on the door, hard. We heard it up here. The walls were shaking. It's a good thing I got down there before he destroyed our house. And you should thank me for convincing my neighbor not to call the police. If it ever happens again—"

"Nachum," Aviva interrupted, "you need a wife who will be happy to serve you in ways I never will be. I'm sure there is someone who will be thrilled to marry you and keep up the traditions the way you want her to. Do you understand?"

Nachum shrugged. "But this doesn't look so good for our family," he said, his voice weak, looking down at his feet.

David stamped his foot on the floor. "Doesn't look good for your family? Does a creep like Eli look good for your family?"

"So you're more concerned with how it looks for your family than how I feel or even how you feel about me?" Aviva said.

"That's it," Ilona said, looking at Nachum, "she is going to do what she's going to do. There is no way we can change her mind—not with this—" She raised her fist and shook it at David. "this *shagetz*[10]. It's all his fault."

"So will you give me the get then?" Aviva said to Nachum.

---

10   *Shagetz* is a Yiddish word meaning a non-Jewish man. It has a bad connotation, as if the man is some sort of miscreant or scoundrel.

Nachum had curled into as close to a fetal position as someone can while standing up. His shoulders were curved inward, his hands wrapped around his body at the midsection, his *peyot*[11] hanging down in front of him like two bouncy pillars. He stood that way for a moment. Then he said, "I think I'm going to throw up."

Aviva took his elbow and led him to the bathroom. She closed the door behind him. Then she went back to David. Several minutes later, Nachum emerged. "You left some things," he said. "At our home."

"I left everything. And it's your home, not mine."

"Do you want any of it back?"

"Not much. Just the photograph books from my parents and my alarm clock. And my stepstool and dressing table. You can keep everything else."

Nachum sniffled. "I'll give it to you," he said. "Everything. And I'll give you the get." He wiped his eyes with his coat sleeve. "You're sure there is no way? No matter what?"

"I told you the last time and I'm telling you now, there is no way I'm ever coming back. My mind is made up."

Nachum hesitated, staring at her, his mouth starting to open as if he was going to say something, but before he could, Ilona grabbed him by the collar. "Stupid girl couldn't get pregnant anyway. Don't waste your tears on her. Let's get out of this place," she said. "It's making me feel dirty to be here." Then she pushed him through the door, and as she went, she turned her head toward David, threatening him with a clenched fist, and yelled, "*Zal dir got sheltn mit di ergst fun di tsen mkhus!*"

David raised his eyebrows at Aviva, who waved at the air as if to blow the curse away. "I'll tell you what it means

---

11   The curly sidelocks worn by ultraorthodox Jewish men and boys.

246   *Rebecca Marks*

later, after we both calm down and can breathe again," she said. Finally, Ilona and Nachum were gone. David craned his head out into the corridor and watched them walk quickly to the end of the hallway and disappear down the stairs. Then he closed and locked the door.

Aviva collapsed on the couch. "Thank you," was all she could muster.

David sat down beside her, and she put her head on his shoulder. He kissed her cheek. "Seriously, what did that woman say to me?" he said, after they'd sat silently for a few moments.

"She said, 'May God curse you with the worst of the ten plagues.'"[12]

"Lovely person," he said, shaking his head.

She looked up at him. "You look a little troubled," she said, rubbing his face tenderly with her hand. "Your forehead is all wrinkled up."

"You mean other than that the woman who used to be your sister-in-law just cursed God's wrath on me?" He snorted a little.

"You can't take that seriously?"

"No, not really. But that's not all."

"What then?" she said.

He sighed, pushed her away gently, and faced her. "Every time I see you with Nachum, I feel—well, I feel a little jealous." He looked down at his hands, turning them over and then back.

"What? Why would you even say that?"

"You seem to have some sort of feelings for him," David said. "I can't explain it, but it makes me nervous, and it

---

[12] A reference to the ten plagues that God sent to Egypt before the Jewish people escaped from slavery there.

makes me a little angry. If what you've told me is true, he meant nothing to you."

Aviva took one of his large hands in both her smaller ones. She remembered the first time she'd let him touch her, when he rubbed her hand gently with his thumb, in the car the day they drove to Boston. It made her feel warm inside thinking about it. She started to rub his hand the same way. "It's hard to explain," she said. "I don't have feelings for him in the way you mean. I don't have loving feelings for him, nor do I miss being with him. You must know that by now? What more could I do to show you how much I love you?"

"I know that," he said. "When Nachum's not around, I don't really think about it. And there's nothing more you need to do for me. But the way you embraced him the last time, and the way you so kindly led him to the bathroom before, touching him." He looked at her, trying to assess what was in her head.

"Sweetheart, I was married to him for two years."

"Unhappily," he said.

"Yes, true. But I shared a bed with him and a house and everything else. And I keep reminding you, he is not an evil man. If what happened with Eli hadn't happened, I'd probably still be with him, as unhappy as I was. And I do have feelings for him—mostly, I pity him and feel sad for him, but I certainly don't love him. I never did, and I never will. And," she added, "I didn't want him vomiting all over our rug. That's why I took him to the bathroom." She poked David in the ribs.

"I know," he said, grabbing her hand and kissing it. "I'm sorry for acting this way. It's just that we got together so quickly, after—And you're so young. Maybe you'd like to have some other experiences before you settle down again."

"Our life together feels so right to me," she said. "I can't imagine being with anyone besides you. I'm old for my years anyway. We've had this conversation."

"Just maybe if you kiss me a lot, I'll get over myself?" He smiled.

"I will kiss you all night long," she said. "But seriously, there are others beside Nachum we should be concerned about. Ilona is hateful but not dangerous. But do you think we're safe? From Eli?" Aviva pulled her head away and looked up at David.

He leaned down and kissed her tenderly on the lips, and she kissed him back. "As safe as we can be without a restraining order," David said, "and you need to get one as soon as possible. I even did some research. I called that Footsteps program. They gave me information about how to get one at Family Court."

"When did you do that?" Aviva was surprised, her eyes wide. "I had no idea." She opened her mouth as if she was going to say something else.

David put a finger on Aviva's lips. "We should have done it sooner. But I told Eli if he ever came back here, I would make sure he would regret it. Hopefully he'll listen to me and believe me."

For the first time since the noisy commotion outside had started, Aviva felt as if she could relax. "My knight in shining armor," she said, turning and squeezing him around the middle, breathing in his smell she loved so much.

"On a white horse?" he asked.

"Whatever color horse you like."

CHAPTER TWENTY-EIGHT

Aviva and David

Their boss wasn't too happy about it, but the next day, David called work and said they'd have to take at least half a day off. He wasn't explicit about why, but he only said it was a family emergency. After some grumbling, the boss said it was all right. After ascertaining that Eli was an uncle by marriage, a helpful clerk at the courthouse walked a shaky Aviva through the Family Offense petition. Once that was filed, they received an immediate hearing.

"No going back now," she said to David, as they walked into the courtroom hand-in-hand.

"Of course not," he replied. "You have to do this. No other choice."

"I'm just a little scared," she said. "He is so volatile. I'm not sure how he'll react."

"Well, he'd be a violent criminal whether or not you got the order, and this way you have the authorities behind you if he tries something again."

The hearing was short and not that difficult, although Aviva didn't feel as if she were quite there. It felt as if her feet were skimming somewhat above the floor, never quite touching it. The judge was a kindly looking woman who appeared to be in her sixties, with short white hair, rosy cheeks, and half-glasses that sat on the tip of her nose. If Aviva hadn't been so nervous, she'd have giggled every time the judge peered over the tops of the glasses to ask a question.

"I am granting this temporary restraining order," she said, after Aviva had explained the circumstances. "You and the defendant will be required to return to court for a hearing on the permanent order three weeks from tomorrow. I see you included his address and contact information on the petition." She looked down at the paper and then over the glasses again.

Aviva nodded. "Yes, your honor."

The judge banged her gavel. "So decided," she said. Then she smiled at Aviva. "Please be safe, Ms. Stern," she said. For some reason, the unexpected words touched Aviva, who began to cry, although she'd promised herself she wouldn't lose her composure. The judge signaled to the court officer, who produced a tissue from a box on the bench and brought it over to Aviva, who wiped her eyes and blew her nose.

"Thank you very much," Aviva managed.

"Next case," said the judge.

It was close to noon when they left the courthouse. "I suspect you don't feel up to going in to work today?" David said. Aviva hadn't said much as they waited for the bus.

"I'm sorry, I just want to go home and recover," she said. "Do you mind?"

"No, I'll stay with you. I'm not leaving you there alone. The business will survive our absence for one day," he said.

"I never thought one human being could have so many tears," she said to him. "I'm tired of crying."

He hugged her. "If you're crying, you must need to cry," he said.

"What did I do to deserve you?" she said. She'd said that many times during their time together.

"I don't know," he said. "Maybe I'll throw you back in the water and catch a better fish?"

Aviva laughed. "Always making jokes," she said.

"How do you know I was joking?"

Despite her worry, Aviva felt a kind of freedom, having taken care of the restraining order. The anticipation of court had been worse than the actual process. The judge hadn't denigrated her story or disbelieved her. She and David were laughing again. And as David had said, Eli was an evil person whether there was a restraining order or not. Hopefully, he would appear on the appointed date, and the judge would make it permanent.

"So what do you want to do for the rest of the day?" he said, as they sat on the bus, going home.

"Maybe after I relax a little, go to the library?"

"Anything but that," he said, wagging his index finger at her.

"Then afterward, maybe we could splurge and eat dinner out?" she said. "I'm not sure I feel like cooking."

"Or I could cook for you," he said. "How about that?"

David was a good cook. He often surprised her with some new vegetarian recipe that was delicious and, he always pointed out, kosher. "If you feel like it," she said. "I thought maybe you'd like to take a break too."

"We'll see," he said. "We'll have a nice day, no matter what. Then tomorrow, back to the old grind."

He'd told her there was another out-of-town gig coming up in a few weeks that would take him away from home for two days and nights. She'd been mildly worried about being alone again, and what had happened the previous night made the prospect of being alone even more troubling, but she hoped now that there was a restraining order in place, perhaps she could let down her guard somewhat. However, she felt as if she were waiting for "the other shoe to drop," wondering when Eli would receive the summons. She wasn't looking forward to the repercussions, whatever they might be.

They whiled the day away, each passing hour helping Aviva to become less tense, as if she could hope life were returning to normal again. As much as she was sure her life here was normal, there was always the specter of Eli hanging over both of them. It was at best unsettling, at worst terrifying, especially after the baseball bat incident. After they ate the dinner David prepared, Aviva felt exhausted. "I think I just want to go to bed," she said.

"I'd like to practice a little, and then I'll join you," he said, hugging her. "Sound good?"

"Of course. I would love that," she said. "I love being—with you."

Aviva went about her business for the next few days on pins and needles, waiting for any indication that Eli had received the summons to respond to her request for a permanent restraining order. But there was only silence from her former family. She had a little trouble relaxing—even sleeping—although with David there, she knew it would be safer than if she were alone. But every tiny noise in the house made her jump, and she actually relished her work time, because if she was around many people, she felt much more comfortable even than if she was at home with David.

"Try not to think about him," David said. "I'm telling you, I scared him off. He's not coming back here. He's a coward—only acts like a maniac with people weaker than he is."

"Hah," she said. "It's impossible to frighten him. He thinks he's the most important man in the world and the most powerful."

"But there's been nothing, right? Not a peep out of them."

"Yes, but he'll fly into a temper tantrum when he receives the summons. I know he will. He might not even come to court."

"Well if that happens, you'll win by default. So don't worry about it. Worry doesn't help anything."

They were lying in bed, David propped up on an elbow looking at her. Every few moments he bent down and kissed her—her mouth, her neck, her breasts. She was wearing only an old shirt of his, completely unbuttoned, and nothing else, and he thought she was the most beautiful woman he'd ever seen. Her blonde hair was growing out nicely now, without the spikes it had had at first. He bent down and pulled her close, running his fingers through the loose curls, and then kissing her deeply, exploring places with his tongue he swore he'd never found before. Each time they kissed, he felt he discovered something new about her, something more delicious that was a revelation.

He pulled the shirt up over her head and stared down at her body. He loved the round breasts, the way her waist dipped in with soft curves, the distinct line of her hip bones. They always made love with the lights on, although Aviva had been a bit uncomfortable with that in the beginning. Now she was used to it, and she admitted she loved to look at his beautiful body as much as he loved to look at hers.

"I love you so much," she said, as he smothered her with another kiss, pulling her body in close. His skin was warm, and she loved the hardness of his muscles and bones, even the scratchiness of his beard and the tickle of the hair on his legs, which often made her laugh.

"I love you too, more than I thought I could love any woman," he said.

"I have no idea how it worked out that we found each other, but I thank God every single day that we did." Those were the last words she spoke, before the perfect merging of their bodies kept her from speaking any more.

"Do you think maybe you're going to be able to fall asleep now?" he asked, after they were both spent from the lovemaking.

"Until I start thinking about—him," she said. "Then I seem to get wide awake."

"Can't you try to enjoy what we just did? Without letting the memory of that man seep into your consciousness?"

"I'm sorry, love," she said. But before she could say anything more, his breathing became regular and he was asleep, his arm still under her head. The breeze from the fan in front of the window had begun giving her goose bumps, so she reached down to the floor, picked up his shirt, and put it back on. She pulled the light quilt over both of them, but she tossed and turned for what seemed like hours before she drifted off to sleep.

CHAPTER TWENTY-NINE

Aviva and David

A week and a half had passed since the court hearing, but there was still no response from Eli, at least to them. Aviva had no idea whether he'd show up at the new date for the permanent order. She was starting to feel less tense at home, starting to eat better and sleep better, but she was worried about facing Eli in the courthouse. She tried to steel herself, knowing she wouldn't be alone there, that David would be with her. David pointed out that if Eli had one of his bouts of fury in the courtroom, it would only make her case look more credible.

"Do you mean the judge might think my story is not credible?" she said. Her lips pulled into a straight line. "Even if Eli somehow manages to behave like a human being?" She felt the three vertical lines forming at the bridge of her nose, as her face contracted into a frown.

"No, no, that didn't come out right," he said, lifting his hand to smooth out her face. She pulled away. "Of course your story is credible. But if Eli pulls some crap in front of the judge, it would simply put an exclamation point after your sworn testimony."

"I guess," she said. At the same time, she was always

aware of the quickly passing days leading up to David's out of town gig. "How am I going to be able to stay here without you when you're gone?" she said.

"I kind of had an idea about that," he said, raising an eyebrow and tapping on the kitchen counter with a pencil he was holding in his hand.

"What idea?" she said. She put her hand on his and grabbed the pencil to stop the tapping, but he pulled his hand out from under hers and continued beating a rhythm with his fingers, even louder.

"Carlos mentioned that he was playing in New York the same time I'm leaving."

"Yes?" she said.

"And Sylvia is coming with him."

"Oh." She walked away from David and stared out the window. There was nothing much to see, except the backs of the houses on the next street.

"So," he continued quickly, "I was thinking maybe they could stay here? You know, so they don't have to pay for a hotel."

Aviva wheeled around. "Are you kidding?" she said. "Sylvia is going to stay here with me, when you're not even here?"

He shrugged, a small half-smile raising the corners of his lips, as if he'd had some secretly delicious but off-color idea and was slightly embarrassed about it.

"Is she going to lecture me again about how I'm ruining your life?" The frown had crept back.

"I'm pretty sure she's had a change of heart," he said, standing up and joining her at the window. He took her hand, leaned down, and kissed it.

"What makes you so sure?"

"I talk to Carlos from time to time. Seems they had a few small arguments about it, and finally, after he made her see how obnoxious she was being, she relented." David didn't let go of Aviva's hand.

"So, her relenting has nothing to do with accepting me then?" She didn't pull her hand away, but she could feel her whole body tensing up. He was trying to intertwine his fingers with hers, but she held them stiff and locked together. The interchanges with Sylvia had been not only unpleasant, but unnerving, almost like the ones she'd regularly had with Ilona. She didn't know why these women didn't like her but admitted she would rather avoid them altogether than having to deal with their constant disapproval. It was enough dealing with the entire debacle of her marriage and Eli.

"No, actually it does have to do with accepting you, really. She sees we're happy and not going anywhere," he said.

"How does she know that?"

"Because I tell Carlos and he tells her."

Aviva cocked her head, raising one eyebrow.

"So this way," he continued, before she had a chance to respond, "you wouldn't have to stay alone in the apartment."

She'd never before brought up her hunch, but she decided this was the time to pull out all the stops, especially if the woman was going to spend a few days with her. "Do you think Sylvia has a—a thing for you?"

"A thing for me? What do you mean by that?"

She pulled her hand out of his and gave him a little slap on the rear. "You know what I mean. She 'likes' you."

"She likes me. We're friends."

"Why are you playing so innocent, my love? You have accused *me* of being innocent when it comes to romance. I do not think you are. I'm pretty sure Sylvia has the hots for you. She was much happier when you were single, because that left her a little hope she might have you."

David slapped his side and laughed. "No way. She and Carlos are solid."

"What's that got to do with it? You're much better looking than Carlos." Aviva wasn't smiling. She was almost positive she was right.

"You're dead serious, huh?"

Aviva shrugged.

"Well, whether she has the hots for me or not, I only have the hots for one woman. David pulled her into one of his sweet, yearning kisses, and then held her tight. "If you don't know that by now, I have no idea how to prove it to you."

"You prove it to me all the time," she said, "but that doesn't mean Sylvia will stop hating me for stealing you away from her."

"You can't steal something from a person if the person never had it in the first place. Sylvia is like a sister to me, that's all. And besides, probably the only one of them who has the hots is Carlos—for you—and I told him 'hands off or else.'"

"Well if that's true, no wonder Sylvia hates me. But you know you don't have to worry about me, right?" She snuggled into his arms, breathing in his heady man smell that she loved so much. "I am a one-man woman. And that man is you."

"I know, baby," he said. "So just stop worrying about her. The longer she sees you and me together, the more she will back off and stop her nonsense, whatever reason she's doing it. And if she doesn't, she'll lose me as a friend. And I don't think she wants that. I know Carlos doesn't."

"So you really think I should have them stay here while you're gone?"

"Only if you're sure staying with them won't be worse than staying alone. Wouldn't it be great to have a girlfriend?"

"I think you're pushing this a little far, aren't you, honey? Last time she talked to me, she invited me to disappear to the far ends of the earth so I wouldn't break your heart. Now you're saying we can be girlfriends?"

"If I'm wrong, I'll splurge and take you to dinner at a great kosher restaurant, and then I'll take you to a Broadway show with seats in the first ten rows of the orchestra."

That was too much for Aviva, who broke down laughing. "What else can I get out of this?" she said, sputtering with laughter. "Maybe if I resist more you'll offer to get me a fur coat and a BMW."

David's face fell. "Do you want a fur coat and a BMW?" he said. "Because it'll be a while before I can do that for you."

"No, silly," she said. "It was just so funny, you bribing me to host Sylvia."

"She'll be in your city, in your home, watching how happy you are," he said. "I only thought—You know, I'll feel better if you're not staying here alone."

"It's all right. If you are sure she will behave, I'll do it. It is comforting to know I won't have to be cringing in my own home for two days and nights because I'm scared Eli is coming to attack me. And I know how close you are to Carlos. The last thing I want is to be at war with Sylvia."

"And anyway, how would Eli have any idea you're going to be alone?"

"I have no idea how he finds these things out, but he always seems to know what everyone else is doing," she said. "Sometimes before they even know it."

CHAPTER THIRTY

Aviva

Work was fairly slow the next day. Aviva found herself cleaning the counters and sweeping the floor a few times. She was bored. After her conversation with David last night, he had called and invited Carlos and Sylvia to stay. Carlos had readily accepted the invitation. She was a little anxious about spending two days and nights with Sylvia, but she was trying hard to put that anxiety out of her head. David kept reassuring her it would work out fine. She was also waiting for the results of the GED exams she had taken. She was almost sure she'd passed them all, but there was always a little germ of doubt. As soon as she got her GED, she could enroll in the community college near their apartment and start taking classes. She couldn't wait. Her mind often wandered to the subjects she was excited to study, where her studies would lead, what she would do after she finished community college and then a four-year college.

"Aviva? Did you hear me? I said there's a phone call for you." Aviva had a scrub-brush in her hand and was squatting over a spot on the floor. Something had apparently dropped and been ground into the wood by people's shoes. She jerked her head up.

"For me? Who would be calling me here?"

Her co-worker shrugged. "No idea," he said, "but the phone was ringing and I picked it up and they asked for you. Pretty sure you're the only Aviva we have here." He held the phone out to her.

Aviva stood and brushed her hands off on her apron. Maybe it was someone calling her with the results of the GED test? But no, that would come in email, not over the phone. Anyway, this was the work phone. They wouldn't even have that number. She ran her hands through warm water in the sink behind the counter, dried them off on her apron, and picked up the phone.

"Hello? This is Aviva."

"Oh, Aviva. Thank God I got a hold of you."

Aviva didn't recognize the female voice on the other end of the line. The voice sounded young and agitated. "Who is this? Do I know you?" she said.

"It's Miriam," the girl said. "Mimi. From work—um, your old work."

"Oh, goodness," Aviva said. She hadn't spoken to her co-worker from the Brooklyn bakery since she'd left. "Are you okay? How on earth did you get this number? How did you even know I was here?"

"Oh, you know," Mimi said. "Everyone knows everyone else's business in this place."

"But—"

"Listen, I have to talk to you. It's urgent. Can you get away and meet me?"

"I'm at work, Mimi. What's this about?"

"I can't talk about it on the phone," Mimi said. "and I'm on a break from work right now. But I have to meet you in person somewhere, in a place where we're not overheard.

Can you come here? To Williamsburg?"

Aviva felt a stab of fear course through her veins. "I'm sorry, I just—I don't feel comfortable going there. Is there somewhere else?"

"I don't know." The girl sounded as if she was about to cry.

"Could you meet me at Grand Central? It's all so impersonal there, you know? You don't have to worry about anyone overhearing us there. They have a big food court. Maybe we could sit over a cup of coffee and talk."

"That might work," Mimi said.

"Seriously, are you all right?" It had been such a strange call, so fraught with anxiety. Even though Aviva had no idea what the problem could be, she found her hand shaking.

"No, no. It's not me. I'm fine," Mimi said.

"Oh, that's a relief," Aviva said. "So, what time do you want to meet?"

They made the arrangements, but Aviva had trouble keeping her mind on anything but the phone call for the rest of the day. After their shift was over, on the way home, she told David about it.

"Well, I'm going with you," he said.

"Maybe I should go alone," she said.

"No, I insist. What if this is some scheme by Eli to get you alone? I don't trust it."

"Mimi is my friend," Aviva said. "I can't imagine she would try to sabotage me. Besides, what can Eli do to me in the middle of Grand Central Station?"

"Well, I'll go. And if she doesn't want me to be there for the conversation, I'll lurk around the fringes. But I'm going."

"Okay, I guess that will be all right. I just don't want to scare her off. Something is obviously terribly wrong."

"She didn't give you any clues?"

"No," Aviva said. "She wouldn't talk about it on the phone. But she wasn't in good shape. I told her I'd meet her at four, so we should just take the Q and go over there now. All right?"

David nodded. At least this was taking Aviva away temporarily from her current worries, which were the court appearance and the Carlos/Sylvia visit. He was glad she'd get a temporary break from that. It wasn't quite rush hour yet, so they got a seat on the subway at seventy-second street, got off at forty-second, jumped on the shuttle, and walked out into the noisy hubbub that was always Grand Central. It was three-forty-five.

"We made great time," David said. He knew Aviva wasn't up for small talk, but he wished he had some way to calm her down. "What do you think it's about, honey? Don't worry so much. I'm sure it's nothing."

"Mimi was freaking out," Aviva said. "What keeps coming back to me is that she was one of the only people I ever told about Eli."

"Oh, I didn't realize you confided in anyone."

"You, my aunt Rachel, and Mimi. For some reason, it seemed safe to talk to her. She has nothing to do with that family."

"But didn't you say Eli was well known in the community?"

Aviva shrugged. "It just came out one day, and she was my only friend, so—"

Aviva led him to the place where she'd agreed to meet her friend, and they sat down at a table.

"Do you want some coffee?"

"How about some iced tea?" she said. "I feel like I have to cool down."

While David was up at the counter getting their drinks, Mimi arrived. She stared at Aviva with a look of disbelief.

"Oh my God, I almost didn't recognize you," she said. Aviva had blown out her hair and was wearing lipstick and some eye makeup. She had on tight jeans and a sleeveless pink blouse with ruffles around the neck.

"It's the same me," Aviva said, standing up to hug her friend. "Just a better version."

"You look—wow, you look amazing," Mimi said.

"David came with me," Aviva said, as he walked toward the table with the iced tea.

"Oh, no—" Mimi's smile disappeared, and the color left her face.

"It's all right. If you don't want him here, he'll go sit at another table. But Eli paid us a visit the other night, armed with a baseball bat, so David doesn't want me going out by myself. I hope that's all right with you?"

David put the glass down on the table and pointed toward a table a few yards away. "I'll be over there," he said. "Hello Mimi."

Mimi slumped into the chair and put her head in her hands. "He's the one who came to the bakery."

"He is. He's wonderful," Aviva said. "So, what's going on that's got you so upset? I'm all ears."

Mimi began speaking in Yiddish. It almost made Aviva laugh at first, because no one around here would have any interest in listening in on their conversation, no matter what language it was in. But she didn't stop her friend. Aviva didn't feel like laughing for long.

"So, Eli is in the hospital."

"*What* did you say?"

Mimi nodded.

"Why?" Aviva remembered clearly the other night when they'd had a visit from Ilona and Nachum. David hadn't said a word about Eli's looking sick, only that he had been well on the way to breaking down the door to their house with a baseball bat, not something someone sick enough to be in the hospital would likely have the stamina or strength to do.

"You heard me. He's in the hospital, and no one knows if he's even going to live."

"What happened?"

"Well, I knew you'd want to hear this, because—" She wiped her forehead with her sleeve and took a deep breath. "It seems he was at the apartment of someone in the community, I don't even know the people's name. He was supposed to be there to discuss something with the husband, some kind of event, fund raising, I'm not sure, but apparently the husband was not around. So the rumors flying around are that he asked the wife where her husband was, and she said he was out for the day."

"Okay, so?"

"So Eli attacked that woman—like you."

"*What?*" Aviva didn't notice her voice had reached a fever pitch. She felt as if Mimi had sucked all the oxygen out of the air. David came running over from the other table.

"Are you all right, Aviva? What's going on here?" He stood behind Aviva's chair, one hand on each of her shoulders. He felt her trembling. Mimi looked up at him, her eyes narrow, her mouth drawn. "Mimi? It's all right. You can say it in front of me. Aviva and I—we're together. I know everything."

Mimi continued speaking in Yiddish. "Would you mind speaking English?" David said.

Mimi repeated the first part of the story and then continued in English. "But while he had this poor girl—um—with his hand over her mouth so she couldn't scream, two of her brothers walked in on them. He had her skirt up and—well—I don't want to say what might have happened. Her brothers grabbed him off her and beat him so badly, it's amazing he lived. They say you can't even recognize his face. He's in the hospital. He has a fractured skull and brain swelling. They just left him and rushed their sister to the hospital, but when they told the hospital what had happened, the hospital discharged an ambulance to go get him. Apparently he was in surgery for a few hours, but he's in a medically induced coma, and no one is sure whether he'll ever come out of it."

For a moment, Aviva was unable to speak. All kinds of thoughts went through her head. Should she have turned him in when he did the same thing to her? Or was she right in thinking no one would have believed her.

"How is the woman?" she finally managed to blurt out.

"Physically, she'll be all right. He didn't actually do anything to her."

"Except scare the living hell out of her and give her lifelong memories of a hideous trauma," Aviva said. "I feel like this is my fault."

"How can you say that?" David said. "You had nothing to do with it."

"I could have told someone when he did it to me."

David shook his head. "You were in the process of taking him to court, honey. And I did tell Nachum and Ilona that time they—um—paid us a visit. Obviously, they didn't pay attention to me or try to stop him. He went out and tried to do it again to another innocent woman. I wonder how many more there have been."

Aviva burst into tears. The whole thing was such a shock, she didn't know whether to feel sad because of all the lives at least partially ruined, or happy that she wouldn't have to deal with Eli anymore, after months of living in fear that he would return to assault her again. She took a deep breath. Mimi had sat there, her mouth partially open, her face white as a sheet.

"I had to tell you, Aviva. The whole community is in shock."

Aviva reached her hand across the table and grabbed Mimi's. "Thank you, Mimi. You can't know how grateful I am. I won't have to worry anymore."

"I think I should get back now, before my parents start worrying where I am."

"Is there any way we can stay in touch? I feel I owe you something for just being my friend and caring."

Mimi shook her head. "No, you don't owe me anything. Honestly, when you told me what happened to you, I wondered whether you were making it up. I just couldn't believe he would—"

"See what I mean?" David said to Aviva. "Please don't feel as if this is your fault."

Mimi stood up. "I'm just not sure how we would keep in touch. I miss you, and I'd like to, but—you know."

"It's all right," Aviva said. "I completely understand. But if you ever feel you'd like to talk, I'm happy to meet you here. It would be so nice to see you."

"Can we walk you back to your train?" David said. "Seems like the least we can do."

"No, that's all right," she replied.

"Can you maybe let me know if you have any more information? You can call me at work the way you did today," Aviva said.

"I'll try," she said. "Goodbye, Aviva." She headed off toward the subway, turned around, and waved to them. Aviva waved back.

"The ice is melting in your drink," David said.

Aviva took a big sip and looked up at him. "Thank you for coming. I love you for taking such good care of me."

David smiled. "That's how people who love each other are supposed to act," he said.

"You have taught me more in a few months than I think I learned over the past ten years," she said.

"I wouldn't say that," he said. "I have a feeling that everything that library did for you is going to give you a passing score on your GED exams."

"I hope you're right," she said.

"I'm always right," he said, sitting down at the table beside her and pulling her gently toward him for a kiss.

Acknowledgments

I would never feel as secure publishing any book without the input and guidance of a series of trusted readers and writing workshoppers, all of whom have donated their valuable time to help me ensure that this book is as good as it can be. In no particular order, I would like to thank my trusted readers—Elaine Lansky (who has read and commented on this book over several revisions), Susan Machler, and Matthew Schneiderman; and Janie Emaus, Julie Trelstad, and Tina Ferraro, a writing group that met "remotely," with members on the east and west coasts, even before the pandemic made that a necessity. And special thanks to Lauren Teichholtz and Cecily Cohen for their advice and counsel. Finally, I would like to give my sincere thanks to Andrés Fonseca Alfonso, a good friend who generously shared some personal stories that inspired some of the ideas in this book.

Author Bio

Rebecca Marks is an author living in New York City. After a long career in the legal and technical writing fields, she paused to fulfill her lifelong dream, which was to write and publish works of fiction. Prior to the publication of this book, Black Opal Books published seven of her novels. Besides writing, she is a devotee of dog training and showing, and a musician and singer who has studied cello, Celtic harp, and classical harp. She currently studies *llanera* harp with the *llanera* harp virtuoso Edmar Castañeda.

Author Bio

Rebecca Marks is an author living in New York City. After a long career in the legal and technical writing fields, she paused to fulfill her lifelong dream, which was to write and publish works of fiction. Prior to the publication of this book, Black Opal Books published seven of her novels. Besides writing, she is a devotee of dog training and showing, and a musician and singer who has studied cello, Celtic harp, and classical harp. She currently studies *llanera* harp with the *llanera* harp virtuoso Edmar Castañeda.

www.ingramcontent.com/pod-product-compliance
Lightning Source LLC
LaVergne TN
LVHW041624060526
838200LV00040B/1419